NIGHTSHADE

Also available by M. L. Huie

Spitfire

NIGHTSHADE

A Livy Nash
Mystery

M. L. HUIE

CROOKED
LANE

NEW YORK

Copyright © 2020 by Michael Huie

Published in the United States by Crooked Lane Books, an imprint of The Quick Brown Fox & Company LLC.

Crooked Lane Books and its logo are trademarks of The Quick Brown Fox & Company LLC.

Library of Congress Catalog-in-Publication data available upon request.

ISBN (hardcover): 978-1-64385-456-4
ISBN (ebook): 978-1-64385-457-1

Cover design by Nicole Lecht

Printed in the United States.

www.crookedlanebooks.com

Crooked Lane Books
34 West 27th St., 10th Floor
New York, NY 10001

First Edition: September 2020

10 9 8 7 6 5 4 3 2 1

For James Dodding

"Sometimes in life you feel there is something you *must* do, and in which you must trust your own judgment and not that of any other person. Some call it conscience and some plain obstinacy."

John Masterman

"If I wasn't an actor I'd be a secret agent."

Thornton Wilder

Prologue

~

1943

Livy Nash sat on a hill above a runway somewhere outside of Manchester and wished she was going to Paris. The summer night air chilled, even though the sky was clear and the moon bright enough to light her plane's way across the Channel. She had to wait for that flight, though. Still two nights before her scheduled departure. She'd spent the last months training for this moment and for what lay beyond, when she would finally find herself on the ground in occupied France. She felt ready. Anxious. Give her a plane, she'd fly the damn thing herself.

But this wasn't her night. It was Margot's.

They'd arranged to meet on this hillside just after the final briefing. Margot was late, as usual. She had a unique relationship with time: they were more casual acquaintances than actual friends. For a moment, Livy wondered if she would come at all. Margot had gone pale at dinner and wouldn't touch the evening rations. Livy'd made jokes about the taste and compared it to her Aunt Rosie's bangers and mash.

"Feed that to the Jerries, and the war is over tomorrow. Can't fight if you're running to the loo every five minutes," she'd said. The joke seemed to improve Margot's pallor. She liked them like that—the raunchier, the better.

What if she didn't come? Livy wondered. It wouldn't be out of character for her friend to miss their final send-off entirely. Always averse to sentiment, Margot hadn't shown up at the goodbye party for Yvette the past weekend. Claimed she had a cold. However, Livy knew her better than that. Knew Margot had made an excuse so she wouldn't have to be there when all the others sobbed and the like. Livy wasn't that type either, but the thought of not seeing Margot one last time chilled her far more than the windy night in the northwest of England.

When she'd first met Margot they'd sat on opposite sides of the table during a training briefing. Both women kept themselves at a distance from the others. But when the instructor began speaking in his thick Glaswegian accent, Livy and Margot both had to suppress laughter. When their eyes met, they couldn't hold it in. The instructor had not been pleased, but Margot and Livy had become fast friends.

God, Margot you can't leave me and not at least say goodbye.

Livy pushed her thick brown hair out of her face and felt the emotion about to erupt. Just as she rubbed her eyes to keep the tears back, Livy felt a hand on her shoulder.

"Look, just because you were the worst at parachute training doesn't mean you should cry about it."

Livy started. "Bloody hell, Margot. You're late. Again."

Margot sat down beside her. The summer wind fanned through her dirty-blonde hair. "Sorry. You know, last-minute briefing before they send me off to save France." Both Livy and

Margot had French mothers, but whereas Livy's accent was strictly Lancashire, Margot sounded like an English girl who'd grown up in Lyon.

"Dunno what England will do without you."

Margot smiled and put an arm around Livy's shoulders. "I don't know what you'll do without me."

Livy felt the tears again and willed them away. Neither of them spoke. They didn't need words.

"The car comes for me in an hour," Margot said. "I'm going somewhere on the coast tonight. They didn't even tell me where."

"Not exactly a holiday, is it?"

"Speak for yourself. I plan to enjoy myself over there." Margot grinned and looked up into the night sky. Livy saw wetness on her cheek, which Margot quickly wiped away. One thing Livy admired most about her friend was her ability to shut off her feelings and get down to work. She saw the transformation happen now.

Margot stood, brushed off her trousers, and helped Livy up. They held on to each other's hands.

"I do have to put my things in a bag. They don't give a girl much time to prepare around here."

"Rude little bastards, aren't they?" Livy kept her voice level, but her insides felt like they might come gushing out at any moment.

Margot let go first. She gave Livy a wink and a smile, then abruptly turned away. Livy couldn't move. Her boots felt frozen to the ground. She watched Margot turn, and felt more alone than she had since the death of her mum. Just as she was about to call out, Margot stopped and looked back at her.

"*A bientôt*, Livy."

Typical Margot. Never goodbye—always "see you soon."

Then she was gone. Livy only saw her back as Margot Dupont trudged down the incline toward the lighted buildings below.

"See you soon, luv," Livy said, almost to herself.

Chapter One

❧

June 1947
London

Geoffrey Collins found nothing at all extraordinary about his workplace except perhaps for its exclusivity. The small cluster of white buildings surrounded by the high wire fence was off limits to most residents of Eastcote, the unassuming village in the west of London. Even the majority of those who showed proper identification to the guard at the front gate couldn't enter the plain, white, boxlike building at the very rear of the compound. Collins, though, was allowed admittance to what on the outside looked to be a perfectly normal storage facility. Each morning he walked down the long hallway lit by harsh overhead bulbs, with a row of eight doors, four on either side, all closed. Eventually he came to the last door, marked 118. Collins often thought that a visitor might mistake it—with its faded numbers and chipped paint around the frame—for the haunt of the resident custodian.

But like many rooms in this building, looks deceived. The plain white structure was the heart of the London Signals

Intelligence Centre. Wireless messages from across the globe were received here, pondered over, and picked apart for the decision-makers in Britain's intelligence services. The building where Collins worked was better known to most at RAF Eastcote as "Station X."

On this morning in late June, at the end of a particularly long shift, Collins sat at his station in 118 and stifled a yawn. Though there were no windows in room 118, he guessed that the first rays of dawn would be peering over the river.

From his chair, Collins could pick up signals from almost a thousand miles away. He could hear broadcasts from Poland and All-Union Radio from Moscow. Some nights he listened to a Spanish-language version of his favorite drama, *The Shadow*: *"Quién sabe qué maldad acecha los corazónes de los hombres."*

This night had been quiet until he heard a strangely familiar sound.

First came the preliminary signal from RAF Gatow near Berlin:

Unknown wireless call sign received 0350. Message to follow.

Then a light tapping, sounding as if it came from inside a tunnel. The tapping repeated. Louder. More present. Immediately Collins recognized it.

N-I-G-H-T-S-H-A-D-E

He'd spent part of the war in much larger rooms at Bletchley Park, with receivers that picked up wireless signals from British agents stationed behind enemy lines. He hadn't heard this particular type of call sign since 1945.

Suddenly it ended. Time for the message now. Collins's pencil hovered over the logbook, waiting. The call sign came again.

N-I-G-H-T-S-H-A-D-E

This operator had a distinctive "fist." A hard touch on the consonant, a pause, and then much lighter for the vowels. Wireless operators during the war perfected individual signatures, so, if captured, the Germans could not replicate their distinctive signals.

But no message arrived. Just the call sign again. The same "fist." Almost as if the operator was repeating a name over and over. Collins held his breath as the signal ended. The silence in his headset felt heavy.

His shoulders slumped. The message had slipped back into the past. Nevertheless, he kept the receiver on that channel until the end of his shift. But it didn't repeat. Then, he scribbled a note beside the record he'd made of the call sign, with his own interpretation. He filed the report and placed it in one of the distinctive blue jackets that would give it priority. Collins wished he could deliver it personally.

*   *   *

Two nights later Ian Fleming sat at his usual window seat at one of the smaller tables of Boodle's gentleman's club on St. James's Street. This location gave him a bit more privacy away from the typical sounds one heard every night here. The clink of cut-glass tumblers, the *tock-tock-tock* of backgammon die in plush cups, the muffled leather of bespoke John Lobb shoes clicking across the marble floor gave Boodle's a unique ambience that comforted the delicate ears of many an aging member.

But Fleming needed time to think. He put down his knife and fork and sat back in the comfortable Georgian armchair. He looked down at the dinner he couldn't finish. The better part of a perfectly cooked piece of smoked salmon lay on his plate alongside asparagus in an exquisite Béarnaise sauce. His mind had been elsewhere all night.

"Sir?"

Fleming started. Hopkins, the chief steward, hovered over his left shoulder.

"Yes?"

"I do beg your pardon, Commander, but there's a gentlemen asking to speak to you, and since he isn't a member, I felt I ought to consult you first, sir."

Fleming smiled. Hopkins's old-world formality as well as his insistence on addressing him by his naval rank pleased him.

"Thank you, Hopkins. I've been expecting Colonel Dunbar."

The silver-haired steward bowed, his shirt still crisp after an evening on the floor, and retreated toward the entranceway.

Fleming's chest clinched. A familiar ache of late. He put a hand to his heart and reached for the two fingers of ice-cold vodka he'd only just poured.

The liquor burned his throat all the way down. For the moment, he forgot the pain his doctor blamed on the stress of work. Fleming glanced at his Rolex. An hour until he was scheduled to meet Anne. Dear God, was he actually counting the minutes? His mind went to the taste of her lips, her scent, and that damned wedding ring on her finger. Again, his chest tightened.

Fleming fitted one of his specially blended cigarettes into his holder and lit it. He drew the smoke deep into his lungs and let it waft out in front of his thoughts. Sleeping with a married woman was one thing, but this level of emotion frankly troubled him. Anne was exactly the sort of woman he craved. But love?

God! Love inevitably led to an altar, and that gave Fleming pause.

And now Henry Dunbar.

It had been almost a year since the deputy chief of MI6 had paid a personal call on Fleming. They'd first met during the war, when Fleming worked in Naval Intelligence. Postwar their paths had diverged. Dunbar ascended the intelligence ladder with speed while Fleming had gone back to journalism.

Despite their commonalities, Fleming considered the man an arrogant prig who'd stab a friend in the back if it meant promotion or an operational win. Dunbar's presence at Boodle's, however, could only mean one thing. He needed something.

"Knew I'd find you here, old man."

Fleming turned in the direction of the voice.

Dunbar forced a smile, surveying the club. "Always did like your comforts."

"Without them, Henry, what's the point of living?"

Fleming often joked that Dunbar was born with his ever-present thick bristly mustache. With steely gray eyes and a mouth perpetually frozen in a determined frown, Henry Dunbar had the dusty, weather-beaten look of a tank commander who'd chased Rommel across Africa.

"But where are my manners," Fleming said. "Despite my misplaced appetite, the smoked salmon here is first rate."

"No need. Didn't come here to dine." The colonel glanced around, dragging a finger across his mustache. Fleming recognized the nervous tic and dismissed Hopkins.

"We can say what we like here, Henry. This is one of the safest places in England for a man to speak his mind," Fleming assured him.

Dunbar settled back in his chair. "Very well, then. Last week a listening station in Germany picked up an old SOE wireless call sign. Two nights later they heard it again. No message. Just the call sign. The boys at Eastcote gave it the once-over, and it appears to be the genuine article."

Fleming lit another cigarette. Henry Dunbar was a born curmudgeon. He exuded cynicism. Tonight, he looked shaken.

"Do you have any idea who might have sent it?"

"The code name corresponds to one of our people. Someone we'd marked captured, presumed dead. The Red Army liberated a few of the German camps at the end of the war and had no scheme whatsoever for repatriation. So, some prisoners were just freed while others were rounded up by the Reds. God knows what happened in that chaos."

"And you actually think the Soviets might still be holding one of our people after all this time?"

Dunbar glanced away. "Could I at least get a drink here?"

Fleming gestured for Hopkins and ordered another carafe of vodka.

Dunbar waited until the steward was out of sight before speaking again. "I think that has to be the assumption given that wireless message. My guess is at the very least they know her whereabouts."

Her. The evening suddenly began to make a bit more sense to Fleming.

Hopkins returned with another glass as well as the ice-cold vodka. Fleming poured. Dunbar downed his in one.

"Look, the thing is, I could use someone on your end," Dunbar said, averting his eyes. "We need one of those creative pieces of misdirection you seemed to pull out of a hat for Godfrey in the war."

Since they began working together after the war, Dunbar had treated Fleming, and his correspondents, as a necessary evil on more than one occasion. Bunglers he had to tolerate. Fleming drew deep on his cigarette. He noted the derogatory lilt Dunbar used. Despite the slight, Fleming nevertheless adored being courted. He swallowed a retort.

"Perhaps you'd like to tell me how my humble news organization could be of service."

"Look, this all might very well end up being a wild-goose chase. If I send an operation like this through official channels, it may well die on the vine. So, I need to farm this out, if you take my meaning. This has to be one of your people, Ian."

"And what sort of misdirection do you require?"

"Yuri Kostin. Do you know him?"

Fleming exhaled smoke and shook his head.

"He's MGB, attached to the Soviet Embassy in Washington. Kostin was on the Eastern Front during the war, rooting out traitors and German spies. The Jerries had a name for him—*Der Rote Teufel.*"

"Ha. *The Red Devil.* How theatrical."

"Thing is we've been looking at having a go at him for some time. He has certain vulnerabilities."

"You think you could turn him?"

More confident now, Dunbar downed another shot of vodka. "Think he might be susceptible to a double agent. Someone who could ingratiate themselves with Kostin. Then, this signal comes along and the timing seems perfect. If anyone knows what happened to British agents in those camps, it would be Kostin. He was in command then right after the war." Dunbar smoothed his mustache at both ends. When he spoke again, his voice was hushed. "Look, old man, things are hot right now in Berlin between the Reds and all of us. The stakes are just too high, so for this I need someone—well, deniable on my end."

There's the rub, Fleming thought, pushing the half-eaten salmon with his fork. *Feel as if you're going to seed? The steel claws of marriage opening to clamp around you? Well, this is the price of staying relevant in the game*—old man. *Deniability. If it all goes wrong, then it's your mess to clean up. His Majesty's Government knows nothing.*

Fleming smiled, a grin that broke out across his broad mouth and lit up his blue-gray eyes. "A gentleman would at least call me a taxi and ring me in a couple of days, Henry."

The quip bounced off the colonel's armor. "If you can't help me, I can always go elsewhere."

Fleming felt a familiar twinge in his neck and residual tightness from his last chest pain. He picked up his cigarette case from the table and slipped it into his coat. "Charming as your company is, Henry, I have an engagement with one slightly more desirable. As I understand it, you need someone who can charm the information we want right out of this Red Devil."

"Thing is, one of your people knows Kostin. Or knew him, anyway."

Fleming put away his cigarette holder and straightened his polka-dot bow tie. "And just who might that be?"

"Well, your girl in Paris."

Chapter Two

〜

Earlier that same day, the "girl in Paris" stood in front of the painting *Les Mystères de la Passion du Christ* in the Louvre and tried to remember all seven of the heavenly virtues.

Livy Nash interrupted her reverent contemplation to check the time. Her agent was five minutes late now. Patience was one of the virtues, but it wasn't one of hers.

She'd been running him for several months. He was a low-lying member of the PCF, the French communist party, who'd turned double when she started talking francs. Despite his status or lack thereof, his information had been top notch. Today, he was scheduled to deliver the *coup de grace*: a list of PCF officials who'd met with Soviet agents after the May elections.

The spot for this particular meet—in front of this spectacular crucifixion mural—had been chosen by the agent. Perhaps, he reasoned, the last place anyone would expect to find a godless Soviet spy would be ogling a painting of Jesus.

Perched on a bench a few feet from the painting, Livy silently cursed the man she knew as Barnard. He'd never been late before. Tension ran down her spine. The sensation felt all too familiar.

Livy knew every nook and corner of Paris. The city felt like a second home. Her mother, sweet Marion, had been born here. When she drank wine, her mother would often break out into a warbly rendition of "Plaisir d'amour." Livy could still hear her voice.

"Plaisir d'amour ne dure qu'un moment
Chagrin d'amour dure toute la vie."

Memories of her mother's voice had helped get her through the war. Dropped behind enemy lines in 1943 as part of a network of British agents, Livy had to learn quickly to deal with the constant anxiety of suspicion and the fear of capture. She knew that someone who looked like an ordinary Parisian might stop you outside a café and ask for a light. *"Bien sûr, monsieur."* Then, the vulnerable moment—match held high—as two others race out of the shadows to bundle you into a waiting car. Next stop, an unlit basement room for interrogation at the notorious Avenue Foch.

Even today, an occasional shiver ran down her back when she walked the streets. The shadows of the Nazi occupiers—vanquished for three years now—still lurked in the city's darkness.

A cry of laughter from a three-year-old running through his father's long legs brought her back to the present. The summertime crowds had recently returned to the Louvre in droves. On this Saturday in late June, lines of visitors dawdled from painting to painting, taking in the art like they had all the time in the world.

Livy felt none of their calm. She rocked on her heels, trying to keep her focus on the painting. Something about this meet didn't feel right. Her nerves felt like icicles.

Seven minutes late now. Where was the man?

Agents weren't late unless they'd been blown or picked up a tail. Barnard—who'd been saddled with the code name "Tempest"—had been a dedicated member of a communist resistance cell during the war. When it ended, he decided to lend his talents to the Russians. Livy'd invested ample time working him, gaining his trust, and making certain for herself that he was what he appeared to be. At first she hadn't trusted Barnard. He lacked the passion of a devout Marxist. His eyes didn't brighten when talking about a global worker's revolt. But when the subject of francs came up, he became a bit more animated.

Behind every good communist is a capitalist looking to negotiate a better deal.

Where was the man? Livy's insides were fit to pop. She felt sweat against her blouse. Dammit, she'd waited long enough.

She rose from the bench and spun on her heel toward the stairwell a good thirty yards away.

There he stood.

Barnard always struck her as a bit like one of Shakespeare's clowns. Comic by appearance and nature, but just obtuse enough you weren't ever quite sure if he was supposed to be funny. He sauntered toward her, his crown of thick black curls covered by a beret of all things. After that—baggy coat, baggy trousers, baggy face. Even a baggy smell.

He stopped in front of the painting and rocked on his heels, waiting.

Livy moved next to him and feigned interest.

"Every time I come here, this is the painting I must see," he said in English. They'd always used French before.

Livy took the opportunity to move closer. *"Monsieur?"*

"It moves me. I don't know why, but it does."

She weighed the pros and cons of being seen in conversation with Barnard. Total strangers discussing art must happen hundreds of times a day. Enthusiasts studying brush strokes and what-not.

Livy'd seen the painting before, of course, but had never stopped to consider it. This was a crucifixion piece unlike the millions that hung in churches around the world. Jesus and the other two men on the hill, nailed to their crosses. Their bodies sagged. A roiling dark cloud hung behind them. This wasn't realism, no. Scenes from the life of the Messiah fought for space on the canvas. In the upper right corner, Jesus ascended into a shimmering sphere along with a multitude of souls, all reaching up.

Barnard couldn't take his eyes off it. "It's breathtaking up close. You can feel the paint, the texture. Like it's alive. Breathing."

Art class needed to be over soon, or she'd leave her suddenly pious Red to commune with his savior.

"It can't be here, you know that," she said, keeping her eyes on the wall.

"What? Oh, I'll go in a moment."

"There's a bench just behind us. I'm going to have a sit—"

He grabbed her cuff and pulled her closer. Livy stiffened. She resisted the urge to push him aside and run. This didn't feel right.

"You're not listening to me," Barnard said, pointing at the three men on the cross. "There, you see, this is so much bigger than us. This makes me feel insignificant, *tu comprends*? Insignificant enough that they just might leave me alone."

Livy placed her hand on his. "Of course," she said. She hoped the gesture appeared comforting, even though she wanted to slap his face and remind him why they were there.

Instead, she asked quietly, "Who is it you want to leave you alone?"

"All of you," he said, turning away from the painting to walk to the bench.

Livy kept her focus on Jesus just long enough for the suddenly emotional Barnard to gather himself on the bench behind her. Pirouetting, she took the opportunity to scan the long gallery and see if Barnard had been followed. A tail would be tough to spot in the Louvre tourist crowds, but once she'd ruled out the families, the lovebirds, and the old folks, that left only a few options. Her pulse began to normalize.

She positioned herself behind Barnard on the bench as if to observe the painting from a distance. Livy's mind raced through the next few moments so quickly she had no answer when a Parisian Lothario, old enough to know better, said to her, "A thing of beauty, no?"

Frenchmen take those Charles Boyer pictures way too seriously.

Nevertheless, the flirtation provided cover. Livy dipped her chin coquettishly and eased back toward Barnard and the stone bench. Once seated beside him, looking in the opposite direction, she unfolded her map of the Louvre and pretended to find her next destination.

"Did you bring it?" she said quietly in French.

"*Oui, oui.* Right here." He patted his baggy coat.

"You seem anxious today. *Vous semblez nerveux.*"

"I'm tired."

He smelled like black market booze. The scent took her back to just after the war, when most nights her best friend was a costly bottle of Polish vodka. She'd ended all that last year. Her life felt different now. Cleaner. But the reminders were always there.

Barnard shoved his big, fleshy hand into his coat and removed a dirty A9 envelope. He studied it. "Will this buy me a little freedom?"

Livy's face flushed. She knew Barnard was prone to mood swings.

"My people will let you know," she said. Livy placed her museum guide on the bench next to Barnard's envelope.

She reached for the larger package and his moist hand fell on top of hers.

"You know there is another way of looking at that painting," he said. "That we all are on a path to the cross."

Livy couldn't remove her hand without drawing attention. Any sudden movement meant they'd be seen, heard, and possibly remembered.

"I was never terribly biblical," she said, forcing a grin.

"It's not that, Miss Nash."

Damn the bugger. Her name now.

"No matter what we do, they get us in the end." He released her hand and pocketed the museum guide. "They always do."

* * *

Before Livy could respond, Barnard pushed away from the bench; shuffled through the crowd, past his favorite painting; and was gone.

She folded the greasy envelope he'd left behind into her purse. No time to check and make sure it contained a list of names and addresses. Nor had he taken the time to count the francs in the envelope she'd brought.

This just didn't feel right.

His hasty departure brought back an all-too-familiar vulnerability. The sensation of being the hunted, with no idea where the hunter might be lurking.

Trying to ignore the panic coursing through her body, Livy turned toward the opposite exit at the end of the long hall. Barnard had limited her choices for leaving. He'd scrambled away in one direction, leaving her only option being the long hallway to her right, which lead to the stairs and then, eventually, the front entrance. She'd just started to scan the crowd that aligned her exit route when two men strolled into her field of vision at the same time.

One man—balding and mustached, a flat cap clinched in his fist—stepped through the tall archway near the stairwell about twenty yards away. He wore a light blue jacket over gray trousers.

Across the way from him, another man. Straw trilby paired with a gray wool suit.

Both looked overdressed for Paris in the summer. Both alone. Both looked like they'd be more at home on holiday in the Crimea than in the Renaissance Hall of the Louvre. Did that little baggy-pants bastard set her up? *They always get us in the end.* Damn him. Practically a warning. Although his behavior had seemed more like that of a condemned man than a nervous double.

No time to think now. She had to get out.

Livy's focus narrowed to the archway. The gauntlet up ahead. Flat Cap on her left. Straw Hat closer on the right. Her heartbeat spiked as she edged closer. She licked her dry lips and took a deep breath. Would they try and take her here? So many people around.

Ten yards now. Flat Cap pivoted to the center of the room, away from an oil portrait. Straw Hat crossed his arms and stepped deeper into the hallway. In ten feet, Livy would pass within arm's length of him. The archway loomed. More tourists entered. A family who looked lost and an older couple, breathless from the stairs.

Straw Hat turned toward her as she passed. Would he move on her now?

Something struck her leg. Livy flinched and grabbed her purse with both hands. The little boy. The three-year-old who'd run between his father's legs earlier rushed past Livy, brushing her skirt, on his way to the archway and the staircase beyond. She gasped. The boy's embarrassed father shuffled past her, uttering a quick apology. Flat Cap and Straw Hat looked at her.

Livy scolded herself. A little boy touches her and she draws attention. *What's wrong with me? Stupid!*

She passed between the two men without incident. Livy tried to bring her breath under control.

They wouldn't have taken her there anyway. A gendarme would have been summoned. *"Constable, these two men suddenly grabbed this poor woman. We will never again tolerate this in Paris."*

She knew how Russians worked. Far more subtly than the Gestapo. Their secret police tactics had been honed for almost thirty years. They would wait until she got outside. So, Livy had to lose them somehow.

Fine, she would be someone else now. Play another part. A woman hurrying to the front of the museum to meet her lover.

A look at her watch. Oh yes, the time had gotten away from her, and he was waiting. *Mon dieu!* She hoped he hadn't been there long.

The little game in her head quickly gave way to more realistic thoughts as she approached the first landing of the winding stairs. There, in the turn, she'd know her odds. She held her handbag tight against her body. The last few steps now. Then, the landing. She turned. A quick glance up.

Straw Hat stepped through the upper archway, unmistakably heading in her direction.

Down another floor, Livy pivoted on the next landing. The flow of foot traffic upstairs thickened, but Straw Hat stuck out. Behind him, maybe ten paces, strolled Flat Cap, his partner.

Barnard had sold her out. No doubt now.

Livy's heel scraped on the edge of a step as a wave of dizziness passed through her. She had to keep moving. If she kept her distance, she'd have an advantage. A small one, but it could be decisive.

Once she reached the bottom of the stairs, the main entrance would send her out into the concrete plaza in front of the great U-shaped museum. Perhaps fifty yards from there to the Tuileries Garden, and then to the crowded Place de la Concorde, where, if her luck held, she might be able to flag a taxi.

No, they'd be smarter than to let her get away. Somewhere between here and the street, they'd take her by the arms, smiling, helpful. From there, a quick walk to a waiting automobile. She'd be shoved into the back before the car sped away, then secreted to an MGB safe house in the city. What then? They'd be smart enough to know that she was much more than a journalist. Self-respecting foreign correspondents don't plan meet-ups with spies in the center of Paris. They might even know about her war background.

So, they'd bleed her. See how much she knew. Lock her in a dirty basement room. Take her clothes. Keep her dirty, hungry, and unsure of what was to come while they waited for her to talk.

Images of the war flashed through Livy's mind. Caught finally by the Gestapo at a roadblock. Then, prison. She still felt the dampness of that cell in her bones. The fear rampant in her veins. Naked, cold, and hungry. Alone. Her face bruised from repeated beatings. Then, the waiting. Wondering when would they come for her. When would it be her time?

Livy's foot hit the floor on the main level of the museum. The sight of the outdoors and sunshine calmed her briefly. She picked up her pace. Forget caution. The fear was a part of her.

Up ahead, the exit and beyond. She could see the light of the afternoon. She glanced back to the bottom of the stairwell. Straw Hat stepped onto the main floor, headed in her direction.

Livy had no plan, no idea what to do. Her resourcefulness— which she'd called upon so often in the past—left her as fear rumbled in her gut. She passed through the entranceway and into the brightness of a Paris afternoon.

She allowed herself one quick turn back. Both men stood near the entrance now. They maintained their distance, not speaking to each other, but Flat Cap and Straw Hat were on the move.

Livy turned and slammed into a tall blue wall. She tried to back away but couldn't. The long arms of a gendarme, one of the tallest men she'd ever seen in Paris, held her tight.

"Pardon, mademoiselle," he said, a broad paternal smile spreading across his face.

Livy resisted the impulse to bolt. Her heart thumped so hard in her chest she felt sure he must hear it.

"Forgive me," she said in English. She struggled for words, a tourist who didn't speak the language, trying to be clear. "I—um—it is my mother—you see, *monsieur*."

The gendarme had her bag in his hand. The snap at the top had come undone. The greasy envelope Barnard had left her peeked out from the opening. The police officer was trying to make sense of it. A woman running from the Louvre. A thief?

How close would her pursuers be now?

"My mother, *monsieur*—very sick." She spoke slowly, voice rising. "I have to hurry, you see." A woman on the verge of tears. She placed a hand on his chest where they had collided. Holding herself up. Lifting her eyes to his. The confused gendarme tipped his kepi and stood aside, holding the handbag out for her.

Livy resisted snatching it from his hand. She snapped it shut. "Thank you—um—*merci, monsieur*."

"Avec plaisir." And the now-gallant gendarme stopped the procession to the exit just long enough for Livy to break free of the crowd.

She dared not look back. The progress of Straw Hat and Flat Cap would be delayed, but not for long. No choice now but to make her way through the gardens and pray a taxi or streetcar would be passing.

Livy ran. The tightness of her skirt tugged at her legs as she shuffled past groups of tourists making their way to the museum. More than one stood aside; many more stared.

At any moment, she expected a hand on her shoulder or the tug at her elbow. What would she do? Shrug it off? No, it would come again. Harder this time, like a vise. She knew how to defend herself. Her training during the war gave her confidence that she could take one man down. But two? A pair of Moscow-trained hoods would have no problem with one woman, no matter how well she could handle herself.

Just bloody well don't let them get you.

Further away from the entrance, the crowds thinned. Keeping her eyes on the horizon, Livy saw a few cars crisscrossing the street ahead. Traffic would be lighter midday, but Parisian taxis seemed to outnumber cars in the capital two to one.

Her lungs strained as she ran harder. She'd gotten soft. She felt it in her ragged breath. Two years on rations, yes, but still she'd had regular meals and plenty of sleep. She should have been ready for this. Should've recognized the weakness in her agent. *Damn Barnard!*

Then, up ahead, her savior.

A black Peugeot cruised along the Place de la Concorde just beyond the gardens. The familiar taxi sign clearly visible on the passenger door.

Livy waved frantically. Still too far away to be heard, but the sight of this escape route ahead gave her legs new life.

Miraculously, the car slowed. She saw the silhouette of the driver's head turn toward her. The taxi stopped.

But for another passenger. The man in the flat cap approached the car from the boot. Somehow he had beaten her there. Straw Hat must be right behind her. How?

Livy stopped. Still another ten yards from the car. But so vulnerable in the open. She had nowhere to go.

Flat Cap had his hand on the passenger door. He turned and looked at Livy.

"No, no, *monsieur*," another voice spoke in a husky Parisian dialect. The taxi driver had rolled down his window. He was speaking to Flat Cap. "The *mademoiselle* hailed me first. Another car will be along shortly, *monsieur*." The cabbie waved her forward.

Her breath uneven, Livy walked the last few yards to the Peugeot. Flat Cap held the door for her. He smiled. Was he embarrassed?

His hand rose toward her. A threat? Livy didn't wait to find out. She flattened the edge of her right hand and slammed it into the man's windpipe. Flat Cap went down hard. Eyes wide as he fell. Stunned.

Livy leapt into the back seat, pulled the door tight.

"Allez, allez!" Livy shouted.

"Mademoiselle," the driver protested.

"Allez, allez, vite!"

The taxi lurched forward. Livy turned to see Flat Cap struggling to his feet, holding a hand to his throat.

As the car picked up speed, Livy saw Straw Hat in the distance. He waited at the edge of the gardens. A small boy in shorts, wearing an American baseball cap, ran into the man's arms. He lifted the child, and twirled him around, laughing.

"Who was that man, *mademoiselle*?" the driver asked. Livy hesitated, watching the men she thought would take her to an MGB safe house. One played with his son while the other, Flat Cap, struggled to get off the pavement.

"Mademoiselle, where are we going?"

Livy had no idea what to say.

Chapter Three

～

Two days later Livy sat in Fleming's London office, fretting over her misadventure at the Louvre. She felt a mess, inside and out, perched in one of the armchairs beside the desk of Fleming's secretary, Penelope Baker. The rainy weather this month caused Livy's normally untamable rat's nest of hair to frizz. She tried to appear at ease as she nervously pushed it out of her face.

Today's meeting was fairly standard. She came back to London about once a month for these briefings with Fleming. It had been her routine for the past year. The trips back gave her time to check on the Camden Town flat and keep her life in some semblance of order before heading back to Paris. But Livy knew this time would be different.

Pen, the über-efficient keeper of Fleming's business time, looked like a cross between Greta Garbo and Lana Turner. She had the healthy good looks of the latter and the former's air of sensual mystery. No wonder that, on her best day, Livy felt a little less put together by comparison.

Livy's usual summer attire of white blouse and navy skirt looked as if she'd bought it with rationing coupons, compared to Pen's Vogue-inspired ensemble. Every blonde hair in place. A wrinkle wouldn't dare be seen in her wardrobe. Livy had her share of admirers no doubt, but a second division team compared to Liverpool is still second division.

Swiping the hair out of her eyes again she sat, legs crossed, trying not to fidget. Livy gripped an envelope in her right hand. She'd spent the better part of last night writing the letter it contained. When Fleming summoned her into the inner sanctum she planned to hand it to him and be done with it.

Livy wondered how many times she'd walked into this office. She remembered the first time she'd staggered down the hallway, half-soused on gin, hours late for a meeting with Fleming and through the doorway marked "Kemsley News Service." That day she'd wondered if this might be just another news organization. How wrong she had been. Later she learned that Fleming ran foreign correspondents for papers like *The Sunday Times* all over the world. Some of those correspondents were actual journalists, and others, like Livy, were essentially freelance agents whose work ended up on desks at MI6.

Now, the embarrassment of that first meeting with Fleming washed over Livy. God, that felt like ages ago. But only a year really. She felt a different woman now. She'd said goodbye to so many things since then. Her nightly bouts with Polish vodka, her dead-end job as a copyeditor at a third-rate newspaper across town and—of course—Peter Scobee. She still thought about him. Her commander during the war. Her friend, her lover. But then last year had changed so many things. She felt a different woman now, and lately Livy wondered if that applied to her work as well.

She took a breath and released the envelope she'd been holding for dear life. Her palms were sweaty.

Livy scanned the outer office, wondering if this might be the last time she'd see it. Thick wood-paneled walls surrounded Pen's clutter-free desk, which was the only substantial piece of furniture in the room. A gleaming Royal Arrow typewriter and a black telephone anchored her workspace. Behind the desk hung a large framed print of Turner's *The Battle of Trafalgar*. Nelson's flagship, HMS *Victory*, dominated the canvas, with the final letters of the signal "England expects that every man will do his duty" flying from the mast.

Every woman too, Livy thought.

"He should have finished five minutes ago. I don't know what's keeping him," Pen said, her voice as smooth and crisp as a summer walk in Hyde Park. She looked at her sleek gold wristwatch, sighed, and turned back to her typewriter.

Pen ran a tight ship and was more than a bit obsessive about keeping Fleming on schedule. Livy knew that beneath her icy blonde glare lay a good heart and a woman who'd do anything for a sack of chips.

Livy again pushed her hair back in place. She wanted to look calm and collected for the meeting but knew her appearance probably matched the rumpled bundle of nerves inside. She'd called London home since the end of the war and still hadn't quite gotten over the bumpkin stereotype many southerners have of working-class people from the North. She'd grown up in Blackpool, Lancashire. Even with an Irish father and French mother, Livy's vowels and lilting cadence betrayed her Lanky upbringing.

"You quite all right today, Livy?" Pen's eyes shifted away from her typewriter. "You have that nervous thing you get sometimes."

"Bit of a rough go in Paris the other day."

Pen stiffened. As Fleming's secretary, she handled the journalistic side of things. Livy doubted Pen had ever signed the Official Secrets Act, the document that bound journalists, spies, or whomever from betraying the knowledge gained while working for His Majesty's Secret Service.

"Right, well after you're done in there, we could pop down to that fish and chips stand on the corner at lunch. I'll tell you all about my latest. Christopher. Mmm. Absolutely spiffing. I'll even buy."

Livy smiled and glanced at the letter in her hand. "Might just take you up on that, luv."

The thick oak door behind Pen's shoulder opened with a great whooshing sound as the rubber seal around the frame dislodged. Fleming stood in the doorway.

Livy didn't go for him at all, although she could see why certain women might. His blue-gray eyes betrayed the first hints of aging, but his wide, turned-down mouth, below a nose that had been broken at least once, suggested the sort of cruel, devil-may-care attitude that made some women lose their train of thought. As always, he wore a navy suit with a white shirt and polka-dot bow tie. But today he looked tired.

"Olivia," he said. "Right." He turned back into his office.

Livy stood and pushed her hair back again. Pen gave her a wink as she headed inside.

Fleming's inner office didn't seem much bigger than the outer, perhaps about twelve feet square. A small picture window dominated the far wall, with a view of neighboring brownstones that stretched as far as Livy could see. In contrast to his secretary's workspace, Fleming's chunky oak desk was buried under newspapers, many dog-eared and lying open. Several carefully stacked piles of papers were kept in order by a cannonball paperweight. Alongside rested a pair of reading glasses as well as a pack of Chesterfields and Fleming's own custom-made cigarettes kept in a small blue box.

The clutter paled compared to the spectacle of the wall-length map of the world that hung directly behind Fleming's desk. The chart stretched from Alaska and North America on the left to Siberia and the South China Sea on the far right. Tiny lights, representing the Kemsley correspondents throughout the world, were embedded in the map itself. Livy guessed there were almost a hundred. The map glowed like an elongated Christmas tree, from one corner of the world to the other. Most of the lights seemed to be concentrated in North and South America, Europe, and Africa, but the occasional single light flickered in Czechoslovakia or Peking. Moscow even had its own small bulb.

Livy's eyes went to the light in Paris. For over a year now that had been her.

"Your man certainly came through for us," Fleming said, lighting one of his special blended cigarettes and placing it in a long holder. "Allard had a look at the list from Tempest. He wired Six this morning to say it all appears genuine." He looked up. "Are you going to stand all day?"

"Sorry, sir." Her heart sank lower as she descended into the chair across from his desk. Anxiety still made her crave a drink. Her eyes strayed to the drink cabinet Fleming kept beside his desk.

Fleming leaned back in his swivel chair and took a long draw of the cigarette. "Olivia, there is something we need to discuss. I'm afraid it's rather—"

"Here. This is for you." Livy held out the envelope. Her hand shook.

Fleming's brow wrinkled. He took the envelope but didn't open it. "And what do we have here?"

"You just need to read that. Explains everything."

"Olivia."

"I need you to read it. You gave me a great opportunity here, and I know when I first started, I wasn't exactly *Sunday Times* material, but that didn't matter—"

"Olivia, please."

"You were loyal to me. I won't forget that."

"What the devil are you on about?"

Livy sat up straighter in the leather armchair. "I cocked it up but good in Paris the other day. I misread the situation and just flat-out lost my nerve."

"I read your report."

"I attacked an innocent man. I put him on the pavement. He was just some bloke getting a taxi and I—it was crazy of me—but I thought he and this other man were following me, and I hit him. I convinced myself Barnard ratted me and I . . . panicked. A year ago, in the same situation, I could have thought it through. But now, I don't know, something's changed."

It hadn't happened overnight. The feeling began around the time she met Barnard, "Tempest." The job had been a new one for Livy. Recruiting and then running an agent. Suddenly the pressure of being responsible for a man living under the enormous risk of life as a double agent caught up to her. She became restless. Her temper shortened and became more volatile. Sleepless nights were soon the norm.

Fleming fidgeted with his cigarette holder, looking more uncomfortable than Livy had ever seen him.

"The work isn't always black and white, Olivia."

"Maybe that's what I need then. Bit of the normal. The everyday. I'm twenty-seven now, sir. Practically every woman my age is married, with a great heap of kids running about. Maybe that's what I need to do, or maybe it's time I just stepped aside."

Fleming's ruddy complexion looked washed out. The wide, almost piratical grin now a grimace of pain. Deliberately, he put his cigarette down and touched his chest.

"You all right, sir?"

He quietly cleared his throat and held up the envelope she'd given him as if it contained poison. "This envelope, I am to assume, is some sort of resignation?"

She nodded.

"So, because of this mishap in Paris, you've decided to settle down and make someone a good housewife, is that it?

"I don't know, but maybe a bit of the quiet life might do me good. I have to stop doing *this* at some point, don't I? I can't keep playing spy until I'm what—forty?"

Fleming looked as if he'd been smacked across the face. He took a drink and threw the envelope on his desk without so much as opening it.

"Do you remember the day I found you in that pub last year? Do you remember the shape you were in? I took a risk that day on a girl who was living every day out of a bottle. I took a risk, and you proved to be more than worth it. But one failure of judgment later and you want to throw all that away and . . . do what, exactly? Make someone a good wife? You?" Fleming practically scoffed. "Well, if you want to leave our business and go off and be one of those women pushing a baby round the park, then I'll accept this letter of yours and have Pen do the necessary paperwork. You can leave this office and never come back. Simple as that."

Livy didn't know how to respond to Fleming's direct challenge. *Was* that what she really wanted? A quiet life? Or was this simply fear talking? Something about her last meeting with Barnard had shaken her. During the war, she'd taken far greater risks, but she could see the pressure of the double life had Barnard at the breaking point, and Livy had feared he just might take her down with him.

"And what about you?" she said. "You never wanted that? Normal life and all?"

Fleming sighed, looked at the dial on his Rolex, and straightened his bow tie.

"The fact is, Olivia, we are the *watchers*," he said, his voice soft and clipped. "We keep the wolves at bay, so the people who lead the quiet lives never have to know. Once you've been in our line of work, it's more than a little difficult to be satisfied with what passes for a normal life."

"Speak from experience, do you?"

Fleming leaned back in his chair. The color was coming back into his face. His blue eyes brightened, "Perhaps the best course of action is to get you out of Paris for a spell. A change of scenery might do wonders for you."

"And what about Barnard?"

"Who?"

"My agent. Tempest."

"Ah yes. Well, I'll pass him off to our head of station there. Allard can handle your nervous little Red, I think."

Livy wondered how the impeccably dressed and mannered Henry Allard might react to Barnard's ennui and fragrant body odor. She glanced down at the resignation letter on Fleming's desk. It seemed embarrassing now. Impulsive and immature. Not to mention arrogant. She'd made plenty of mistakes before and would again. But Livy hated each and every one, deep in the pit of her soul. She fixated on blunders on nights she couldn't sleep.

She picked up the envelope and slid it onto the chair beside her like an offensive thing that had to be hidden.

"So, if not Paris, then where?"

Fleming's grin widened. "I do have a job for you. And quite a serious one at that."

Livy's skin tingled. His words alone thrilled her. No more running Barnard. Relief swept over her. She sat up straighter. The perfect attentive student.

Fleming now held a small card in his hand, which he gave to Livy. It bore a Greenwich address and the name "Anka" at the top. Livy took the card, sensing her boss's discomfort. It felt as if he wanted to say something to her but couldn't.

"Anka is expecting you tonight." Fleming said in a barely audible whisper. "Listen to what she has to say. If you're still interested, I'll be in the office tomorrow morning."

"That's mysterious enough."

Fleming slid open a drawer in his desk and removed a small square package wrapped in fine brown paper and stamped with the word "Morlands."

"This is a gift for her. A treat. Hopefully, it will make her a bit more . . . stable."

Chapter Four

Darkness followed Livy as she took the thirty-minute train ride to south London. By the time she reached the small platform where the rail disembarked, night had fallen.

Fleming had sent her on a number of wild-goose chases over the last year. There was the assignment to locate a gold ring last seen on the finger of a Luftwaffe pilot who'd been dead for four years. Then, the brief excursion to Istanbul. That particular memory made Livy laugh and tremble at the same time.

Anka in Greenwich? Fleming had said nothing else. Just go, and then decide.

The train ride gave Livy time to consider the future, but all along the route signs from the recent past confronted her. The summer had brought much-needed warmth to a city still dealing with the remnants of the one of the worst winters in London's history leading to one of the wettest Marches. Buildings with flood damage stood beside still unrepaired office blocks crushed during the Blitz. Union Jacks dotted the urban landscape, as if the real Britain was trying to emerge from the rubble.

The train pulled into the station just after eight thirty. Livy had always liked the quiet of Greenwich. Far enough away from the torrid pace of central London, with all the trappings of modern urban living. She remembered one or two pubs near Greenwich Park particularly well.

She followed a gaggle of businessmen away from the train to the stairs at the end of the above-ground platform. She twirled the card marked "Anka" in her right hand.

What was she doing? Not ten hours ago she'd almost resigned, and now here she was on her way to talk with a stranger. About what exactly? Fleming had been unusually cryptic. Something about all this reminded Livy of another visit she'd paid a stranger last year in Kensington, when she'd encountered Emma Sherbourne, the woman she came to know—not without affection—as The Great Actress. But that had been training. She sensed tonight's visit was something else entirely.

Yet, she kept going, surging ahead with the crowd of men getting home late from work, headed to their flats or wives or sweethearts to steal a few hours of normalcy before getting back on the same train the next morning.

The stairs ended in an alley between two hotels that bordered the Greenwich station. The night felt cool against Livy's legs as she turned left on the High Road.

A couple of the men looked back at her, their expressions suggesting they wondered where a single woman could possibly be going this time of night. Livy wondered that herself.

The card had only the name, an address, and the added direction: *Behind St. Alfege's*. Livy had once interrogated an informer on a bench in Greenwich's massive park, so she was familiar with the location of the church.

After a few blocks she saw the grand tower and high walls of the parish chapel. A construction rope still blocked the front steps of the building. The charred roof served as another reminder of the beating the city had taken during the Blitz. The structure appeared sturdy enough, but the interior looked burned out, gutted.

The address on the card said Turnpin Lane, which was a narrow street tucked in behind the church. Number 110 stood off the road slightly. The house looked a typical English-style cottage. Asymmetrical with narrow windows—curtains drawn, of course—and a gabled entranceway. It was small but beautifully maintained, fronted by a well-kept garden with the right amount of green, a concrete bench, and a statue of Cupid with honest-to-God water draining from the cherub's stone mouth into an ornate basin on a pedestal.

So posh.

Livy stepped up to the door. She reached for the knocker. It was one of those brass jobs with a low ring and some bloke's face in the center. It reminded her of the ghost of Jacob Marley. She hesitated.

The door opened.

A tall, very thin, blonde woman stood on the other side. She wore an off the shoulder summer frock that seemed a bit youthful for someone who looked to be on the downside of forty. A gold watch hung loose on her right wrist, just above a bracelet with some sort of inscription. The whole thing smelled like the vault of the Bank of England.

The woman saw Livy and plastered the most insincere smile across her pinched face.

"May I help you?" Her accent sounded vaguely Austrian with a thick coating of the BBC. She also didn't sound in the mood to help anyone.

"Mr. Fleming sent me."

"Of course, of course. Well, don't just stand there."

Livy stepped into the foyer, which, although dimly lit, looked like the outside. Old money and lots of it.

The blonde woman closed the door behind her. Somehow she'd managed to produce a Walther P38 from inside her cute little summer dress. Livy'd seen enough of those in the war, usually on the belts of Wehrmacht soldiers.

The woman smiled at the gun, as if surprised it had somehow ended up in her hand. "You must excuse me. I live alone and tend to be a very cautious woman. You have identification of some sort?"

Livy opened her unfashionably large handbag and fumbled for her Kemsley News card. The woman kept the gun on her the whole time. Finally Livy found it, handed it to her, and waited. The woman seemed satisfied and lowered the Walther.

"Please, come into the parlor, Miss Nash."

Said the spider to the bloody fly. But Livy flew on regardless.

The parlor looked every bit as elegant and tasteful as the foyer. Livy didn't know much about furniture, but the loveseat in the corner seemed older than her grandmother, as did the two armchairs facing it. The servants must have recently beaten the rug. Pictures of rolling hills and landscapes dotted the walls, so the overall effect led Livy to believe that anyone in England with money would feel right at home here.

"Please, sit down," the woman said, making the pleasantry sound like a command. Placing the Walther on the sofa cushion, she made herself at home in the center of the loveseat.

"You brought something, yes?" the woman asked.

"Right," Livy said, digging into her purse. She leaned forward with the package stamped "Morland's."

The woman took the box and unwrapped it hungrily. Once the brown paper had been torn off and tossed to the floor Livy recognized one of the special-blend cigarette boxes Fleming always had on his desk. The woman opened it and removed one of the cigarettes with three gold bands, sniffing it luxuriously. She then produced a gold Ronson lighter from the side table and flicked the flame to the tip. She drew the first smoke deep into her lungs and exhaled with a rapturous smile on her face.

Engulfed by a haze of smoke, the woman opened a decanter of something very dark and poured a shot's worth into a cut-glass tumbler. Straight. No mixer. She swirled it in the glass and took two dainty sips.

"It's piss," she said, swallowing, "but what can you expect." She took another long draw on the cigarette, and her eyes wandered over Livy from head to toe. Not in a sexual way. More like a boxer sizing up a sparring partner.

"How long have you known dear Ian?"

Livy felt the beginnings of a headache. The tension of the day had caught up with her, and she lacked patience for an interrogation.

"You're Anka, then?"

The blonde woman's eyes narrowed to slits. "Of course I am. Don't be silly. Now, answer my question."

"He hired me last year."

Anka scoffed. "I met him during the war. So, five years for me. He is a very charming man, of course. And also a cad. I must say you don't exactly look his type."

Under normal circumstances Livy would've walked out. She hated this pretentious little nook of a house, and its mistress even more. She decided to give it two more minutes. Then, gun or no gun, she'd leave.

"I work for Mr. Fleming. That's all."

"He has never asked you for a drink or flirted with you?" Anka's blue eyes fairly twinkled.

"As I said, it's just about work, he and I."

"Of course it is."

It had been a while since Livy had taken an aversion to anyone this quickly.

"So, why did he send me here? You have something to tell me?"

Anka shrugged and lit another one of Fleming's cigarettes.

Livy's eyes shifted to the gun. She had the impulse to reach for it. Anka didn't look particularly agile, but with the Walther beside her, she held the upper hand.

"I'm not here to be evaluated," Livy said. "You have your cigarettes, and frankly, I'm a little tired of being given the once-over."

The woman just stared and smoked.

Livy stood. If Anka cared, she didn't show it. So, throwing a bit of caution to the wind, Livy turned and headed to the door. She wondered if the gun might now be aimed at her back.

"He wants you to be a double."

Livy looked over her shoulder. No gun.

"A double?"

Anka laughed, deep and sneering. "A double?" she repeated, mocking Livy's voice. "Where exactly is it you're from?"

Livy ignored the insult. A double agent, she meant. Her mind raced back to Barnard. She remembered the fear and anxiety that he wore like his baggy overcoat the last time she saw him. A servant of two masters. Caught between them both.

A double.

Livy answered. "I'm from England. The side that won the war."

No laugh this time. Anka crushed her cigarette in the ashtray and grabbed another.

"I worked for Ian. For England. During the war." The flame sparked the tobacco, and Anka's hand shook ever so slightly.

"Yes? And?"

"Miss Nash, if Ian asked you to visit me, then it means he is considering you for the type of work I did for him. I'm one of its few survivors, you might say."

"You were a double agent for our side?"

"For Ian, to be precise. I passed false information to the Germans in Vienna. For almost two years."

The smoke haze that now covered the chintzy sitting room seemed to clear ever so slightly. Two years undercover behind the lines. Livy's stint with the SOE had lasted just over a year. At times she had pretended to be someone else in confrontations with the Germans, but many days had consisted of playing cards in an abandoned shop, waiting for signals from back home.

"And you were never captured?" Livy asked.

Anka shook her head. She picked tobacco from her thin bottom lip and flicked it across the room. "No, I was very good. The best, Ian said."

"Two years is a long time for that sort of work."

"One week is a long time for that sort of work. But I didn't have a choice. It was the war."

Livy took a hesitant step back into the room. "We all did things then we'd rather not remember."

Another husky laugh. "You're right, Miss Nash. Remembering is the problem." She reached for the decanter and poured another two fingers in the tumbler. "And forgetting is the only tonic."

Livy watched her down another glass. She didn't say so, but Anka could have been speaking for her. It felt a bit like looking at a version of herself just after the war, when all she could do was drink away the pain. Livy wondered if this was how she would have turned out if she'd continued.

"This gun was not meant for you, but I tend to be a little more nervous these days."

"Even now?"

"Two years is a long time, and it doesn't leave you so quickly." Anka picked up the Walther and placed it on the side table with the liquor. Livy wondered if one day she might use the gun on herself. Her heart broke for this woman who survived on cigarettes and booze. She considered how many other Ankas there might be out there all across Europe.

"Do you enjoy the theatre, Miss Nash?"

The question surprised Livy and brought her back to the moment. "I do."

"Then, perhaps you know something about how a great actress submerges herself in a role. It's a facade, of course, but when it's done well, it appears the part consumes her. Replaces who she is with someone else entirely."

"I wouldn't put it quite like that, but yes."

"That's what it was like. What Ian had me do. Play a part. Always onstage. Always in the spotlight. But never quite sure if I'd got the lines right and how they might play for my audience. Do you understand me?"

"I think so."

"But even in this play, this long play, you must find time to be offstage, you see. Somewhere you can relax. Otherwise you lose yourself entirely. And that is very frightening, Miss Nash. I had a book that I read when I was alone, and as I read it, I remembered my own thoughts, and the part left me, yes? It was my favorite book, of course. A book from my childhood. It was my talisman, you might say."

Livy listened as Anka smoked and talked, the words spilling out of her almost automatically. She dared not interrupt, nor move even. This was a test, she decided. Fleming wanted her to hear Anka's story. To carefully consider what he had in store for her. He'd said the next assignment was "quite a serious one at that." So Livy took it all in, and tried to picture herself in the lonely, dangerous world Anka described.

"Because they won't believe you at first, you see," Anka continued. "Why would they? You offer them information or secrets and they suspect you. They think, 'Oh, she's a spy, of course.' So before you even start, they don't trust you. You have to win them over, and that takes time and patience. But even once you have it, you are always so close to catastrophe. Like you are dancing on a precipice. You can't slip up. You can never allow yourself to relax. It's actually quite thrilling at times. Exhilarating. The energy is almost sexual. It makes you feel you can do no wrong, and that—that is the moment when you are the most vulnerable. A part of me wanted to confess it all, Miss Nash. To the Germans. My contact. We had developed an intimacy, you see. I wanted to tell him the whole thing. Who I really was. It was such a great weight to carry, the burden of the deception."

Her cigarette burned down to her finger. The ash fell on her summer frock, bringing Anka back to the present. "Goddamit! Why didn't you warn me? This dress wasn't cheap, you know."

Livy held still. Drink and recalling the past had made Anka volatile. Never a good thing when a gun was within reach.

Anka snatched another cigarette and held it between her fingers, as if waiting for a light. "You might think I am very silly, talking all this nonsense, but you don't understand. They—the men who sent me—never understood. Of course they were all full of praise and congratulations, but they don't really know how it feels to be someone else entirely."

Livy didn't want to ask the obvious question. She knew the answer might terrify her. Anxiety crept up her neck like a spider. No choice. She had to know.

"Well, how does it feel, then?"

Anka's eyes half-closed and her voice became very soft. "It feels like you are a small child walking into the shadows. Alone. No one there to hold your hand. But that's not the hardest part. No, the hard part is walking back out. If you're not careful, you might lose yourself in there."

Livy saw it quite clearly, what the spy game had done to this woman. She looked years older and acted a bloody wreck. Nervous. Paranoid. Chain-smoking. Livy gritted her teeth and told herself that no matter what Fleming had in store, she wouldn't end up like this.

"But you did get out," Livy said.

Anka's lips curled into a snarl.

"A part of me remained. A part of me will always be there. You can't change who you are with the flip of a switch. Hah. But they didn't care—the men. I only did it for Ian."

Livy knew no clean way to extricate herself from this smoky pity parade that could go on well into the evening. Trickier still since the pitiable had an automatic on the cushion next to her. She stood. "Well, I should probably be off."

"You're all wrong for it, you know." Anka stabbed her cigarette out and crossed her long, thin legs, kicking her foot nervously.

"Beg your pardon," Livy said. She tried to keep her eyes away from the gun.

"For what Ian wants. You're wrong. That country voice of yours, the way you walk. You lack—subtlety."

Livy pivoted and turned toward the door, trying to ignore the challenge. "Thanks again for your time," she said. This sideshow had just gotten stranger. Anka's voice pitched higher, demanding to be heard. "You have too many weak spots. I've seen them all in fifteen minutes. The Russians won't need that long."

Halfway to the door, Livy stopped and turned back. Her head felt light. She hadn't eaten the whole day. Maybe her wobbliness contributed to it all, but somehow she felt like her future seemed to teeter in this moment. She'd woken up thinking she was done with Fleming and Kemsley News. Did she ever want "the quiet life," or did she just want out of running Barnard and the chance to put herself back in control of things? Honestly, Anka's words chilled her. Livy could go back to Fleming and tell him no. Maybe she should.

Her eyes flicked over to the gun that still lay on the sofa. Anka's lithe foot kicked like a metronome.

She felt the danger in the air, and it made her tingle. Livy Nash hadn't sat on the sidelines when the whole world was fighting, and she'd be damned if she'd let this woman scare her into that now.

Anka looked to be spoiling for a fight, and Livy wanted to give it to her. She wanted to refute everything Anka'd said and then slap her thin little mouth with the back of her hand. But she broke the stare; spun on the heel of her cheap, serviceable shoe; and went back out into the night.

She didn't go to the train station immediately. She spent much of the next two hours walking London. Now that she was away from Anka, that gun, and her vitriol, Livy could think more clearly. She found the emptiest streets and strolled with no particular direction, trying to see the path forward. Fleming wanted her to be a double. He sent her to a wreck like Anka to show her the consequences of such an assignment. It was a warning. And a damned good one at that. Part of Livy wanted to hand in her resignation again rather than run the risk of ending up as another Anka.

But why had Fleming warned her? The question nagged. When had he ever flinched from giving her a tough assignment? Fine, he'd said this one was more dangerous, but why give her the opportunity to say no? Had her bad judgment at the Louvre caused Fleming to lose faith in her, to doubt her ability? No, that didn't make sense. He'd had this planned. He thought several steps ahead. Of course he did.

Livy stopped, looked around. She didn't recognize this block. Pubs were closed, lights out everywhere. No tube stop in sight. How long had she been walking? And where the hell was she? She might be lost, but she'd managed to get clearer about what this all meant. Fleming wanted to warn her because he knew there was a reason Livy would leap to take this job. That reason had to be very compelling. And the stakes higher than she imagined.

She walked down the block, trying to find a street sign in the dim light. Really had no bloody idea where she was.

Eventually she found a taxi and took it back to her flat in Camden Town. The events of the last few days—from the Louvre to the surreal encounter with Anka—swirled in her head like the haze of cigarette smoke in that Greenwich cottage.

By the time Livy reached her own bed, she felt more exhausted than she could remember. Her stomach ached from hunger. So she fell asleep, fully dressed, knowing that what she learned tomorrow in Fleming's office might change the rest of her life.

Chapter Five

~

Livy went right back to Fleming's office on the Gray's Inn Road the next morning. As usual, she sat in the armchair across from Pen Baker's desk and waited for the summons.

Finally, the seal around the big inner office door opened with a whoosh, and Fleming stood in the doorway, cigarette holder between the first and second fingers of his right hand. Livy stood up, smoothed her skirt, and considered the ten feet between her and the door. Once inside, there would be no turning back. "The quiet life" would have to wait.

"Olivia, I'm glad you're here," Fleming said, pivoting to allow her inside.

Livy stepped in and hoped she knew what she was doing.

Fleming sat at his desk, the lights on his map of correspondents glowing behind him. He fumbled lighting one of his special-blend cigarettes with three gold bands around the tip. His usual practiced air of nonchalance now seemed to mask a trace of nerves. She'd never seen the man so anxious.

"You saw Anka?" Fleming said. His steel blue eyes twitched slightly.

Livy nodded. "Why are you trying to scare me off this one?"

Fleming picked up a black folder on his desk, considered it, and carefully placed it on a stack of books.

"Because what I am asking you to do—what I need you to do—comes with considerable risk. And despite your reservations, if I show you what's in this folder, you'll agree to do anything. Despite the danger."

Livy figured as much, but she had to know.

"Right then, better give me that folder."

Fleming's hand slapped the desk. "It's not that simple." He smashed his cigarette out, half-smoked, and went over to the credenza beside his big desk, removing the top from a bottle of gin.

Livy took a breath. Did the man start drinking this early every morning? She felt uneasy, watching her normally unflappable boss behave like this. But how could she leave this office without knowing what was in that folder?

"Look, sir, it seems to me you sent me to Anka as a warning, but also as a sort of test. Well, I heard what she had to say. All of it too. I didn't have to come back here. But I did, and we may as well get on with it."

Fleming poured a thimbleful of tonic into half a glass of gin and dropped in two ice cubes. He swirled the drink and studied her.

"Your impertinence doesn't lessen your charm."

"Your reluctance to show me that folder only makes me want to see it more. And you know that."

Fleming took a long drink. He swallowed hard, as if it burned his throat. Must be strong gin to make a world-class drinker like him cringe.

Then, he said, "You knew Margot Dupont?"

"I did. We trained together before the war. We were mates."

"And have you seen her since?"

Livy shook her head. "I heard she was captured. They listed her as missing, presumed dead not long ago."

"Last week someone at RAF Eastcote decoded her wireless call sign. It came again two days later. Same fist. Apparently the same person."

The enormity of Fleming's words washed over Livy. Her mind raced back to the last moment she'd seen Margot on that hill near Manchester. Even though she'd not seen her in years, Livy still considered Margot the dearest of friends.

The news that she hadn't been captured and was listed as missing after the war fairly devastated Livy. First Peter Scobee gone, and then Margot. The double punch of those two losses had sent Livy into a spiral that ended in a bottle.

Now came the news she might be alive. If so, that meant she'd been held captive since the end of the war. The thought of it made Livy's stomach turn over.

"We have to find her," she said.

The words surprised her. They'd come out almost involuntarily. The hell with Anka. The hell with the consequences.

"I have been asked to try to do exactly that," Fleming said, sitting again.

"Right. Do we have any idea where this signal came from?"

"The original was picked up at Gatow, our base near Berlin. So we presume it originated inside Germany. More than likely from the Russian sector."

Livy knew this was the worst possible circumstance. Since President Truman's speech back in March, offering aid to any country threatened by Soviet aggression, tensions between East and West had intensified. Many feared Stalin would close down the Soviet sector of Germany for good.

"If we don't act soon, sir, she could be gone forever."

"Olivia, yesterday you sat in that chair and told me you longed for something different. A normal life. If there is any part of you that truly wants that, then you have to get up and—"

"We're not just leaving her there," Livy said. "A prisoner. For two years now. Wherever she is, I want to help find her."

Fleming finished off the gin and picked up the black folder. His hand shook ever so slightly as he held it out to her.

The thick paper felt heavy in Livy's hand. Her fingertips hesitated at the edges. She got control of her breath, leaned forward, and opened it. Inside, paper-clipped to the top of a standard MI6 dossier, was a five-by-seven official Soviet military photograph.

The man in the photo looked about forty years old and had a gleaming smile. He wore the standard uniform of a Soviet NKVD officer, but the medals across his chest, including an Order of Lenin, lifted him above the rank and file. The NKVD had been Soviet secret police during the war. But this man looked like he ought to be in a film opposite Betty Grable. He had a V-shaped face with a strong Italianate nose and a wide, mischievous smile that caused his face to appear lopsided. While the grin seemed boyish, the deep dark eyes challenged the camera. They seemed to say, "I'm here. Take my picture, but be quick about it." The dichotomy between the smile and the message the eyes gave was striking.

Fleming studied her. "You know him, don't you?"

The photo was yet another shock. Her mouth went dry. The man's undeniably handsome face brought back memories of some of her lowest times after the war. Livy took her time answering. Her stomach clinched. She turned away as heat rushed up her neck, flushing her face. It galled her that somewhere at MI6 a file existed with information on her lovers. Suddenly her visit to Anka made that much more sense.

"I *knew* him. A few years back."

Seeing Yuri Kostin's face again took her back two years to just after V-E Day. She'd met him at a big party thrown by a few lads from the old Firm. In those heady days of victory, there was no East and West. Livy didn't remember many specifics about the soiree, but it had been an international affair attended by Brits, French, Yanks, and even a few Russians. She and Kostin had vodka on a balcony with a spectacular view of St. Paul's. Of course she'd been taken with him. They drank. A lot. And ended up in bed. The affair continued for almost two months before he left London. Kostin knew how to respond to women, and frankly, he was thrilling in bed. Livy sank into a bit of a depression when he left.

In hindsight, that year was a low point for Livy. The memories of the war had driven her to drinking. Black Market Billy and his endless supply of booze kept her going most days. Kostin supplied the vodka, however, and had the added bonus of being a damned good-looking Russian with that charming crooked smile.

"What does Yuri Kostin have to do with Margot, sir?"

"He is a major in the MGB now. Moving up in the Soviet hierarchy. Special diplomat at their embassy in Washington. At the end of the war, though, he was in charge of the rather meager attempt at repatriation of the concentration camps liberated by the Red Army. Margot was at Ravensbrück."

The name felt like another gut punch. Ravensbrück had been the German concentration camp for women. Few survived and those that did suffered at the hand of Nazi doctors. Fleming went on.

"She's one of a few the old Firm couldn't account for after the war. So if anyone on their side knows where she might be—anyone we might have access to, that is—it would be Kostin."

"I don't understand. Why would the Russians want to hold her, sir? It makes no sense."

"I asked the same question," Fleming said, scoffing. "We do know they rounded up large numbers in their march to Berlin, but no one can be certain of how many. And yet this is her call sign. Nightshade. We've received it twice now. With her signature. If she is alive out there sending us signals, then Yuri Kostin is our best chance at finding her."

Anka. Kostin. Margot. It added up now. Her best friend might still be alive, and to find out where she was being held she had to rekindle this—what? Was "flame" the right word for what Kostin meant to her? The ghosts of the end of the war and her past had come calling for Livy again. And what choice did she have? She couldn't possibly measure her own fear at what lay ahead against Margot's two years or more in a foreign prison.

Livy took a breath. "I want the job, sir."

Fleming crushed his cigarette in a large glass ashtray buried in the clutter that engulfed his desk. He didn't speak for the longest time, so the only tangible sensation in the room was the smell of tobacco that lingered in Livy's nostrils and the fabric of her clothes. He sat back and regarded her. He looked tired and sad.

"You were chosen for this, obviously, because you have history with Kostin, but also because of your background. Your run with SOE is perfect cover. A young woman who gave every-thing for England but returned home only to be shut out of the intelligence community. A woman who feels betrayed by her own country."

"Betrayed" felt a bit strong, but Livy remembered a time when she wasn't given the time of day by men like Henry Dun-bar, who transitioned into a cushy chair at MI6 right after the war. She had to admit the role fit her. Fleming was the play-wright creating a starring role for Livy as leading lady.

"I don't have to tell you that the best cover always has ele-ments of the truth. You could play this role quite well.

"Everything we have on Kostin is in there," he said, flicking a finger at the folder in Livy's lap. "Despite your intimacy with him, you should have no illusions about his toughness. His war-time reputation could best be described as fearsome. But he has certain traits we feel can be exploited. Apparently, he's some-thing of an Anglophile, obsessed with Sherlock Holmes of all things. Loves women and as many Western comforts as can be allowed a Soviet agent of his stature. That's what you'll have to exploit if you're to gain his trust."

Livy listened. She'd had no real feelings for Kostin even two years ago. He was like alcohol, a way to deal with the pain. So how would she regain the trust of an old lover? Her emotions bounced back and forth between thoughts of Margot and her own creeping anxiety about what this new assignment meant.

"You'll be working with FBI counterintelligence. They'll provide you with the information you'll give Kostin. He has to believe you're more than just an old flame. That your feelings of being left behind by your own people have pushed you not only back into his arms but into betraying your own country. In a way, it's how a new lover must believe you no longer have feelings or desire for your old one. He has to trust you."

"I think I understand how it works, sir."

"No doubt. But once you earn his trust—and understand that will take time—then and only then can you start to work him for information on Margot's whereabouts. You have to move him to a point where he is willing to give you the information and give it freely."

"Oh, I'll get it, sir. Count on it."

Fleming leaned forward, the devil-may-care insouciance replaced by an uncharacteristic severity. "You can't force this, Olivia. You must be surgical. Anything less and they will make you disappear. Do you understand me?"

"Is that what you told Anka?"

"The circumstances were different. She's Austrian. Sent here to spy on us during the war. We caught Anka, turned her, then forced her to work against her own people. If she'd failed, then . . . she'd have been one less Nazi spy."

"I'm flattered. I think."

"Dammit it, girl, this is no time for your bloody cheek!" His eyes flashed and he smacked the table again. "I'm sending you into a viper's nest."

"Not for the first time, sir."

"No. I'm just hoping it won't be the last either."

"Makes two of us."

"Fine, let's get on with it."

Fleming pulled a black Mont Blanc pen from his desk. Even when his underlying stress seemed to be showing, the man was so preoccupied with gadgets and the other trappings of status. He scribbled an address on the paper and passed it to her.

"That's where we're having dinner tonight. About half-past nine I should think."

"Dinner?"

"The two of us. Another couple will join us. And, with any luck, one or two chaps from the Soviet Embassy here. This is opening night, my dear. The true challenge of this operation is for the Russians to believe that Olivia Nash, formerly SOE, former copy girl for the lowly *London Press and Journal*, and now sometimes correspondent for Kemsley News, would actually betray her country. You must have sufficient motivation, you see. So, we're meeting for dinner and drinks tonight at The Ivy, a somewhat over-rated restaurant in the West End that is nevertheless frequented by theatricals as well as one Dimitri Grimov. He's what we call a talent spotter. Recruiter for Moscow. Typically you'll find him planting stories in leftist papers or cozying up to academics, but he also has his fingers on the pulse of the artistic community here. Tonight you and I will be putting on a show for him."

"What sort of show, sir?"

"One that might make our Russian friend believe you're unhappy with your job and employer."

"I'm guessing you have something in mind, then?" Livy said, a tinge of excitement in her voice.

The twinkle had returned to Fleming's blue eyes as well. His wide mouth expanded in a grin worthy of the Cheshire cat.

"Nothing so obvious, my dear. At some point in the evening, I will make a rather public pass at you. Behave accordingly. Make it good for our Russian friend."

"Shouldn't be a problem."

"Good, then. Oh, and wear something a bit provocative," Fleming said. "You do have something not entirely drab in your wardrobe, don't you?" His nose wrinkled as if he wasn't quite sure the answer would be yes.

Chapter Six

Livy Nash grew up a backstage baby. She remembered birthdays where greasepaint filled her nostrils instead of the scent of cake and candy. Many nights she slept on a cot in a narrow gap between wooden flats and the floor of the Tower Circus, the resident attraction in Blackpool. Her father performed on the high wire, which wasn't quite as high as people thought, but nevertheless gave her mother fits every summer when the season started and her sweet Archie performed twelve shows a week for nine months of the year. But Livy adored being behind the scenes. The smells, the makeup, the sweat all made worthwhile by the energy and appreciation of the audience. Even though Livy'd never gone onstage, she felt like show folk were her people.

So she felt a little extra swagger in her walk as she made her way out of the cab toward The Ivy. Livy's somewhat meager salary didn't allow her to frequent as many West End shows as she would have liked. She and Pen Baker had gone to see *Can-Can* last year. It did not impress. She'd managed to get tickets for Olivier's *King Lear* as well, and adored it. Such a mature play, and this had been a full-blown production, with Alec Guinness and Margaret Leighton. Olivier was too young for the role, but that didn't matter onstage. Livy sympathized with the fever pitch of the lives of Shakespeare's characters.

So tonight, as she strolled toward the first entrance of her starring role as the mysterious double agent, Livy felt more than a few butterflies. Her lines had to be perfect because these critics would be savage.

The Ivy resided in a building that resembled a blunt triangle with the name of the restaurant at the top. Green awnings marked the entrance as Livy swayed past theatregoers scurrying to catch post-show trains or duck into one of a number of pubs.

Livy, of course, had never eaten at The Ivy, or for that matter, any of the best restaurants in London. Much less one with the reputation of being a favorite post-curtain destination for the West End's most notable. But this wasn't the first time an assignment had caused her to feel like a fish out of water and in a saucepan. She pulled the gray silk wrap tighter around her shoulders and tried to shrug off the feeling that Livy from Blackpool would be rubbing shoulders with the elite of the theatre world. Tonight, she took security in the part she was about to play for God knew how long. The role of the double agent—the women who would betray her country—countered her very real working-class neuroses.

A doorman, a sure sign of this place's posh credentials, gave her a grin and whisked open The Ivy's thick wooden door. Livy breezed in like she owned the place. The restaurant felt intimate inside. At nine thirty the theatre crowd had descended. Men, dressed in navy and dark wools, smoked in the corners. Women clustered together all in black, deep burgundy, and grays. No pastels for the denizens of the night here.

"Livy!" Her name rose from amid the sea of diners. The mass parted, and a petite blonde appeared out of the sea of navy blazers. Pen Baker looked more marvelous than Livy could have imagined. As in the office, everything was in its place, tucked and lifted where appropriate. In this environment, though, she seemed to glow, from her delicate nose down to her smooth golden ankles.

Every male head turned as she sauntered past.

Pen grabbed Livy by the arm and pulled her into the crowd, careful not to make eye contact with the gaping boys. One small glance, Livy knew, and they'd be devoured instantly.

"Darling, Mr. Fleming has the best table for us all," Pen said, speaking loud enough to be heard. "Now you can finally meet Christopher. He's so marvelous. You'll love him." Her voice softened. "I'm dying for chips, but joints like this just ruin them."

Livy listened as her friend chattered away. So Pen and her man were "the other couple" Fleming had mentioned. That meant Fleming's personal secretary would be front row for whatever saga of betrayal might unfold tonight. Livy forced a smile as they walked. She had to hand it to Fleming. Brilliant move. The veracity of this evening would be verified by Pen's honest reaction tonight as well as afterward. Livy wondered whether whatever happened tonight might damage her friendship with Pen.

Right, Livy thought, *put that aside.* She had a part to play and couldn't anticipate the next scene.

They emerged from the throng and entered a dining room that looked like the set of a Noel Coward play. The space itself felt crowded, but the thick white linen cloths on every table enlarged it. Carved Greek figures hung from the walls, and although each table had a small ornate lamp, the light in the room felt designed. The tables glowed warm and soft. Darkness hung around the edges, so the waiters seemed to appear out of the blackness.

The real ambience of The Ivy was its customers. A vision of beautiful people eating, laughing, drinking, smoking, and whispering overwhelmed Livy as Pen pulled her through the big room. Finally, at a small round table near a window, she saw the familiar figure of Ian Fleming. He wore his "uniform"—a simple navy suit, polka-dotted bow tie, and white shirt—and a grin that betrayed nothing of the coming scene they were about to play.

Pen's Christopher stood beside Fleming. He looked just as Livy'd imagined. Tall, dark hair, solid chin, deep blue eyes, barrel chest. The Jerries must have surrendered just looking at this one.

Greetings were exchanged. Fleming held Livy's chair for her and said, "You look exquisite tonight, Olivia." His eyes roamed over her red dress, cinched at the waist and perhaps a bit shorter at the knee than she'd usually ever wear. *Provocative enough?* The way Fleming's eyes wandered down her body gave her the answer.

Pen attached herself to the rugged Christopher. She gave a wink across the table to Livy. The table beside them erupted in laughter. She craned her neck to see the cause of the ruckus, and when she turned back, Ian Fleming had his hand on her thigh.

"Christopher, we've been decidedly less than chivalrous. These girls need libation," he said, tapping a spoon on one of two martini glasses on the table in front of him. The black-tied waiter appeared. "Waiter, schnapps for the blonde, and I think another round of martinis for the more charming side of the table." Fleming laughed and threw his arm around the back of Livy's chair.

He's laying it on a bit thick, Livy thought. She countered by catching Pen's somewhat shocked gaze and rolling her eyes as if to say, *The boss is soused.*

Livy actually felt thankful for Fleming overdoing it. It forced her to step up and leave fear behind. She was playing a new version of herself right now and hadn't quite gotten the character down. She wasn't holding up her end just yet.

The drinks arrived. Livy stared at hers. She hadn't really had alcohol in more than a year. Once she found her way out of its reach, she'd never gone back. But Fleming's martini sat before her. She picked up the glass. Ice glistened on the surface of the drink as a twist of lemon danced around the edge.

Their eyes met. Fleming's gaze immediately shifted three tables over. Livy's followed to see two middle-aged men, both in double-breasted gray suits, smoking and talking over the remains of their dinner. These must be the Russians, the intended audience for tonight's pantomime. The one who sat facing Livy had small, close-set eyes that enhanced his resemblance to Peter Lorre. He seemed to be holding court with his guest, talking nonstop as he gestured around the room. Plus he had a perfect view of Fleming and Livy. This had to be the talent spotter, Grimov. The Russian scoured the room, which might be suspicious elsewhere, but when you factored in The Ivy's famous clientele, anyone could be excused for keeping an eye out for Vivien Leigh or Leslie Howard.

Finally, Livy took a sip of her drink. The bitterness of the gin felt good on her tongue. She desperately wanted more.

Instead, she wrinkled her nose, pursed her lips, and pushed the martini away.

"That has to be the worst drink I've ever tasted," she said. Her glare challenged Fleming. "What sort of a place have you brought us to then . . . sir?"

Fleming smirked. Touché. "It's my own concoction. I shall make this martini famous one day. People will drink them all over the world."

Christopher chimed in with "Hear, hear." Pen cut her eyes at Livy. Her brow furrowed.

They ordered three courses, which began with creamed chicken and coconut soup. Livy had salmon with mousseline sauce, or at least that's what Fleming called it. She thought it tasted like eggs smeared in butter. The salmon, which was tender, with a delicate smoked flavor, would have been fine on its own. Then, the final course: a truly scrumptious toffee pudding with a slightly sweet cream sauce. If Livy's stomach hadn't felt tied in knots, she would have thought the dinner—as they said back home—proper *reet* grand.

The dinner conversation centered on the war mostly. Christopher, who had a cleft chin, had been a Navy man like Fleming and served on a destroyer. So the boys traded sea tales while Pen ate everything in sight. Livy wondered where she put it all. Between bites, Fleming's secretary, who seemed beyond bored with the war stories, gave Livy meaningful glances. Livy felt pleased that her disaffected act seemed to be working. But anxiety about the path forward troubled her. Did everything change here tonight?

"Olivia was stationed in Paris just after the war," Fleming said through a haze of cigarette smoke. "Knows the city better than I possibly could. Isn't that right, darling?"

Livy put down her fork and gave him a stern look.

"Paris is really like a second home to me," Livy told Christopher, avoiding Fleming's leer. "My mother was born there."

"Your father was English then?" Christopher said. Livy could see why Pen liked him. Good listener, this one.

"His people were from County Kerry, but Dad was born and raised in Blackpool."

Fleming snorted. "Well, that explains it."

The quick jab floated around the table. A familiar joke between coworkers. Livy played it as an insult. Her jaw stiffened into a deep frown. She took her cloth napkin and dabbed the corners of her mouth, as if to say she wanted to leave. In doing so she made eye contact with the Russian Grimov. But, no, he looked over her shoulder. Someone new had arrived.

Applause began back in the lobby and made its way into the dining room as a tall, dark-haired man and a petite redhead maneuvered their way through the throng. It took Livy a moment to recognize the man. Big teeth and big hair. It was the American, Howard Keel, who had been playing the lead in the smash *Oklahoma*. Pen had bought tickets for the musical a month into its run and had invited Livy. Apparently, the other diners at The Ivy had been more impressed with the show; the restaurant burst into applause. A few patrons reached for the tall man's hand as he passed, and he shook theirs with grace.

Eventually, the star and his guest found their table. A small spot for two along the inside wall. A lover's romantic dinner in full view of adoring fans. The bigger the star, the cozier the table.

As the spectacle subsided, Livy looked past Christopher to the Russians nearby. Grimov leaned back in his chair, casting glances at the newly arrived couple. Then he whispered to his tablemate. His eyebrows rose as if passing along juicy gossip. The man with his back to Livy broke out in laughter and turned toward the young couple's table. This Russian had thick dark hair and jowls that sagged under his cheeks.

Whatever Grimov shared with his comrade didn't seem particularly innocent. They liked gossip and had apparently come here to take in the scene. Subtlety wouldn't work on these two.

Despite Livy's earlier protestations, Fleming ordered another round of his special martini for the table. By her count, he'd managed to put away at least four of the drinks. All through the evening he edged his chair closer to hers and found every opportunity to touch her arm and shoulder. Each time, Livy made a slight show of removing her body from the boss's grip.

She ignored her new martini, feigning boredom each time Fleming spoke. The final act approached. How would it happen? Fleming would make the initial move, but her response would be the climax.

The cracked face of her watch showed nearly midnight when drinks were finished and the check handled. Fleming, of course, did the honors. In one corner of the restaurant, the tall, dapper West End star nestled with his redheaded friend while in the other the Russians looked ready to make their own departure.

It had to be now.

Fleming stood first, staggering ever so slightly as he played up the tipsy cad. Christopher, who'd stood drink for drink with Fleming, helped Pen up, draping a wrap around her shoulders. As he did, Pen turned into his big chest, kissed her finger, and placed it on Christopher's dented chin.

Fleming seemed to take that as his cue. He put his left arm along Livy's hip and leaned down, pressing his lips against hers as he—quite obviously—grabbed her bottom with his roving left hand. The authenticity of the kiss surprised her. The man knew what he was doing, but this was no time for slap and tickle.

She placed her hand against his chest and shoved. The gesture moved Fleming back, although he kept his hand on her backside. Livy grabbed her full cocktail glass and threw Fleming's soon-to-be-world-famous martini right in his face.

It was a direct hit. Fleming was soaked.

"Livy!" Pen called.

"Steady on," Christopher added.

She felt others in the room register the moment. Heads turned. People stopped eating. They had everyone's attention.

Finally, Fleming released her, picked up his napkin, and dabbed his wet face. He turned away in the direction of the Russians and said, "Maybe it's time for you to go home, you damned silly little girl."

Livy adjusted her dress. She resisted giving a glance to the corner table, in whose honor she had given a command performance.

"Maybe you'd better learn how to handle your drink . . . sir," she spat back, turning toward the entrance. Livy shoved past the nearest table, intentionally bumping into one of the diners for added effect. She sashayed her way to the door. Making sure that, if anyone had somehow missed the scene, they'd certainly remember her exit.

* * *

The next day Livy received an urgent call from Pen that Fleming wanted to see her that afternoon. Playing her part now, she decided to make him wait. Livy finally showed up at the office three days later. She wandered in at the end of the business day, looking as disheveled as she could without giving Pen the impression that she'd taken again to drinking.

Fleming didn't miss a beat. Instead of inviting Livy into the inner sanctum as he always did, he dropped a file on Pen's desk and left the office without so much as making eye contact with his delinquent correspondent.

Worry creasing the skin under her bright blue eyes, Pen gave the file a cursory look and held it out for Livy.

"He's pulling you out of Paris," she said. "Sending you to the States." Pen's typically cool exterior vanished. Her heart sank a bit as she swiped the file from Pen's manicured hand. Livy didn't read a word. She hated seeing the questions and pain on her friend's face, so she shoved the file under her arm and stormed out of the office, slamming the door behind her.

That afternoon on the street, she noticed a dark blue recent-model Nash shadowing her as she walked from the office to the Kings Cross Station. When she stepped out of the Camden Town stop about ten minutes later, she saw no sign of the car, nor did it appear on the walk back to her flat.

A short while later, a messenger appeared at her door and pushed a plain brown envelope under it. As expected, the parcel contained the documents for the next phase and a plane ticket for Washington, DC, on BOAC tomorrow morning, from London Airport. Just before bed, she looked out her window. She felt almost pleased to find the very Nash that had followed her from the office now parked up the block alongside the curb. Seemed someone had noticed her act with Fleming a few days ago.

Right, then. Time to take the show on the road.

Chapter Seven

∽

The next morning Livy stepped out of her flat. She stopped, her hand on the doorknob, and wondered when she might be back home. She pushed the thought away, locked the door and turned to hail a cab. As she hopped into the back, she spotted the reliable Nash sedan as it came around the corner and followed her taxi.

The International Departure Lounge at London Airport had the feel of a waiting room in purgatory. Livy never liked flying, and the rows of gunmetal seats filled by departing strangers waiting grimly to be called only added to its netherworld atmosphere. She tried distracting herself with a copy of *Look* magazine that featured an interview with none other than Joe Stalin inside. She planned to get to the interview but kept getting sidetracked by the very American adverts.

More Doctors Smoke Camels Than Any Other Cigarette.

He's helpless in your hands with the New Hinds hand cream.

Just as she was getting to the exclusive interview with Uncle Joe, a familiar figure caught the corner of her eye. A man had moved into the seat next to her. At first she only registered the round face, shiny black hair, and beady eyes, accompanied by an overdose of one of the more obvious men's colognes she'd ever had the misfortune to smell.

It was Grimov, the talent spotter. The man she'd performed for in the restaurant a few days ago, and more than likely a passenger in the Nash sedan. Even though she'd have been disappointed if he hadn't come, tension crawled up her back and into her neck. It was showtime again.

She gave him a quick glance. His eyes scanned today's edition of *The Times*. Just before he could have become aware of her look, she turned and went back to her magazine. He gave no indication he was there to see her, but what other explanation could there be? So, she'd made an impression at the restaurant. Fine, then. If he was there to see her, then she'd wait for him to make a move.

She deliberately flipped past the Stalin interview and tried to lose herself in an article called "The Truth about The Stork Club."

The echoing voice over the Airport Tannoy announced the imminent departure of a flight to Paris. A woman and her male traveling companion, to Livy's left, stood and shuffled off to their gate. Livy pulled her legs in so the couple could get by. In that moment, the Russian made himself known.

"Pardon me, miss. Do you have the time? My watch has stopped." He might have looked like Peter Lorre, but his silky voice betrayed no accent.

Livy glanced at her mother's old watch and answered him.

He smiled and feigned a pretty disingenuous look of surprise. "Forgive my impertinence, but you seem very familiar. I feel certain we have met before."

"I hear that a lot. Maybe I have one of those faces." Livy excelled at playing hard to get. Back to *Look*.

"No, no I have an excellent memory. I'm sure I have seen you before. Perhaps—no—wait. Yes, now I remember. Of course. After the theatre the other night at The Ivy. The restaurant. You had some trouble, as I recall."

Livy couldn't blush on cue, so she lowered her chin and kept focus on the magazine. "You must be thinking of someone else. My plane leaves shortly, so if you don't mind."

"Of course, of course, my apologies." He turned away and buried his gaze in the financial section of the paper.

For a moment Livy wondered if the brush-off she'd given him had been too much. He didn't speak or look at her for what seemed like several minutes. No, if this man had been keeping tabs on her since the other night at the restaurant, it made sense that he was at least interested. She had to be ready and then make her case.

Grimov indeed bided his time. Several more minutes ticked by. Livy sweated each passing second. Then the voice came once again over the Tannoy, this time announcing the departure of the BOAC flight with a final stop in New York City. Livy closed her magazine and stood to go. Grimov jumped up beside her. His voice different now, lower, soothing.

"I am not mistaken. You are Olivia Nash, and you work for Mr. Fleming and his news service. Or at least you did until the other night, when you made such a show of your displeasure with him. But perhaps that displeasure was merely a . . . performance?"

"Followed me here to tell me that, did ya? Must not be too good at your job, comrade."

Grimov's eyes searched hers. "Then, let us assume I am wrong and that you have actually turned your back on work. And what precisely was the nature of your business with Fleming?"

Livy grinned. "Nice try, but I've no intention of betraying an oath in the middle of an airport."

"Betrayal is a strong word."

"It is. Sometimes it goes both ways."

"Is that so?" Grimov didn't look convinced, but he was listening.

"Look, I have a plane to catch. And a job to do. I'm being sent to America to write about fashion. Bloody dresses."

"This is a punishment then?"

"Maybe if I'd slept with the boss I'd be doing something worthwhile."

"You sound like a woman who has been underestimated."

"You underestimate *me*. I'm a woman who's done with that lot."

Again the voice over the Tannoy announced Livy's flight. "I believe they are calling you, Miss Nash."

Livy put a hand on Grimov's arm. She leaned in close. His scent was stifling.

"You know who I've worked for, and you know what we do. What you saw the other night had been a long time coming, you see. During the war and even now—they treat you like a servant. I don't ask much. Just want my work appreciated."

The Russian smiled. "And all I ask is to trust the people who work with me."

The noise of the departure lounge rose in pitch as others stood to make their way to the gate. The tinny voice again announced the BOAC flight's imminent departure.

Livy pulled away. "Trust is important in any relationship. Even one that might just be beginning."

She felt his hands graze the top of her coat pocket. He'd dropped a business card inside.

"If you wish to speak again once you reach your final destination," he said.

"I'll talk to one man and one man only. Yuri Kostin. Tell him it's for old-time's sake."

She turned and walked away, wondering just how that bit of theatre had played with the skeptical and over-cologned Mr. Grimov.

* * *

The whining roar of the DC-3 propeller engines diminished to a steady hum as Livy's flight settled into cruising altitude about twenty minutes after takeoff. Thoughts of her encounter with the talent spotter Grimov had left her as soon as the big plane began its rumble down the runway. Air travel had never been especially comfortable for Livy, though she'd spent the beginning of the war driving RAF pilots to their planes at Blackpool Airport. She'd even slept with one of the flyboys, but always on the ground.

Two hours into the flight, the plane bumped and shook. Livy'd been through much worse turbulence, but something about the illusion of safety on this flight caused her stomach to lurch as the plane did.

Livy smiled as she thought about how her mum might have reacted to that airborne hiccup. The furthest distance her mother had ever traveled spanned the English Channel from Calais to London. Livy reckoned that to be no more than a hundred miles. Now her mother's daughter was going to America for the first time.

She could still smell Grimov's pungent scent. If her little act in the departure lounge had gone over, then chances are word would soon filter to Kostin in Washington. Would he remember her? How would he treat the news that his former lover's frustrations had given her cause to reach out to a foreign country? No doubt he'd be skeptical. Livy knew she would have to be even more persuasive once she met Kostin again. And then what? The lingering thought nagged.

She glanced at her watch. Two hours until the stop at the airport in Shannon, and then on to Canada in the morning, and finally New York City that afternoon. Livy leaned back in her seat, closed her eyes, and tried not to think about the long journey ahead and all the intangibles of the future. It was at times like this, moments of stress, that memories of the war flooded her brain.

The war had taught her many things. Fear of flying was perhaps the most innocuous. SOE, the Special Operations Executive, which some public-school types jokingly referred to as the Ministry of Ungentlemanly Warfare, came calling in '43. Livy, finally, had found the purpose that had eluded her. The Firm—as everyone called it—recruited French speakers like Livy, assuming they would be more suited to work behind German lines in occupied France.

Parachute training was mandatory with SOE. Women from every walk of life—secretaries and farm girls—were taught to pack a 'chute, stand in the hold of a plane, and jump. No one leapt out of a plane without fear, but Livy could never get over the height. Her phobia became so great, it interfered with other aspects of the training.

Margot Dupont got her through it.

Margot and Livy slept in bunks next to each other at the training camp in Scotland. Margot's parents had moved to England from Lyon a few years before the war. Her English could best be described as a work in progress.

Livy was never one to make friends easily, but there was something about Margot—other than their shared mix of French and Anglo heritage—that drew them to each other. So many of the other girls kept airs even while learning to pick locks and to kill a man with one blow. Not Margot. She was refreshingly authentic. Many nights she made Livy laugh hard with her garbled pronunciations. Dirty jokes often kept them both chortling well past curfew. Margot had more slang words for male genitalia than even Livy had ever heard, *le cyclope* being her absolute favorite. Livy corrected Margot's English, and she in turn helped Livy perfect her own French.

Both women knew what lay ahead of them. The trainers made no bones about the dangers they faced. When the six weeks ended, they'd be flown to France on a moonlit night and dropped into occupied territory.

The bond they'd made there during training—as they learned how to jump out of planes, clean and fire a gun, and kill someone with the edge of their hands—held long after they'd separated.

As the plane, and Livy's stomach settled, her gaze landed on a woman two seats ahead. Thin with blonde hair. A cigarette dangling from a manicured hand. Her restless mind went back to Anka and her home in Greenwich, thick with paranoia and cigarette smoke. Was that to be her lot in life now? Had Fleming given her a glimpse into her own future. Well, she'd made her choice and she bloody well wasn't Anka. Livy had one job, and it wouldn't take her two years to get it done. She'd go in, find Margot, and get out.

Deciding to stop feeling sorry for herself, Livy opened her handbag and pulled out a creased paperback copy of *Hamlet*. Anka's suggestion to keep grounded with some sort of talisman had registered with Livy. She loved Shakespeare, and to her way of thinking, there was no greater story or more beautiful writing to be found in the English language. She stretched her legs under the seat in front of her and opened it somewhere around the middle. Of course, it was "To be or not to be."

> "Thus conscience does make cowards of us all;
> And thus the native hue of resolution
> Is sicklied o'er with the pale cast of thought,
> And enterprises of great pith and moment
> With this regard their currents turn awry,
> And lose the name of action."

The words resonated. Too close to her own life.

What else was she embarking upon if not an "enterprise of great pith and moment"? All this chatter from her conscience— the "pale cast of thought"—did nothing but turn her into a coward. Made her question everything, fret about the future, and therefore become much less decisive. That was her strength, she knew. How many times during the war had Livy just taken the bull by the horns? She wasn't one to sit around and let things happen to her.

The hell with the "pale cast of thought." If only Hamlet had taken a cue from Livy, God knows the play might've been an hour shorter.

Deciding she'd had enough of the melancholy Dane, Livy put her head back and listened to the soothing hum of the engines. Tomorrow she'd be in the United States for the first time in her life.

Chapter Eight

~

After a stop in New York City and then a ride on a PRR train the next morning to Union Station, Livy finally arrived in the American capital.

By the time she collected her luggage, it was well after two PM, and her stomach rumbled. As soon as her feet hit the pavement outside Union Station, a wave of American heat and humidity engulfed her. She'd just left an abnormally warm London summer, but the American version felt hotter and certainly wetter. A part of her suddenly longed for that year's brutal London winter.

Her feet had just reached the edge of the curb near a row of idling taxis when a door opened, and a tall man in a straw porkpie hat appeared beside her.

"Yer lookin' for a cab, miss?"

"Yes, um, thank you."

"Right this way. Where ya headed?"

"Statler Hotel at Sixteenth and—"

"K Street. I know where it is. Fancy, fancy." He looked at her and grinned from ear to ear. "And don't worry, you'll get used to the heat. It ain't killed nobody yet."

Minutes later Livy sat in the back of the stuffy Diamond cab, feeling as if every item of clothing she was wearing had been glued to her body. She wiped sweat from her brow and inched closer to the window to catch the breeze as the cab sped up Massachusetts Avenue. She'd hoped for a view of the city's famous scenery, but this route only afforded her a glimpse of shops and a few drab government buildings.

She marveled at how, here, life seemed to have moved backed to normal after the war. Cars filled the streets. Pedestrians hurried across intersections. The buildings were all intact. No physical reminders here.

"What brings you to Warsh-ington?" the cabbie said.

Livy hesitated before answering. She had a part to play, and even here, in this stuffy taxi, she was onstage.

"Oh, I'm just a writer, a journalist, you could say, although I'm here as support for someone else. I run around and get the details. Then the real writer does the story."

"Tell you what," the cabbie said, grinning. "For someone who's a gofer, they sure got you stayin' at a nice place."

The cabbie didn't exaggerate. The car pulled up along a sidewalk lined with perfectly trimmed green hedges. The Statler Hotel, located in the center of Washington, took up almost half a city block. The building itself looked not unlike the boxy government structures she'd passed on the way in—cold, sleek, and angular. Livy gave the cabbie thirty cents for the fare and an extra ten because she appreciated his friendly smile and walked toward the big front glass doors. The Stars and Stripes hung limp in the breezeless heat from two flagpoles on either side of the hotel entrance.

A tall, thin, redheaded woman, who looked as if sweat had never touched her body, smiled at Livy from behind a front desk that stretched almost the entire width of the lobby. Several big black phones dotted the long counter. Hundreds of mailboxes, many filled with envelopes and papers, dominated the wall behind the redhead. Livy checked in, playing the gruff, tired foreign reporter to the hilt. After she'd signed several forms, the woman behind the desk told her that a gentleman from "the office" had asked about her earlier.

"Don't even let you get checked in before they crack the whip, do they, luv?" Livy groused and took her key.

She walked across the lobby toward a line of lifts down the hall. A bit overwhelmed by the size and breadth of The Statler, she reckoned two of London's finest hotels could easily fit in this one. The American prairie: wide-open spaces and blazing heat. *Yee-haw.* Truth was, Livy always felt a bit uncomfortable in places like this. Like an imposter. But then that's exactly what she was now.

Her room was on the tenth floor. She plodded down the long, carpeted hallway, turned the corner, and found two men in gray suits, standing on either side of room 1080. Her room, of course.

"Afternoon, ma'am." The taller, thinner one spoke. Height and weight were the only distinguishing features between the two. Square heads. Buzz cuts. Same suit. Like Laurel and Hardy minus the fun.

"Can I help you?" Livy said, keeping her distance.

Laurel reached into his jacket and produced FBI identification. "We'd prefer to talk inside, if it's all the same to you."

Livy unlocked the door and led the way in. The room looked brand new. The soft gray carpet opened into an interior that spread out like a dance hall floor. A queen-sized bed, with night tables on either side, took up one wall. An oak credenza desk, on top of which lay hotel stationery and a Statler Hotel fountain pen, stood opposite. In between—nothing but space.

Laurel closed the door and nodded to Hardy.

"He needs your suitcase, ma'am."

Livy dropped it on the big bed, and Hardy opened it without a word and began to rummage through it.

Welcome to America, Livy thought.

After a thorough search that must've lasted five minutes, Hardy stuffed her clothes and things back into the case and closed it. He nodded to Laurel, who held out an envelope for Livy.

"Inside you'll find instructions from Special Agent Keller and the location of a meeting place in the District where he'll discuss things with you tomorrow. I need you to look this over and commit it to memory."

She opened the envelope and found nothing but a Georgetown address written in block letters on a white sheet of paper.

"Got it."

"I'm going to need for you to burn it while we're still here, ma'am."

"I know how it works, luv. Match?"

Hardy produced a pack of matches from his pocket. Livy touched the end of one to the edge of the paper and then let it crumble in an ashtray on the credenza.

"Very good. Enjoy your stay, ma'am," Laurel said, and without another word, the two FBI men left her alone.

Livy walked to the room door, slid the dead bolt across, and kicked off her shoes. She threw open the thick curtains and looked down on the streets of the American capital. Bright sunshine. Big cars. Everyone bouncing along the concrete sidewalks. She craned her head to the right and caught a glimpse of Lafayette Square. Further on would be the White House itself.

Here she was, deep in the heart of the US of A. The welcoming committee had been less than welcoming. Now all she had to do was cozy up to a Soviet killer and save a young woman she'd not seen in almost four years. The whole thing seemed impossible.

How much was Livy risking on a prayer that Margot might still be alive? And if she were, what would her life be like? More than two years a prisoner. If she was being held in the Soviet sector of Germany, Margot stood a solid chance of never getting out. Tensions were high enough on both sides right now.

She could be lost forever.

The thought made Livy flush. Sweat creased her forehead. *This place is a bloody sauna.* She looked down. Her knees bumped against a steel box built into the window. A vent protruded from one end alongside two knobs. Air-conditioning. The cabbie had mentioned it.

"Only hotel in Washington that can keep you cool when it's this hot," he'd said.

Livy twirled the knobs, and the box began to whir. A few seconds later, cool air poured from the vent and rushed up her body, hitting her face. The air soothed every sweaty pore like a long bath after a hard day's work. She lifted her face and arms and let the coolness take her.

Two years a prisoner.

And here I am, she thought. *Soaking in the cool air in this posh room because my clothes feel a little sticky.*

Livy switched off the air conditioner and threw herself on the bed. Tomorrow couldn't come quickly enough.

Chapter Nine

She slept fitfully, woke up early, and was dressed and ready before seven. To Livy it felt much more like noon.

Precisely at eight she placed a call to the chief Washington correspondent for Kemsley News. He was a man called Wilson Price, with a whiny sort of New England accent.

"Mr. Fleming sent me over to be your stringer."

"Oh yes, got a thing about that in the post the other day. Well, I don't really need anyone—"

"I'll do some background for you. Bit here and there on Mrs. Truman. That's what they sent me for. Woman's touch."

"Well, sure, um, I suppose that could be—"

"Let me know what you need. You have the number? Right, then." *Click.*

The whiny Mr. Price sounded taken aback by the brashness of his subordinate. And a woman at that.

* * *

Her meeting with Special Agent Keller had been scheduled for eleven. The address she'd committed to memory led her to a small brownstone off the beaten path in Washington's fashionable

Georgetown neighborhood. After another taxi ride, this time with a much less entertaining cabbie, Livy found herself outside a nondescript little walk-up that wouldn't have looked out of place in Camden Town. For the first time since she'd arrived in America, after all the air-conditioning and the wide-open spaces, the comfort of the brick-and-mortar building made her feel a bit less alien.

Livy walked around the block again to make certain that Grimov hadn't had her tailed since her arrival in America. As she passed the walk-up's drab facade, she remembered something Anka had told her. This would be backstage for her during the assignment. Her sanctuary.

Satisfied she hadn't been followed, Livy got a closer look at the safe house. A grimy brick stoop led to a brown door flanked by two square windows. The white paint around the entranceway was chipped. Inside it looked dark and gloomy. Honestly, as havens went, it was lacking.

The door of the safe house suddenly opened. A man in his thirties, with short sandy hair and wearing a rumpled gray suit, stood on the other side.

"Can I help you?" His voice sounded tired, with a hint of a Southern accent.

"The Kemsley News Service sent me," she said. He gave no sign of recognition. "Get it fast, but get it right," Livy added.

The man held the door open and let her in.

* * *

The man with sandy hair turned out to be nothing more than the warm-up act. He knew the code phrase and little else. The house itself looked as if it might have been the home of a recently deceased widow, judging by the amount of knickknacks cluttering various shelves and sideboards. Worn blankets had been left on armchairs in the front room. Livy even noticed a few spill stains on the Turkish rug. Perhaps the FBI bought the place at auction and kept the decor as it was in case anyone peeked in off the street.

The man, who didn't give his name, made her a weak cup of coffee and stood around making awkward small talk. After recounting, in detail, the experience of her flight, as well as describing the opulence of the Statler Hotel, Livy's patience ended.

"Is there something we're waiting for, exactly?"

He almost blushed. "Oh, yeah, Mr. Keller got held up at the office. He just said he'd be a little late."

"Held up?"

"I should've—gosh—yeah, he'll be here very soon—just any—um—did you want another cup of coffee there?"

* * *

An hour and a half later, and two more cups of what passed for coffee, the back door opened and another man swept into the front room, where Livy waited with her minder. He was about the same age as the fair-haired man, but that's where the similarities ended.

He was a big man, tall and broad-shouldered, with a slight paunch that pushed at his belt buckle. His blue eyes and strong jawline gave him the sort of face that could only be American. He reminded Livy of someone who might play the sheriff in one of those cowboy B movies.

"You can go now, Hunter," the newcomer grunted, barely looking up from the files he cradled in his arms.

The minder stood, nodded at Livy, and headed out the back. The other man didn't speak. He thumbed through the papers in the file on top of his stack, eyes roaming sentences. He didn't look up, even when he said, "You're Miss Nash?"

"I am."

Thumbing through more pages, he glanced at his watch, an old, no-frills timepiece with a scratched face and frayed leather strap. A far cry from Fleming's immaculate Rolex. Livy wondered if the newcomer's watch was set five minutes fast. He seemed like the type. He'd had a long day already, judging by the heavy circles under his eyes. Tie undone. Shirt collar twisted. Coffee stain on his lapel. Cuff unbuttoned on his left sleeve. Wedding ring. Baby at home, maybe? Up all night with the squalling?

Finally, he looked up and took her in for the first time. He studied her. He sniffed, dropped the files on a side table, and plopped down into the armchair across from her.

He picked up the minder's used mug. "Coffee any good?"

"Not a bit," Livy said.

"That's a problem." He crossed his long legs and held Livy's gaze for an uncomfortable amount of time. Then: "I'm Keller. Did he—Hunter—tell you? No. 'Course not. Anyway, Sam Keller. I'm running this one, and about a hundred other operations. So . . ."

Keller looked back at the stack of files. Livy shifted on the sofa.

". . . that's the file from your Ministry of Defence. I have to be honest with you, Miss Nash, your reason for being here is strictly off the radar. About as unofficial as it gets. We don't—well, my bosses at the Bureau—think this is pretty much a wild-goose chase."

"I know that, Mr. Keller. But that wireless signal was verified, and the call sign is the same one used by—"

Keller put up his hands. "Wait, wait. I think we have a misunderstanding. Our stake in this thing really isn't about that. It's Kostin. Both of our countries have their hands full with Berlin right now, and trying to make sure the Soviets don't launch an invasion of Europe tomorrow. Yuri Kostin is set to be the next *rezident* at their Berlin station. He's one of their top people. If we can get rid of him before he takes over in Berlin, then that gives us and your people a helluva strategic advantage."

The waiting, the bad coffee, and the time change combined to make Livy's temples ache. She could feel something worse building behind her eyes.

"Maybe you should make it clear what it is you're expecting from me," she said.

"I want the bastard completely discredited. I want him shipped back to Moscow in disgrace."

Livy put her cup down and rubbed her forehead. She'd left London thinking she only needed a lead from Kostin about where Margot could possibly be, what prison in the Soviet sector of Germany might house a British POW. Now it felt like she had to climb Mount Everest to rescue a snowbird. She took a breath and crossed her legs. The American's expression hadn't changed.

"You think that's possible, do you Mr. Keller?" Livy asked, trying to keep the Lancashire sass out of her voice. "You just said he's one of their best."

"Damn right, he is. Kostin's a highly decorated MGB officer. Frankly, I thought it was ridiculous to send someone like you, whose greatest achievement in the field of intelligence can best be described as enthusiastic amateurism, to take on a hot shot like Kostin. But those are the cards I've been dealt, apparently."

Livy had, of course, heard it all before. *SOE: Churchill's amateurs.* She couldn't hold back.

"Some of us *enthusiastic amateurs* helped win the war. A number of us died trying."

Keller sighed. "Fair point. Look, I don't question your commitment. But this is a whole other ball game."

All during the meeting, Livy wondered why this was feeling so familiar to her. Finally, it made sense. The way Keller looked at her reminded her of the way her Irish uncle, her father's brother, regarded Christmas presents from the family. Always too big or the wrong color, and just not at all what he wanted.

Keller flipped through the stack of files and handed one to Livy. She opened it. Clipped to the top was a business card with a phone number for a beauty salon in Fairfax, Virginia. "You can call this number anytime. It goes straight to an operator who'll get the message to me."

"Does that come with a free permanent?"

Keller's eyes twitched, but his expression remained glum. Distant.

"You'll also find a ticket to the National Theatre tomorrow night. The Russian delegation has been invited as well as the staffs of a few other embassies. That means Kostin will be there—and so will you."

Livy reached into her skirt pocket and produced the plain card Grimov had given her back in the airport. "Their man in London gave me this. Told me to call if I wanted to speak further."

Keller glanced at the card, crumpled it in his hand, and threw it on the coffee table.

"I don't know who might answer that number, but it sure as hell won't be Yuri Kostin. We don't have that kind of time to slowly work you into their system."

Livy almost smiled. Finally they agreed on something,

"Typically, in situations like this, the contact makes himself available to the target first. Offers them something. Then, if the bait is taken, there's a testing phase where the other side will basically make sure you are what you say you are. That's a pretty damn tenuous time, as you can probably guess." Keller spoke quickly, the words coming out by rote, as if he didn't believe them or think they would do any good.

"During that stage—the testing—you'll need to win over his confidence. If, by some chance, you can make Kostin trust you, then—who knows?"

Livy cleared her throat. "You don't sound especially confident in this operation, Mr. Keller."

The American leaned forward, smiling. He really wasn't a bad-looking sort. Nice hair, good eyes. But right now he looked like he was about to explain nuclear physics to a child. Livy wanted to slap him.

"Kostin is a good target. He had a hard war. Every Russian did. He was a solid intelligence officer before, but the Eastern Front turned him into an animal. Now Stalin is talking tough again, so a career officer like Kostin might be a little war weary after what he's been through. He's older. He's comfortable here now. He likes the food, the bars." Keller looked over his folder again, then up at Livy.

"You slept with him in London, right?"

She'd expected the question, but the bluntness of the delivery still surprised her. Her gaze hardened. "Correct."

"I see. Well, Kostin can't get enough of British culture—and women. And those weaknesses are the only reasons you're sitting in this room, Miss Nash."

Livy sat up, smoothed her skirt, and smiled at Keller. Her head ached, her stomach churned, and deep down she wondered if she was in way over her head. But she'd never let this Yank see that.

"So, what's the play then?"

Chapter Ten

～

The play was, much to Livy's chagrin, the musical *Oklahoma*. The night of the performance felt a bit less muggy and sticky. By showtime, temperatures had cooled to almost sixty degrees. She'd packed a tailored black pencil dress, which fit the bill for a swanky theatre performance three blocks from the White House but didn't provide much relief for a sweaty Brit getting acclimated to a humid American summer. Perspiration would not attract a Russian major who looked like a movie star.

Livy arrived by cab half an hour before curtain. The driver got as close as he could but had to settle for dropping her off about a quarter mile from the front door, behind a long line of limousines. She gave the cabbie an extra dime and started shuffling toward the front. Livy hated heels. Even worse was the feeling that she was showing a bit more hip sway in this tight dress as she hurried to get inside the theatre. She hoped to spot Kostin before the lights went down.

She passed the line of cars. Men in double-breasted tuxes opened doors for women whose perfectly coiffed hair and made-up faces must have taken them the better part of the afternoon. The men, most of whom had deep foreheads, with very little hair to show for their years of service to their country, seemed more interested in glad-handing the other men than escorting their wives to the theatre.

A few threw looks Livy's way. She ignored them. The big fish waited.

By ten minutes after eight, Livy found herself inside the lobby, being politely jostled by the elite of Washington, DC. When she was a kid, her parents' idea of a holiday often meant seeking out the best theatres of England and Ireland in order for their only daughter to get a "cultural education." She'd seen Gielgud at the Old Vic, and plays by Synge and O'Casey at the Abbey in Dublin. How she'd loved those, along with the raucous pleasures of the Christmas and Easter pantos in Blackpool.

So while the plain gray facade of the National Theatre didn't have much to recommend it, other than a glittering marquee that lit up the rather dark streets of the capital, the lobby promised an evening of glamor and splendor. Two glittering chandeliers hung over the heads of the wealthy and powerful as they stepped up to the will-call booths. A smiling blonde at the coat check took a few shawls from well-dressed women who'd ignored the heat, in the name of fashion. Across the way, a lithe redhead, costumed in a frilly skirt and Annie Oakley straw hat, filled glasses of champagne faster than you could say, "Give 'em hell, Harry." No doubt the bubbly was provided to make the night feel celebratory, but Livy thought moonshine might be more appropriate.

She handed her ticket to a red-coated usher and stepped down into the orchestra seats. Livy still hadn't spotted Kostin, much less a Russian contingent. Frankly, she worried they wouldn't show. Before coming to the theatre, she'd read an article in the morning's *Washington Post* about a former Soviet official breaking ranks with the Party to tell the U.S. Congress that Soviet diplomats were really spies and that Stalin wanted anything but peace with the rest of the world. Livy knew that sort of thing could easily derail "feel-good" diplomatic events such as this.

She made her way down to row M, taking in the ornate carvings of the balcony rails and the deep red curtains that separated the guest boxes from the rest of the theatre. Livy took a program from the usher, scooted over the legs of two chattering ladies with coiffed blue hair, and settled into her seat. Follow spots danced across the plush main drape onstage as the last few empty seats filled. For two hours, the campaigning and handshaking would come to a mandatory halt.

Livy twisted and turned, as if looking for a date running late. How hard could it be to find a good-looking Russian in a crowd composed mostly of old white men and their overdressed wives? Livy figured an important man like Kostin wouldn't be stuck up in the last row of the balcony. He'd want to be seen.

The crowd began to quiet as the house lights dimmed. She checked her watch. 8:20. Would the Russians be fashionably late? A gnawing dread crept into Livy's practiced cool. She could try to find him at the interval, but a foreign dignitary just might use that time to retreat, especially if he'd just been called out as a spy on the front page of the newspaper.

She pushed the hair out of her face and tried to take a deep breath in the damned tight dress. First day out of the gate, and she worried the job was already a cock-up. Livy could imagine the look on Keller's face when she told him she not only didn't make contact with Kostin but didn't so much as lay eyes on him.

The aisle lights glowed bright as the house went dark. The orchestra began with a burst of sweeping energy, moving from one peppy song to another. After about five minutes, the main drape began to open, revealing a colorful, almost cartoonish American farm with a woman happily churning butter. From upstage a tall cowboy with a bright smile wandered onstage, singing the show's first big hit, "O What a Beautiful Morning." The audience broke into polite applause.

Livy's heart hammered. She craned her neck, scanning the audience as the score vibrated through the theatre, and spotted him in profile as Kostin turned and looked down the aisle.

Two rows ahead and three seats over. He was right there.

Livy recognized the distinctive shape of his V-shaped face as well as the gray-black hair swept back above his ears. Kostin stared at a big man in an ill-fitting gray suit, awkwardly shuffling down the row until he finally found his seat. The Russian sniffed and returned his attention to the stage.

An older woman with her son sat to Kostin's left, and a young man, twenty perhaps, on the right. Kostin seemed to be alone. *Odd that. Why would he be alone?*

She liked the idea of being able to watch the Russian without his knowledge. The line of his neck, the cut of his suit, the way he shifted in his seat. Livy was surprised how familiar even such small things seemed to her after two years.

Eventually Livy turned her focus to the play. She'd never taken to musicals. Too artificial. But soon the colors of the set and the charm of the leading actors grabbed her as they had the rest of the audience. Maybe there was something about the event itself. Watching a very American play perpetuating America's own mythology in the American capital.

With a contingent of Russians.

Livy's gaze returned to Kostin. From behind, he seemed engrossed in the show. His stillness held her attention. The fearsome Soviet agent with a big heart. Captivated by the romance of cowboys. She'd keep an eye on him in case he had to wipe a tear away.

Oh, this business has made me cynical.

After nearly three hours, the country charm had worn off, and Livy's nerves jangled as she watched Kostin. At the interval, he kept his seat and read the program, leaving Livy no opportunity to approach him.

Onstage, the cast harmonized the final number, and then came the bows. The applause was enthusiastic from the American side and a bit tepid from the foreign dignitaries. But eventually, as they always do, the audience rose to its feet.

Kostin stood as well, applauding deliberately, but as the clapping began to fade, he quickly pushed his way toward the end of his aisle.

This was her chance. She excused herself, slipping past the elderly women on her left. Kostin had reached the aisle, seeming in more than a bit of a hurry. Livy told herself to stay calm. A single woman couldn't exactly flee a theatre without attracting attention. The Russian would have to linger in the lobby for Livy to have any hope of making contact.

The crowd, still under the spell of Rodgers and Hammerstein, was slow to leave. Kostin, up ahead, moving quicker, was almost at the exit.

Livy found herself in a tangle of black jackets and sequined dresses. Clumps of politicos with plastered smiles, turning to shake hands, blocked her path. Then, ten feet from the house left exit, an opening. A clear view of everyone near the door marching obediently. But no Kostin. Brushing past a big man in a too-large gray suit without a word, Livy found herself in the lobby scanning the backs of heads. The square shoulders and black-silver hair she'd spent much of the play watching was gone.

For the second time in one night, just at the moment of despair, she spotted him. Yuri Kostin stood chatting with the Annie Oakley redhead who dished out free champagne.

Now, the approach. The big entrance of Livy Nash of the Kemsley News Service, soon to be traitor to His Majesty's Government. The rest had all been rehearsal.

Chapter Eleven

～

"Don't mind if I do."

Livy whisked the last flute of champagne off the redhead's tray and surveyed the meager contents. She shot the bubbly girl a look and—giving it the full Lancashire twang—said, "Couldn't trade this for a bit of gin, could I, luv?"

Kostin, who had been turned to face the exiting crowd, pivoted at the sound of her voice.

She took a second glass of champagne and remembered some theatrical advice her father used to repeat whenever he drank whiskey.

"Livy, if you're going to make an entrance, then for God's sake, make a bloody entrance."

Kostin made eye contact. He was better looking than she remembered. Eyes slightly hooded and sleepy, which hid his intensity and intellect. His suit was immaculate, the lines accentuated his shoulders and tapered waist. But his age showed a bit tonight. He looked tired.

Livy giggled. "The Yanks lay it on a bit thick, don't they?"

"I suppose," he said. Her accent had grabbed his attention, but he seemed distracted. *Change tactics then.*

"The way I see it, Jud wasn't so bad. And he was a much better dancer than the cowboy."

Livy thought she saw a hint of recognition in his blue-gray eyes. Drink had been a constant companion of their fling, but still, how could he not remember her? There had been intensity to their affair. It had burned for a month and then died. But what a month it had been.

"If you can call that . . . dancing." His accent was subtle enough that he didn't stick out.

Kostin turned, put down his champagne flute, and slid his hands in the pockets of his jacket. He looked everywhere except at her. Nodding to someone across the room. Glancing at his watch. Then another tall, gray-haired man in a brown serviceable suit brushed past him, murmuring something only Kostin could hear. The Russian turned quickly and, with the doors mere feet away, he was gone into the night. Lost among a sea of limousines and taxis, without even a final glance at Livy.

* * *

Blending into the mass of the well-dressed exiting the National Theatre, Livy tried to fend off the sense of failure by replaying her brief chat with Kostin. She went over every gesture, every wrinkle of his brow. Had he recognized her? It had been two years since they'd first met. Of course she'd changed since then, but what could have prevented him from remembering her? The Yuri Kostin she'd known would have been thrilled to see her.

The luxury all around her had forced Livy to consider Margot. Where was she tonight? What sort of hell had she been through just to stay alive? The world had celebrated the end of the war while Margot likely moved from one prison to another.

Livy felt the urgency of her job. *You'll have to do better than tonight,* she said to herself.

She stopped on the sidewalk, away from the crowd, and looked for a taxi. Four cars down, a Diamond cab waited, its yellow light blinking behind the row of limousines. Livy put up her hand.

Ten steps ahead of her, the passenger door of one of the limousines opened. She stepped around the car, pushing toward the taxi. A voice stopped her.

"You look like someone who needs a ride."

She looked into the open door. Kostin reclined in the leather back seat, a broad smile across his V-shaped face.

"I did not recognize you at first. My mind was . . . bothered. You must forgive me, Livy." It came out "Lee-vye" when he said it. The pronunciation stirred in her several sensations. Some sweet, others more than a little bitter.

"I can take you wherever you like."

Livy pushed the thoughts of Margot away. She tried a smile like Rita Hayworth's in *Gilda.* Charmed and slightly carnal.

"You always were a gentleman, comrade," she said and eased into the big black car.

Livy kept her distance from the Russian, which wasn't difficult since the rear seat of the Cadillac felt as spacious as her hotel room. Wood paneling on the doors and even a carpeted footrest in the floorboard. Yuri was a communist with style.

"Where am I taking you?" he asked.

"My hotel. Of course," Livy said, grinning. "The Statler."

Kostin smiled. "Not far from our embassy. Convenient." He spoke to the driver in Russian. The big car eased into the line leaving the theatre.

"It will take us forever to work through this traffic. We don't have such problems in Moscow."

"That's because no one has a car in Moscow," Livy said. "Certainly not a Cadillac. What would Uncle Joe say about his boys driving around in a posh car like this?"

Kostin looked like a different man now than before. Here, in the car, Livy thought he seemed more relaxed than in the lobby of the theatre.

"I am sorry for my behavior earlier. My delegation can be a bit exhausting."

"The Yuri Kostin I knew would never have treated a lady like that."

"It has been two years. We all change. Even you have changed in a way."

Livy feigned mock hurt. "I'm an old hag now, Yuri, I know. No need to rub it in."

His wide mouth stretched back to reveal maybe the cleanest, whitest teeth she'd ever seen on a Russian. That smile would probably make a lot of girls weak in the knees. She'd been one of them once.

"No, no, Livy. You are beautiful. Always. So authentic."

"Authentic? That the best you can do?"

He laughed, long, relaxed, easy. "I mean that you seem—I don't know—maybe wiser, more settled now." He glanced down at her hand. "Still not married, I see. Hmm, and yet you seem like a woman who knows what she wants."

"Well, when we you met me, I was a mess. So, yeah, I imagine I've done a bit of growing up since then."

The car turned down a side street, leaving the traffic behind. Now, the awkwardness settled in between them. Neither knew what to say. The Cadillac's engine hummed.

"You are working in America now?"

"Just for a few weeks. I'm with a newspaper service."

"Ah, a foreign correspondent." He made it sound mysterious and romantic.

"Nothing but an assistant, really. They give the big jobs to the boys."

"And that is why you are so dissatisfied with your work?"

Once again she wished she'd worn something that would allow her to breathe. She could use a bit more air at this moment, because it felt very much like her message to Grimov might have gotten through.

"It's not just the work."

"Of course not. The reasons people turn their back on the familiar are always complex."

"Is that what Grimov told you?" Livy's directness was a risk. She held his gaze. No smiles. He searched her eyes for a long moment. Then his left hand, suntanned below the cuff of the pressed white shirt, reached out to hers. The gesture felt at once intimate and restrictive.

"Livy, I am thinking what a—what is the word?—a coincidence, yes? What a coincidence that we meet again in such a way. Don't you find that odd?"

Streetlights flickered across his face. He looked even more wolfish than she'd remembered. The moment demanded caution. But she'd never been the cautious type.

"That's because it's not a coincidence at all."

"Ah yes," he said. His eyes flashed. Curious. "This Grimov you speak of. Maybe I know someone with that name. It is not uncommon in Russia. But how did you know I would be at the theatre tonight?"

"The people I work for know how to find boys like you."

Kostin tilted his head. He opened his mouth, about to speak, then reconsidered. His eyes bored into hers. The gap between them narrowed. Time and space seemed to compress as he leaned toward her.

"Who?" The word came out almost whispered.

Livy shifted her eyes in the direction of the driver.

"Him?" Kostin said. "No English. So . . . tell me."

"Now, Yuri, you're a smart one. You know what foreign journalists are up to these days. It is, after all, the world's second oldest profession."

Kostin pondered her face like a carnival mind reader desperate for a clue. The silence lingered, but Livy could tell her admission had pulled him in.

"There are always too many secrets between old lovers. So, I ask myself, why are you sitting in the back of my car telling me all this now?"

"Can't figure it out?" She gave him a sexy grin, whatever the hell that was. But it usually worked.

He leaned in close enough she could smell his cologne—probably French—and make out the design of his gold watch—utilitarian Soviet.

"There are so few women a man can truly understand."

"Let me spell it out for you then." Livy leaned closer. "I have something you want."

He glanced at her mouth. Their faces inches apart.

"The same old Livy. Always to the point. So? What do I want?

"Information, Major. I'd say anyone who could fill in the gaps on the Allies designs on Berlin is at least worth a drink. Maybe even two."

The moment deflated slightly. Kostin looked down. The watch again. "If you have something, you can bring it to my embassy."

Livy reached out, touched his lapel with the tips of her fingers. Closer now. She spoke quietly, eyes on his. "I need to make sure it gets into the right hands. I could be—very vulnerable. Look, Yuri, I'm done with them," she said. Her body arched toward his. "Done with all of it. I'm tired. Just so tired."

She knew when a man wanted to kiss her, and Yuri Kostin seemed to be practicing remarkable self-control. But then he would.

He removed her hand, gently, from his jacket. The air in the car changed. Kostin checked his watch again. Livy played the moment. A desperate young woman about to do something unthinkable. She stared at him, her breath quickening. He wouldn't return her gaze.

Finally, he spoke. "You know Ford's Theatre?"

"I can find it."

"President Lincoln was shot there."

The car began to slow. Yuri said something else to the driver and pointed off to the right.

"Tomorrow afternoon at three. Bring what you have. Wrap it in the front section of the *Washington Post*. There's a bench in front of the entrance."

"That's less than twenty-four hours. I don't know what I can get for you by then."

"Then, I wish you luck during your stay in Washington."

The Cadillac eased up to the curb and Livy saw the brightly lit exterior of The Statler. Livy reached for the door handle.

"You'll be there at three? Tomorrow?" She hoped her eyes looked pleading.

Kostin didn't even look at her. "You'll forgive me for not seeing you to the door, of course." He barked something in Russian at the driver, who hopped out of the car and came around to Livy's side. By the time he arrived, she'd stepped on the curb.

The driver gave a curt nod and made his way back around and into the car before it peeled off into the night. Livy wondered if this mission was over before it had even started.

Chapter Twelve

"What the hell is his game?" Sam Keller looked like he'd spent another sleepless evening when he met Livy at the Georgetown safe house the next morning.

After Kostin dropped her at The Statler, Livy had checked her messages with the front desk. Price, the Kemsley reporter, needed to speak to her pronto. In her air-conditioned room, she put in a call to the Fairfax Beauty Salon before going to bed. The line rang and rang. No answering service. The lack of a response showed Livy exactly how much priority the Americans had given this particular job.

Despite the comfortable mattress, which enveloped her body like angel wings, Livy had trouble sleeping. But the light breeze from her open window kept her cool all night long.

By eight thirty AM, the number in Fairfax picked up. It took another hour and a half for Keller to meet her. He seemed his normal helpful self.

"I'll bet that kid didn't make the coffee either." His voice rose when he was angry and he sounded a bit like Joel McCrea in one of those screwball comedies.

Livy allowed the American to storm around the house for a few minutes, throwing open kitchen cabinets, and tossing coffee grounds all over the counter in a blustery attempt to satisfy his need for caffeine. By the time he'd finished, Keller seemed a bit more relaxed. The corners of his mouth evened out. His eyes opened a bit above the dark circles.

He poured two cups and placed them on the scarred wooden table in front of the sofa where Livy sat. The coffee looked like mud. She decided to pass.

"Tell me how he behaved toward you. What did you notice?" Keller said, taking a long sip from a chipped white cup.

"First, he didn't seem to know me. But he was surrounded by his people, so that might explain it. Later, he did. He was relaxed, at first, but then looked like something was bothering him. He was distracted. Maybe he was expected somewhere else. I don't know."

"Did he make a pass at you?"

Livy hated the detached way Keller asked about such things. Like he was asking about the score at a baseball game. Maybe that was for the best. She could already feel the pull of the job on her.

"Not at first, no. But I pressed him. We got closer. I thought he was going to kiss me, but he pulled away. That's when he gave me the ultimatum."

Keller downed the last of the coffee. "What did you offer him?"

"I told him I had information. That I was tired of it all. Vulnerable. That bit, you know."

"Gotcha. So, he's not buying it." Keller rubbed his eyes, looking like a man who'd almost reached a breaking point. "A man like Yuri Kostin would take one look at you and know this was a setup. The Reds play the double game better than anyone."

Livy crossed her legs and looked away from the taciturn FBI man. Everything she said he disputed. It was as if her job was to woo both men, Russian and American. No, Livy'd be damned if she was going to kowtow to this one.

"And yet he's giving me a chance, isn't he?"

"Look, we can't possibly come up with something by—what time did you say? Three o'clock? Today?"

Livy leaned in to press her point. "Look at it from his angle. Assuming Grimov got word to him, he sees me as a woman fed up with it all, bitter with my own country for shoving me to the back of the line after the war. In that scenario, if I knew a man like Yuri Kostin, wouldn't I go out of my way to find him? He's an experienced agent, yes, but he's also a man, Mr. Keller. He has an ego. A part of him wants to believe that, after all these years, I've come running back to him. And that I'd throw myself at him and give the Union Jack the "up yours" to be with him."

Keller's expression remained sour. "Look, there is just too much at stake right now for both sides. Tensions are high here and in Germany. The Soviets see the Marshall Plan as a provocation. This could all blow up in our faces. We need Kostin to come over. And, don't take this the wrong way, but you're not exactly Rita Hayworth."

"So what part of that should I not take the wrong way?"

The remark seemed to disarm Keller's bluster. For a second, Livy believed he might laugh. Instead, one side of his mouth curled. Livy thought she saw something behind his brief grin.

The sleep-deprived Mr. Keller was also a man with an ego. Right now, he stood in her way.

So, she smiled in return and said, "Thanks for the coffee, by the way."

"It's shit."

"And now it's lukewarm shit."

Keller walked to the window. It was so quiet outside it felt as if they could be in the country and not in the heart of the capital of the United States. Keller pulled the lace curtains closed.

"I'll see what I can get for you."

"It needs to whet his appetite. Make him want more."

"Like I said, I'll see what I can get."

*   *   *

By 2:50 that afternoon, Livy arrived by cab on Ninth Street NW, the block behind Ford's Theatre. The Diamond cab had all its windows open as the sun blazed down on the roof of the car.

No wonder Americans are so aggressive, she thought. *Who wouldn't be in this heat?*

She paid the cab fare and walked south on Ninth. She carried a copy of the morning's *Post* under her left arm. Two mimeographed sheets had been carefully placed between the pages of the sports section. The papers were copies of a telex sent from the Pentagon to MI6, outlining notes from the Conference of European Economic Cooperation held last month in Paris.

Keller said the information had been altered, but called it "legitimate enough" to be believable. When she left the safe house, he'd wished her good luck, but she could tell he had little hope for the outcome. Livy even wondered whether Kostin would come at all.

Livy turned right on E Street, heading west. Despite the heat, a crowd of suited men and women in dresses surged past her.

Another right and she was on Tenth. The theatre would be just ahead. She passed the Potomac Electric Power Company. Beyond it, festooned with American flags, stood a building that had the distinct look of another time. Its facade was brick. Not the deep red of most, but more a dark pink.

Everyone else walked past the building without a second glance, but Livy was taken by the moment and the place. She wondered if Kostin had chosen this spot for some sort of symbolic purpose? Everyone in the world knew the story of Lincoln's assassination. Murdered by an actor, a rebel, as he sat watching a play. Is that what Kostin had in mind when he chose this spot? The beginning of another rebellion against a perceived tyrant?

God, get it together, she told herself. *It's all an act. A performance. It's even in front of a bloody theatre for that matter.* Yet, here she was, about to pass intelligence to a Soviet agent.

The front of the theatre loomed. Livy wiped sweat from her brow and knew this was more just than the Washington humidity. Everything about this moment felt wrong. A voice inside her screamed, *You can't possibly pull this off.*

She stopped in the middle of the sidewalk. Closed her eyes. And breathed. Just for a moment. And in that instance, she pictured Margot—her mischievous smile and big laugh. She tried to remember one of her friend's bad jokes. "You know why Belgians don't have ice cubes? They lost the recipe." She'd hooted at that one. Then, Livy opened her eyes, and her steps felt more purposeful and determined.

Up ahead—just beyond the theatre entrance—a flashing neon sign read "J.C. Harding Electrical." There, across from the glass door, an ordinary wooden bench was bolted to the ground beside a blue metal trashcan. The bench was empty.

Livy glanced at her watch: 2:55. The paper under her arm felt moist. She took it out and held it tight in her hand. The role of double agent hung heavy on her shoulders as she edged closer to the bench. Ten feet away, she stumbled. Trouble with the heel of her right shoe. She feigned a slight limp, as if a pebble had worked its way into her heel.

A young man in khakis and a straw hat stopped and turned toward her.

"You okay there, miss?"

"Just a rock in my shoe. I'll be fine in a moment. Thank you."

He tipped his hat and bounced off down the sidewalk.

Dammit! The last thing you want during a live drop is to be noticed. The cheeky little boy might have done just enough to throw Kostin off. Livy kept her head down as she searched through the lining to find the imaginary rock. She placed the newspaper on the bench beside her. If she was being watched, she wanted to let him know she'd come prepared.

As she fussed with her shoe, she glanced at the time. Past three now. She couldn't sit here forever.

Livy decided to give it two minutes. No more. Then what? Wait for Yuri to contact her? Go back to Keller and ask for more time? In a day or two, the intelligence he'd given her might be old news.

Livy slipped the shoe back on, brushed her hair aside, and unsnapped her handbag. She'd check her lipstick once. Maybe even reapply it before giving up.

The double doors of Ford's Theatre opened at once. A wave of young people, all dressed in black, poured out onto the sidewalk. They chatted excitedly. Most of them appeared to be in their twenties. Some looked younger. The women wore black dresses, and the men were in black tie. They all carried cases under their arms, over the shoulder, or at their sides.

An orchestra.

The young people split almost equally, some heading north and others south. A young woman with jet-black hair stopped near the bench, chatting with a tall man, who seemed older and carried a large cello case. After a moment, the man left, and the young woman looked at her watch and turned to Livy.

"Do you mind?" she said.

Livy looked up. "Not at all." She scooted over as the young woman sat down. She placed her violin case on top of Livy's newspaper. She opened the case, took out a pack of Lucky Strikes and a book of matches, and lit one of the cigarettes.

She offered the pack to Livy, who declined.

The young woman was striking. Her lustrous hair looked thick and dark in the sunlight. She had high cheekbones and a firm chin below perfectly shaped lips. Livy thought she looked more like a ballerina than a violinist.

Lipstick in hand, Livy reapplied slowly. She feared the moment had passed. The intrusion of the boy and then the smoke break taken by the gorgeous violinist would have been more than enough for Kostin to call it off. Closing the lipstick, she stashed it in her purse.

The violinist put out her half-smoked cigarette with her shoe.

"Hot day," she said.

"Hmm."

Livy snapped the handbag shut.

The young woman dropped the Lucky Strikes back in her case. Livy's copy of the *Post* now lay on top of the violin, inside the case. She latched the case shut.

"He'll be in touch," the young woman said. She took her case and stalked away.

Livy stood, trying to keep her breathing under control. She watched the young violinist stalk confidently away. The moment swept over Livy. Kostin had followed through.

Now, the waiting began.

*   *   *

Back at her hotel, Livy left a message with the Fairfax Beauty Salon that her friend had been quite pleased with that afternoon's appointment. She wondered what the ever-doubtful Mr. Keller's reaction might be when he heard the news. Now, she just had to hope Kostin came back for more. The woman's parting words couldn't have been clearer. *"He'll be in touch."*

After a late lunch in the hotel restaurant, she hurried back to her room because she'd forgotten to ring Price, Kemsley's man in Washington. He picked up on the second ring as if waiting for the call.

"Miss—what was it again?—That's right, Nash. Now listen, I need you to do a bit of fact finding for me."

Livy pulled a Statler Hotel monogrammed notepad from the bedside table and doodled as he spoke. His nasal whine grated on her nerves.

"The thing is, Mrs. Truman is a very different sort of first lady than our last one. She basically shuns the press, but women here are interested in what she has to say, especially with next year being an election year. I mean, of course, girls are concerned with which man can keep the peace and create jobs, but they want to know more about the First Lady, too. You know that old saying: 'Clothes make the man.' Well, why don't we turn it on its ear and size her up by looking at Mrs. Truman's fashion sense? I mean she certainly wasn't born yesterday exactly, but . . ."

Livy threw in the occasional "mm-hm" and drew concentric circles on the notepad until Price got to the point. He wanted a thumbnail of Bess Truman's contribution to American fashion. He'd set up an interview tomorrow for Livy with a prominent design expert in the city.

"Make sure you get her bonafides. Can you make it at two? That's swell."

And so on and so on.

She wrote down the address, the time, and *Get her bonafides*.

Livy ordered room service and read the *Post* while trying to finish one of the largest turkey sandwiches she'd ever seen. She ended the night with a glass of milk and was in bed before ten. Thoughts of Yuri Kostin having a knife fight with Curly from *Oklahoma*, Margot in prison, and her own two weeks in a Gestapo jail fought for space in her head until she finally succumbed to sleep.

Sometime later, she woke up. Light spilled through the bedroom door from the living room. She didn't remember leaving that light on. Before she could glance at the clock to check the time, something at the foot of her bed moved. It stood.

A man.

Chapter Thirteen

Livy bolted upright, her heart hammering.

Yuri Kostin walked along her bedside and turned on the lamp. Livy shielded her eyes from the brightness. The first thing she saw when they reopened was a pistol dangling from the Russian's right hand. The bedside lamp lit half of Kostin's face, leaving most of the room in a deep blue shadow.

"What the hell do you think you're doing?" she blurted out. The shock surged through her nerves. Under the sheet, she clenched her right hand in a fist, but before she could make a move, Kostin sat beside her and put a finger to his lips.

"Don't wake the other guests." His voice was soft and level.

Her hand burst up through the sheet and knocked his gun hand to the side. At the same time, she slashed the hard edge of her right hand toward his neck. The Russian caught her wrist with his left hand and shoved her back against the headboard. Her head slammed into the carved wood. By the time she recovered, the black barrel of Kostin's weapon was pointed at her chest.

"I told you to be quiet. Did I not?"

Livy didn't like this. Beyond the fact that a man with a gun had broken into her hotel room in the middle of the night, something about Kostin's calm demeanor worried her. She felt vulnerable, cornered, and that made her want to fight to the end.

Kostin stood and backed away from the bed, keeping the gun on her.

"What we say here is private?" he asked.

"Yes." If there were bugs in the room, the FBI hadn't told her. Not that they would.

"You're sure?"

"I imagine you checked when you broke into my room, so you know the answer already."

Kostin grinned. He wore dark trousers, a black shirt, and a light gray houndstooth jacket. Livy figured he was the best-dressed Russian she'd ever seen. Even at—what time?—3:18 AM.

"What you gave us—we checked it. It was genuine, if a bit dated."

"You didn't give me a helluva lot of time."

"No, I did not. But you see, if we work together, Livy, we have to learn to trust each other."

"Says the man with the gun."

The Russian laughed. "I always liked your accent. So charming."

"I'm even more charming after I've had a bit of sleep."

"Yesterday before you conveniently ran into me at the theatre, the U.S. Congress heard testimony from a traitor. He told the world that all diplomats are spies and that Comrade Stalin wants war."

Livy leaned back, pushed a stray hair from her face and let that sink in. She'd read the same story in the paper. But should she tell him that? No, the question now was whether Livy—or the Livy she pretended to be for Kostin—would know.

"I'm a newspaper girl, Yuri, I don't work in Whitehall. But I read what your man told the Yanks, and we both know what he said was mostly true."

Kostin shook his head. "You sound like a politician."

"I just think sometimes you lot don't have a clue as to how to sell your 'worldwide revolution'. But then I'm sure Uncle Joe knows best."

"You do not sound very much like a woman who's—how did you put it?—'done with them.'"

Livy's head felt clearer now, less panicked. But still on edge. She realized Kostin's late-night visit had had been very purposeful. A surprise interrogation when she was at her most vulnerable. What had Keller called it? The testing, yes. She hoped Kostin hadn't brought that nasty automatic along in case she got low marks.

"Luv, I've been done with them since before the end of the war," she said, managing all the world-weariness she could muster. "They took what they could get from me, and from a lot of other women as well, and then put us back on the bottom rung of the ladder to clean and sew and wash the dirty dishes. I'm done with taking orders from them. For nothing."

If Kostin believed her, he didn't show it. He held the gun steady. "Then, you won't mind telling me how a journalist such as yourself happens to have access to classified documents."

"Because I'm not just a journalist." Livy had to be careful here. She had to be selective with the truth. "They use me. They use us all. MI6. Whitehall. It all goes back to them. We may be making notes for a story, but all the raw material gets sent back to the big boys, and they sift through it for whatever they want."

"You didn't answer the question."

"What? Where did I get that? I stole it. I report to the embassy here. There's material marked 'Confidential' lying on secretaries' desks all the time. Sometimes girls get careless with the files, you see. You get them talking about their Saturday nights and they forget. So, that bit I gave your violinist yesterday I took from an office and made a copy to give to you. I didn't have much time, so I took what looked most current. Give me a little more notice, and I'll see what I can get."

Kostin's finger tightened slightly on the trigger.

Livy felt pinned down, trapped. Like she might be sick all over the bed. But she said, "That's going to wake the whole hall, you know."

"I want to believe you, Livy," the Russian said, sighing. "People betray their countries for many reasons. Money. Love. So, what is it you want in return?"

"Right now I want you to put that gun away."

"This is not a damned joke," he snapped.

"No, 'course not," she said, softly. The time had come when she had to deliver the perfect line. The silk of the sheets felt tight against her legs. She wanted to get up. Pace the floor. But Kostin's gun kept her confined to the bed. She took a breath. This would be the most important line in the show so far. She'd rehearsed it in her mind over and over. She hoped the audience bought it.

"I guess, I still think about the war. All the lads who died. On both sides. And what did it get us? We're in the same exact place again. Only now the Yanks have a bomb that can kill millions in an instant. Your lot will probably have it soon. Then what? We all just wait to see who blinks?

"So what do I want?" She paused. Livy'd watched a few top-flight actresses milk such a moment. They filled the empty space with every emotion in the book. She put her head back against the headboard, pulled her knees up, and crossed her arms. Defensive. Vulnerable. Aching.

"The same bloody thing I wanted two years ago when we first met, Yuri. Escape. It's all that's left."

Kostin shifted back, waiting for more. "You think selling out your country will give you that?"

Livy leaned forward in the bed. The sheet fell. She had one pair of soft, blue silk pajamas. Fortunately she'd worn them tonight. No skin, but she knew they hugged her in the right places.

"What am I going to do now—is that what you're asking? What's left for me? Think my plan is to find some bank clerk and have babies. Ha, after what I've been through? I'm sick of being a gofer for someone who spent their war behind a desk. If they don't want me, then the hell with them. With all of them." The words came out naturally because that's exactly how she felt a lot of the time. Having to justify her work to tossers who looked down on her. Maybe Fleming was right when he said this was her part to play.

"Guess that's why I'm here and why I came to you."

Livy saw his finger on the trigger relax. So slightly.

"And so this information was a peace offering. A gift?"

"What else do I have to offer you, Yuri?"

Kostin took another step back and sat down in the chair at the foot of the bed. He kept the gun up, but Livy could see him thinking through it all. The puzzle pieces would be a jumble in his head, but perhaps a rough shape had formed. A shape that might make sense to a man like him.

Livy didn't give him time to think about it too much. "I may not be the one with the gun, but I've a question for you."

He lifted his eyebrows as if to say, *Go on.*

"Why did you come here tonight? You could have waited. Could've sent someone else for that matter."

"You're right," he said. "You're not the one with the gun."

Livy pushed hair from her eyes again, giving it a little Veronica Lake flourish. *Can't lay it on too thick.* She smiled and said, "And I thought we had to learn to trust each other."

"I need to know more about this aid plan of Truman's and how your people will be involved. What else can you get for me?" He spoke quickly. The mood changed. Had she gotten too close? Too familiar?

"I can't go back to the embassy tomorrow. It would seem suspicious. Maybe the day after."

"Every minute counts right now."

"I thought you were recruiting me. Aren't we still in the wooing stage, luv?"

He blasted out of the chair. "I need as much as you can give me, or I let you go. You understand? There is too much risk. For me."

Livy nodded, playing the chagrined, understanding confederate. Too much at risk for him? She'd bet the house he hadn't meant to let that slip.

"I'll try, Yuri. Give me an extra day, and I'll get everything I can."

Her words seem to soothe him, and the tension appeared to dissipate in his body. Kostin kept the gun pointed at her, but the lines in his forehead relaxed, as did his grip on the trigger.

"We both thought we were done after the war," he said. His voice sounded tired. "At some point you wonder, 'What else is there?' Conflict that never ends? Perpetual war."

Livy leaned back in bed. "It's what they want. The politicians, the generals, MI6, the Yanks."

"Do you know what we call them now? The Americans? The main adversary. It *was* Hitler. Now, Truman."

Kostin had moved along the side of the bed. The black hole of the barrel pointed at the floor. His eyes seemed to have a bit of the gleam Livy remembered when they'd first met. They gave his long face dimension and life. She'd been madly attracted to him then. She'd craved him. Now? Even though she agreed with many of the things he said about the never-ending conflict and the weariness of it all, she'd never be that woman again. That poor Livy Nash who'd come home from France so damaged she could only find refuge in a bottle of bitter vodka.

"It's late and I should let you sleep."

Kostin's words hung in the air. What the hell could Livy say? She knew what he wanted to hear. Every moment felt like another test.

"How do I contact you after tonight?"

"You don't. I find you."

"Ah, so I should just leave the door unlocked in case you want to stroll in here with your little gun tomorrow night?"

His smile widened. "Different places, different times. No more nightcaps."

Livy wanted him out, but even more so she wanted the gun back in his belt or on a table. *More charm. Keep the moment alive.*

She stretched underneath the sheets followed by a yawn that sounded more like "mmm." "So, when I least expect it?"

Kostin nodded and dipped the gun to the bed just below her chest. With the black barrel, he dragged the sheet down her body slowly. The metal pulled the bedclothes over her stomach, her hips, and down around her thighs. The right corner of his mouth turned up.

"I knew those were silk," he said.

Every part of her wanted to kick him across the room and pull the covers up to her chin. Instead, she lay there and said, "You know how good silk feels. Against your skin."

Kostin laughed, ran a hand through his graying hair, and shoved the gun in his waistband. "You said your information was worth a drink or two."

"Bit late for room service, though."

He pivoted, bent down in front of the bed, and brought up a bottle of vodka. Condensation shone on it even in the dim light.

"I could not keep it at the right temperature in here, but it's cold enough." Kostin put the bottle on the table and turned to fetch two room glasses from the credenza.

Livy smiled, but inside her stomach quaked. She hadn't had vodka in over a year. Kostin may have put away his gun, but he'd brought out another weapon in this skirmish. A weapon Livy knew too well. The bottle called to her like a lover from the past. She knew the first drink would go down hard. The second would awaken the craving. The third?

Kostin poured and held one glass out for her. Livy swung her legs off the bed, wanting to feel her feet on the ground and not the unsteady softness of the mattress. Her toes burrowed into the thick carpet. She wanted to sink into it.

"Let us drink to trusting each other," the Russian said.

Livy's mind flashed back to Anka—now a paranoid drunk—and wondered if her journey into the shadows had begun in a similar fashion.

"Livy?"

She took the glass. "To trust," she said—and drank.

Chapter Fourteen

London

At precisely nine fifteen AM the next morning, Ian Fleming walked through the frosted door and into the outer office of the Kemsley News Service. He wore his usual single-breasted dark suit with a white Sea Island cotton shirt and blue bow tie. The morning was warm, so he didn't have an overcoat. Fleming nodded at Pen and then took in the visitor who sat in the outer room.

Fleming pegged him as a courier immediately. He wasn't dressed in a typical messenger uniform, but wore a dark suit and tie and had the no-nonsense air of a sergeant major in the Royal Army. He sat ramrod straight in the armchair, holding a thick black envelope across his lap, with both hands.

The breath caught in Fleming's chest. At the moment, he had several correspondents spread across the world, doing intelligence work, but none of them were involved in anything as volatile and dangerous as the mission he'd assigned Olivia Nash. Without betraying his concern, Fleming cleared his throat and gestured for the courier to follow him into his office. He allowed the courier to go first, then turned to his secretary.

"Make sure we're not disturbed, Pen."

Fleming disappeared inside, closing the secure door behind him. By the time he made his way around his desk and to his chair, the courier had prepared the delivery for exchange. A standard MI6 document, which served as an acknowledgment of the receipt of the courier's package, lay on Fleming's desk.

A bit more quickly than he intended, Fleming withdrew his Mont Blanc pen from inside his coat and signed his name across the bottom. He'd been through this particular ritual on many occasions, but today his pulse throbbed against the band of his Rolex as he scrawled his name. He wanted the courier gone and the package to be his.

Exactly one minute later, Fleming found himself alone in his office. The padded envelope had been taken away by the courier, and a plain manila folder lay on his desk. A paper ribbon with the inscription "Top Secret" sealed the delivery like a present.

Fleming looked down at the folder with a sense of dread. Which one of them could it be? Harrison in Prague? Sewell in Buenos Aires? His mind kept coming back to Livy. He felt the familiar ache in his chest. His doctor would not approve. *"Cut back on the cigarettes and the alcohol,"* he would say. *"Perhaps your work is too stressful. Have you considered a holiday?"*

Fleming listened to the familiar droning voice in his head and then promptly poured himself two fingers of Old Grand-Dad bourbon, and lit one of his specially blended cigarettes from Morland's. He drew the smoke into his lungs and savored the first tang of the whiskey, sighed, and picked up the folder.

He used a Fairbairn-Sykes fighting knife from the war as a letter opener. He slit the paper ribbon across the folder, placed it on his desk, and opened the cover.

He saw the photograph first. It was a man lying on his side. His face was a mess. Blood surrounded the upper half of his body.

Fleming breathed a sigh of relief.

He took another sip of the drink and looked more closely at the image. The man in the photograph was obviously dead. He wore a black suit that seemed almost two sizes too big for him. His hair was thick and dark. The body appeared to be lying in an alley. Fleming saw cobblestones underneath and a scattering of cigarettes butts at the man's feet. The blood in the photograph seemed to originate from the man's face and the back of his head. Fleming had seen enough such pictures to presume the victim had been shot at least twice in the face.

That told him almost all he needed to know.

He slipped the photograph aside and found a typed, page-length report. The memorandum began with *From Station F, Head of Station Allard*. Dennis Allard, Six's man in Paris. Thorough as usual.

Fleming scanned the text for the most salient points. His eye stopped on one word: "Tempest." The code name popped in his mind. This had been Olivia's agent. The one who she said seemed so nervous at their last meeting in the Louvre.

Fleming's replaced the grisly photograph and closed the manila folder. He put the cigarette holder to his lips and drew in the smoke. His mind returned to the dark place it had inhabited prior to opening the delivery.

This man—Barnard she had called him—worked as a double and must have been found out by his other masters, the Soviets. In true Moscow form, the traitor had been executed with two bullets to the face. They liked to make it messy as a warning to other potential traitors to the state.

Fleming wondered if the results for Tempest would have been the same if he had kept Olivia as the man's handler. Had he sacrificed a nervous double so that he could do a favor for Henry Dunbar?

And what about Olivia?

He'd half-expected the file to have just such a photograph of her inside. Fleming had shipped her off to America to do precisely the same sort of work this man Barnard had done. He knew it wasn't a stretch that one day soon he might receive another folder with the very picture he had imagined he was about to see this morning. He'd done everything he could to warn Oliva of the risks of this job, but dammit, the fact was he wanted her to take it. *Needed* her to take it. Henry Dunbar didn't often come to him with assignments as juicy as this. His correspondents dealt with informational intelligence. Rarely had he been authorized by MI6 to oversee an elaborate operation like the ones he'd supervised during the war. If this one was a success, then there might be more. But the question lingered. Had he sent Olivia to her death just so that he could stay in the game?

The thought gripped Fleming's chest like a vise. He stubbed out his cigarette and wiped a strand of sweat from his forehead. He felt his pulse throbbing against his temple and behind his eyes.

A knock at the door. "Sir?"

"Yes, Pen."

"Your nine thirty's here."

Fleming downed the last of the bourbon. Too early for drinking. He put the glass away and stashed the folder in the top drawer of his oak desk. Straightening his tie, Fleming stood up and tried to remember the name of the person he was about to see.

Chapter Fifteen

~

After a nearly thirty-minute drive, Livy's cab pulled up in front of a large white building just off the Jefferson Davis Highway somewhere in Northern Virginia. It could have been one of any number of colonial-style homes in the area except for its bright orange roof and a gleaming marquee on the front lawn that announced "Ice Cream—28 Flavors."

Livy paid the cab driver and stepped out into the late morning heat. The Howard Johnson's looked like it was built yesterday, and befitting its status as new kid on the block, most of the spaces in the parking lot were taken.

A young woman, wearing a blue dress with a clean white apron, cheerily greeted her at the front door. She held a serving tray on her hip and said, "Just sit anywhere you like. There's a booth in the back."

Livy took off the ten-cent sunglasses she'd bought that morning while waiting for the cab. The night had been sleepless, even after Kostin left. She'd called the Fairfax Beauty Salon at eight and asked for the first possible appointment. Assuming she might have a tail she took a taxi to the National Mall, walked several blocks to the Highway Bridge, and picked up another cab near a hotel. She gave the driver a destination in Alexandria. Halfway there, she apologized, saying she had been confused by the address, and asked him to take her to the Howard Johnson's.

After being greeted by the waitress, she scanned the restaurant for Keller. Of course he was late. She walked down an aisle of booths stuffed with men in suits, chatting loudly over steaming coffee, and young mothers trying to get their well-dressed toddlers to take a bite of their bacon. She looked out the window for any late-arriving cars.

There was one free booth at the very back of the restaurant. Two dirty plates and glasses had been left on the table, along with a couple of dimes. Another waitress, wearing the same blue uniform, swept in behind Livy.

"Let me get that out of your way, honey," she said, stacking up the dishes and pocketing the change. "Just have a seat, and I'll get you all cleaned up."

Livy sat down and pulled a plastic menu from behind the salt and pepper stand. The waitress came back, swabbed the table with a wet cloth, and then pulled a thick pad from her clean apron. Although tempted by the puzzling egg lemonade drink on the menu, Livy settled for coffee.

She looked over the menu but couldn't concentrate. The thought of food made her stomach churn even more. Instead, Livy counted the number of drinks she'd had last night. Four. They'd stopped after four, and then she'd told Kostin to leave, that she had work tomorrow, had to sleep. So just four.

The vodka felt as if it was still rumbling around in her stomach. She didn't want anything to eat. Her face felt hot. The skirt and blouse she'd thrown on that morning felt too small, like someone else's clothes. She recognized all the classic signs of shame.

She could have told him, "I don't drink anymore, Yuri. That was a bad time." But the vodka had sealed the pact of trust between them. Now, Livy wondered if she could trust herself.

Keller plopped himself down in the seat opposite her. Livy started. How had he slipped in without her noticing him? *God, it's already started.* The moment took her back two years to the middle of the downward slide, when all she'd cared about was the next drink.

"So, what's good today?" He grabbed a menu, glanced at Livy. "What happened to you?"

"What?"

"You just look like—"

"What can I get you, sir?" The waitress reappeared.

"Um, coffee and orange juice. Toast, bacon, and two eggs over easy for me. Make it the same for the lady."

"Easy enough," the waitress said and hurried off.

"Ordering for me now, are you?"

"Well, you look like you could use something on your stomach," Keller said, rubbing his eyes. "And so can I, for that matter."

Livy replaced her menu and sat back in the booth.

"You took precautions coming here, I assume?" he said.

"Very astute, Mr. Keller."

The waitress dropped off Keller's coffee and juice. He splashed cream into the cup, stirred it three times, and took a long sip. "Okay, so what's so important?"

Livy told him about Kostin verifying the information and the Russian's impatience for more.

"That quick? Damn. Well, good, we've got him on the hook. How did he contact you?"

"He showed up in my bedroom in the middle of the night."

Keller put the coffee down. "You let him in?"

"No." Livy took a sip of her own coffee. The hot liquid burned on the way down and seemed to settle on top of her vodka-soaked stomach.

"He just let himself in? For a chat?"

"Something like that. He had questions for me. Suspicions. He seems to want to believe me, though."

Keller demanded details. He wanted to know everything. What was Kostin wearing? What was his mood? Personal details about the Russian. "And, after the questions, he left?"

The implication caught Livy off guard. Of course, Keller would assume she'd slept with Kostin. She'd done it before. Why not now?

"Yes," she said. Livy left out the vodka. She couldn't admit it out loud. And even if she did, she doubted Keller would care.

"I see."

Livy wondered if the news pleased him. Did he want her to sleep with Kostin? No one had mentioned the possibility to her. Not Fleming and not Keller. Yet. But her past with the Russian and her undeniable use of the tactic of sexuality led in that direction. She felt her breath quicken, so she rubbed her eyes and pushed the thought away for now.

Keller finished off his coffee and turned to look for the waitress. He had a light brown stain on the shoulder of his black suit. She knew enough young mothers back home to recognize the distinct color of baby spit-up.

"You've got a little something right there," Livy said.

"Huh?"

"On your coat. Here." She pulled a paper napkin from the stainless steel dispenser by the window and wet it with the tip of her tongue. She had to stand to reach his shoulder and the stain. Keller seemed mildly irritated, and then embarrassed.

The waitress came with the pot of coffee, assured them their food would be "comin' right up," and then was gone.

"Girl or boy?"

Keller began his now familiar coffee ritual once more. Splash of cream and three careful stirs. "A boy."

"Your first?"

"Yep."

"Must be exhausting."

"Damn right it is."

"You don't seem to want to talk about it."

Keller sipped the coffee while the fingers of his left hand nervously drummed the table. "We're not here for chitchat, Miss Nash."

Livy's face burned. Her life now seemed topsy-turvy. She craved something, anything normal. *Tell me about your kid.* *What's your wife like?* But instead, she nodded, had another sip of the burning coffee, and didn't speak.

Their food came, and they ate. Keller devoured his while Livy stuck with toast and jam. Her stomach regarded the runny egg yolks with caution. She wondered if he knew. Could he see the night of drinking written all over her face?

"You okay?" he asked, wiping the corners of his mouth.

"Bit tired. That's all."

Livy watched one of the suited businessmen put a coin in the big, lighted jukebox near the front counter. Perry Como began to croon "Prisoner of Love."

Keller moved back to Kostin. More questions. "The thing is we have to be careful now about what we give him. Kostin's a big fish, and he knows bait when he sees it. The next batch of stuff will be juicier. Once he's all in with you, then we'll start feeding him a little truth and a lot of bullshit."

"He's anxious about Truman's aid plan."

"The whole damn world is." Keller bit into a greasy strip of bacon. "Do you plan to sleep with him?"

There it was. On the table now with the Howard Johnson's breakfast. Livy glanced around at the other diners. She felt shocked by his casual frankness, so she picked up her toast and smeared it with what passed for strawberry jam.

"That something you need to know this morning, is it?"

"I need to know everything."

Perry Como's voice filled the silence.

Livy felt sick. She took another bite of the bland toast and chewed.

"I'll let you know then."

After a few more minutes of silence, the waitress dropped off the check.

Livy said, "I promised him something for tomorrow."

"Tomorrow? You arrange a drop?"

"He said he'd find me."

Keller absentmindedly picked up his empty coffee mug for a sip. "I'll have a courier bring something to your room tonight. Make sure you're there at eight."

"Shouldn't be a problem."

Keller put his hand on hers. The sudden move threw Livy for yet another flip in a breakfast that had already been a bit like a gymnastics routine.

"You need to be careful, Livy. I'm just a little surprised by how fast Kostin is taking this. Recruitment is usually a slow process. Feels to me like there's something else going on."

Livy regarded this sudden tenderness with suspicion. But she didn't move her hand. Truth be told, she appreciated the comfort of his touch. "I'll be careful."

"We'll meet at the house the day after tomorrow, all right?" Keller said, his voice low and reassuring. "I'll get someone on the Fairfax number. Night and day. Something happens, you call. Okay?

"I really should get going. I have an appointment this afternoon. For my real job." Livy got up, more to calm her nerves than anything. If they served vodka at Howard Johnson's, she'd have ordered a double. Keller grabbed the check. He paid at the counter and asked the waitress to call Livy a cab.

He smoked a cigarette outside the restaurant as they waited. Keller brought up sports. He'd grown up a Cleveland Indians fan. She talked Blackpool Football Club. It felt like he was trying to find some common ground. But it felt pushed. Like an automobile salesman who wants to be your mate. He was playing her in almost the same way she was playing Kostin. Still, the ordinariness of it all felt like an oasis in the midst of her turbulent assignment.

The cab came. Keller held the door for Livy and paid the fare. She didn't protest. She played the game, thanked him, and even smiled when she left.

Chapter Sixteen

⁓

"The fact is that even though she might not seem it, given her age, the First Lady has actually set trends in fashion."

The woman who sat across the polished wooden table in the bar of the Mayflower Hotel certainly looked the part of "fashion expert" with a slight touch of sadist. Livy knew next to nothing about trends in women's clothing; she liked what she liked. But Mrs. Allison Prentiss's outfit hit all the right notes. Her ensemble said season with its color, business with the cut of her skirt and light jacket, and of course style. Livy thought she looked like a department store mannequin come to life.

"Mrs. Truman embraced the new look for women after the war when she started wearing sleeveless gowns at White House functions. So, although I'd never refer to her as a style icon, she certainly hasn't shirked her duty as role model for the women of America."

Livy looked up from her notebook. "She's a role model because of sleeveless gowns?"

"That's right," Mrs. Prentiss said. She peered across the table at Livy's notebook. Her type was always worried about being misquoted. "That's something we take quite seriously in America. Your readers in *The Times* might find that enlightening."

"They just might."

"There is a photographer coming as well, isn't there?" Mrs. Prentiss had a gin and tonic in front of her, which she hadn't touched.

"That will be up to Mr. Price, actually."

"I see." Disappointment dripped from her reply.

Livy's fifteen minutes with Allison Prentiss had felt about three times as long. The glass of water, loaded down with ice, sweated on the napkin in front of her. She took a quick sip, trying to ignore the smell of alcohol, the bar sounds, the oeuvre of drinking.

They sat at a corner table about twenty feet away from the bar. The counter and tables had been built from dark wood. The long mirror, which ran the length of the entire bar, filled the space with a kind of silver glow. Even at four in the afternoon, the room had the feeling of midnight.

"And what about her apparent disdain for the press? If she's a role model, as you say, shouldn't she speak to the people through folks like me?" Livy asked.

The mannequin began to pontificate again. Livy leaned back in her chair, pencil scribbling in her reporter's notebook. She turned her head and checked the end of the bar. A balding man in a rumpled gray suit still sat there. Looking back, she nodded and murmured in appreciation of Mrs. Prentiss's expertise. Her mind, however, wrestled with the problem of the Gray Man.

About fifteen minutes after leaving Keller at the Howard Johnson's, Livy had noticed a blue Packard following the cab as it wound its way back into the district. She'd had the cab drop her off several blocks away from the Mayflower. On her circuitous route to the hotel, she stopped at a newsstand and waited.

She watched through the reflection in the window of an office building as the blue Packard slowly cruised past.

She waited until the car turned the corner at the next block, and walked in the opposite direction. It took her another ten minutes to reach the front doors of the hotel. Still early for her meeting with Mrs. Prentiss, Livy found a seat in the spacious lobby that had a view of the street. Minutes later the blue Packard drove by, but it didn't stop.

She felt certain no one had followed her on the way to meet Keller, which led her to believe that the blue Packard was FBI. However, the Russians had even more reason to keep tabs on her. Kostin's insistence on moving quickly with Livy meant the Soviets would have much to lose if she proved to be a double. They'd want to know her every move.

Once Mrs. Prentiss arrived and they'd adjourned to the fancy bar, Livy had noticed the Gray Man come in and take a seat a good distance away, but close enough that he could keep an eye on her through the bar's prominent mirror. A single man at a bar in a major city didn't strike her as unusual, but something about the man's clothes—the slump of his shoulders, and the functionality of his shoes—didn't quite fit in with the other pin-striped, double-breasted men who drank beside him. They exuded power. He looked like someone at the end of a surveillance shift. Something about him seemed familiar, although she couldn't quite pinpoint what.

So as Mrs. Prentiss droned on now about how much she admired Thomas Dewey's wife, Bess Truman's likely First Lady opponent in next year's presidential election, Livy considered the Gray Man and how she might react to him. It didn't matter if he was Russian or American. A tail needed to be dismissed as quickly as possible. She couldn't tolerate him babysitting her in such an obvious way.

"I'm sorry, Miss Nash, but is everything all right?"

Livy turned back. Mrs. Prentiss looked peeved.

"Yes, of course," Livy countered. Pencil back to notepad. "You were saying about Mrs. Dewey?"

Mrs. Prentiss tilted her head, studying Livy. "You keep looking at the bar."

Livy'd interviewed a lot of people over the last year, but this woman took the cake for overbearing.

Livy put her pencil down. "Mrs. Prentiss, I do apologize. I don't mean to appear unprofessional in any way." She leaned forward, affecting a conspiratorial tone. "The truth is, I know the man at the bar. The fellow in the gray suit with his back to us."

Mrs. Prentiss shot him a look, her arched eyebrows like predatory commas.

"I really shouldn't be saying any of this. I mean you are clearly a very perceptive woman and could tell I was just, well, a bit upset by seeing him here. But please, I apologize. This story is very important to my paper. Could we get back to—"

"Who is he?"

Livy cleared her throat. "Well . . . um . . . he's . . . he's a detective."

Mrs. Prentiss took her first sip of the gin and tonic. "Go on."

"You don't want to hear all this."

"Miss Nash. Go on."

"All right. Well, my husband—he's an American—and we separated after the war. He . . . um, it's very personal, Mrs. Prentiss, but let's just say I could no longer tolerate certain . . . indiscretions."

Allison Prentiss, fashion expert, didn't look shocked. She looked angry.

"So, naturally, I couldn't stay married to a man like that. After all those times. But my husband couldn't accept it, I suppose. You know how men are. Like little boys if they don't have their way. Anyway, that was last year. Then, about six months ago, I started seeing that fella out and about." She glanced at the Gray Man. "I'd see him out on the street when I went shopping. Or when I went to a picture with the girls. He was everywhere. Finally, I confronted him. He told me he was a private detective."

Not even the ice in her drink could have been as cold as the expression in Mrs. Prentiss's eyes. "Your husband is having you followed?"

Livy nodded.

"Even when you're working?"

"Yes, and he's probably around a lot more than I know. Anyway, as I said, please forgive me. I didn't want to intrude on our interview."

Mrs. Prentiss put up a hand. "Don't." Then she snapped her fingers twice for the bar waiter. A college-aged kid in dark pants, pressed white shirt, and a black vest scurried over. She said something quietly to the waiter, who then hurried off.

"Mrs. Prentiss, I'm very sorry—"

"Wait," she commanded.

Less than a minute later, a very sleek man, who looked a bit like George Sanders with a pencil-thin mustache, waded through the bar tables toward theirs. He took Mrs. Prentiss's hand and gave it a familiar kiss. She whispered in his ear, gestured toward the bar. He nodded and took his leave.

"Now," Mrs. Prentiss said, turning to Livy, "we may continue."

Livy, playing the puzzled, naive newspaper girl, shook her head and opened her notebook. "Um, what would you expect from Mrs. Dewey if she became—"

Before she could finish the question, two burly men in navy double-breasted suits strolled up to the Gray Man. Their arms bulged through their suit jackets. One leaned down and said something quietly. The Gray Man listened, gave each man a look, and stood up. The two muscular house detectives remained on either side of him as the Gray Man buttoned his jacket, picked up his slouching fedora, and followed them to the exit. He gave Livy a parting glance. No malice. Just the briefest of moments to say, "I see you."

Livy didn't need to act shocked—she was. The last thing she'd expected from the fashion expert opposite her was this kind of moxie.

Mrs. Prentiss smiled and took another sip of her drink as the three men disappeared into the lobby. "That was off the record, by the way."

*   *   *

Livy had an early dinner that night at one of the Statler Hotel restaurants called The Embassy Room. Despite Mrs. Prentiss's intervention, the encounter with the Gray Man left her more than a little bothered. There'd been an implied threat in the way he looked at her before leaving. Odd. The last thing a tail wants is to be seen. This man's gaze felt like a direct challenge.

She ordered a steak, a Caesar salad, and something called steak fries. Livy found the meat undercooked and the thick, finger-like fried potatoes far too much. She picked at her salad and thought about Margot. She wondered if there had been any more signals, or had they stopped completely? Was the signal even from Margot? The listener had identified her distinctive wireless signature, but he could have been wrong. For a few moments Livy picked at the bloody meat and considered that this whole misadventure might very well be a fluke. False leads and futile missions were far more frequent than any intelligence agency would ever admit. The idea that all this could be for nothing clung to her like the guilt she still felt from last night's vodka shots.

After dinner she returned to her room. Someone knocked on her door at exactly eight PM. The courier carried a rectangular box, wrapped in brown paper, and wore a neatly pressed gray uniform and peaked cap.

"Your dry cleaning, ma'am," he said.

Although she knew the courier had been sent by Keller, she tipped him.

The box had a sticker on the top corner, which said, "Dupont Circle Cleaning & Laundry." She tore open the box and found a plain gray file folder. It contained two typed sheets of white foolscap topped by the letterhead for the United State Department of the Air Force. A stamp at the bottom indicated the documents had been transferred to the Embassy of the United Kingdom.

Livy threw away the box and the file, folded the typed pages, and put them into her purse. She turned down the lights in the room and sat in an armchair by the window overlooking K Street. She needed escape.

She found her heavily worn copy of *Hamlet* in her case and thumbed through it. The play had been a gift from her father.

Although he'd been a circus man and of Irish descent, Archie Nash always referred to Shakespeare as his "favorite Englishman." As a child, Livy had played Horatio in an all-girl production at her school. Reading the lines now, as the prince teases an overzealous actor—"Speak the speech I pray you . . ."—helped to ease the tremor she had noticed in her right hand.

She recited the lines out loud, giving them a bit of emphasis. But the anxiety remained. Putting the play down, she fell to the carpet and began doing press-ups. That didn't ease her tension either. She knew the one thing that might allow her to get a moment of restful sleep tonight was waiting for her downstairs.

After an hour of reading and exercising, Livy fixed her hair, tidied her blouse into her skirt, and took the lift to the lobby. She sat as far away from the bar of the Embassy Room as possible. Her voice quivered slightly when she gave the waiter her order. "An old-fashioned, please. With Old Grand-Dad bourbon if you have it." She'd heard Fleming place that very order many times.

The waiter came back with the drink. Livy looked into the deep amber of the whiskey and promised herself that she and Margot would be back home soon.

Chapter Seventeen

"I'll be with you in just one minute, dear. Take a seat. Won't be a tic."

The young woman sitting behind the second desk at the entrance to the British Embassy looked to be about Livy's age, perhaps a couple of years younger, and sounded Yorkshire to her core.

Livy stepped away from the desk. The embassy compound, which took up a wide swath of Massachusetts Avenue, felt distinctly English among the American style of architecture that typified many homes in DC. Livy stood in the main hall in the center of the U-shaped brick building. Discreet lace curtains on the ground-level windows filtered sunlight through the entranceway. The marble floors added a touch of elegance, but the utilitarian furniture assured visitors that austere Britain was not footing the bill for the glamorous life on this side of the Atlantic.

"How can I help you, dear?"

Livy approached the desk. The woman behind it wore a smart, light blue blouse with a dark skirt. She had big brown eyes, matching hair, a pointed nose, and a jaw that would keep her out of boxing if she were a man. The ID tag pinned to her chest identified her as Alice Dawson.

"We're doing a follow-up on some of the missing from the war." Livy showed her passport and press credentials. "I have a couple of names I'd like to see if you have files on."

Alice's mouth turned down. "We're not really accepting press requests for that sort of thing. The files of the missing and all. Between you and me, they like to keep it quiet, you know, about the girls who fought and didn't come back. Morale and all."

Livy's heart sank. The night before, as she sat in the hotel bar, she'd thought about Margot and tried to remember her face. Maybe it was the bourbon, but she couldn't readily picture her friend's features. She wanted a photo of her. That was the talisman she needed. That, she told herself, would get her through.

No press requests? Fine. New tactic.

"Hmm. West Yorkshire, I'd say. Somewhere in the vicinity of . . . Huddersfield?"

Alice's wide jaw broke into a grin. "Further north. Halifax."

"I knew it."

"And you? I sussed you as Lancashire first thing. But I'm no good at guessing towns, so you'll just have to tell me."

"Blackpool."

Alice eyes widened. "My mum and dad took me there every season before the war. The Illuminations. Oh, and the circus. But then I suppose Lancashire has to have something to offer." Her eyes widened as Livy registered the playful slight.

"Oh, that's the way it is?"

For centuries the two English counties had waged a mostly peaceful rivalry that extended to food, scenery, as well as hundreds of years of history.

"I mean we have you lot beaten in size—certainly in cricket championships—and Yorkshire pudding travels a bit further than hot pot." Alice smiled.

Livy quickly parried, "I'll give you the games and the food, but we won the War of the Roses."

"Ancient history, dear," Alice fired back. "But your football club is downright formidable."

Livy dropped that her dad had been an acrobat in the Blackpool Tower Circus, and Alice's day was made.

"Oh my, I do miss home sometimes," she said.

"Is it always this bloody hot?"

"Summers are misery here."

Livy checked her watch and sighed. "The thing is, luv, my boss—he's a Yank—he wants a profile of one of these girls, and the only one I could find is . . . um . . . let me see." Livy fiddled about in her handbag, pushing past the folded classified documents she carried for Kostin, and pulled out her reporter's notebook. "Dupont. Margot Dupont. Her father was something in the Foreign Office and was stationed here for a bit in the thirties. Thought you might have something on her. Just background, you know. I'm on a bit of a deadline. Otherwise, I'd let you show me if there's a place to get a decent English breakfast round here."

"Tell you what. Let me see if we have a file, and maybe you could sneak a peek, Okay? Be a dear and watch my desk. Won't be a minute." Alice laughed. She turned and trundled down the long hallway.

Livy felt a bit bad laying it on so thick for homesick Alice. She seemed like a nice girl. Truth was, Livy knew exactly how she felt.

*　　*　　*

She left the embassy with a promise to meet Alice the next morning at a pub owned by a man from Leeds who catered to ex-pats and embassy workers. Alice promised "a better English breakfast than you've ever had in Lancashire." Margot's file would have to be pulled by an archivist, but Alice promised to bring it when they met, and let Livy have a look.

Her plan was to hail a cab to Price's office in Georgetown, but Alice suggested the streetcar, so Livy walked along the edge of Dumbarton Oaks Park to Wisconsin Avenue to wait for the car. The nerves from last night had returned. Her right hand shook only slightly as she surveyed the area, wondering if the blue Packard might make another appearance.

Kostin had said he'd find her today. She assumed the most likely place might be her hotel, but depending on his level of caution, he could prefer something more public. Livy half-expected the Russian to walk up behind her at any moment.

Always onstage, she felt the "performance" taking its toll only a few days in. Her mind went to Anka. Now she saw her as a woman trying to cope with the stress of her war. Livy'd had her own battles overcoming the past, and she wondered if perhaps she was living in a moment she'd again struggle to put behind her.

It wasn't even noon and she wanted another drink. *This is how it starts.* Experience told her that. She had to be disciplined. But how the hell else was she supposed to cope?

Waiting for Kostin. Livy hated feeling like a pawn in someone else's game. A part of her wanted to take a cab to the airport and go home. Tell Fleming to stuff it and then curl up in her own bed for days.

The visit to the embassy hadn't settled her nerves her as much as she hoped it might. Livy prayed Margot's file would contain a photo. She needed to see her. Remember her. Needed that part of the operation to be real. It had to feel like more than just a pipe dream that she could reach across the world and the years to try to bring her back home.

The rumble of the approaching streetcar brought her back to the moment. The green, blue, and white car, with its snubbed nose and sleek design, reminded Livy of a rocket ship out of Flash Gordon. She climbed aboard. The noon lunch crowd packed the car, making it standing room only. A wall of men in gray and blue suits, with big slouching hats, crowded the center of the aisle, leaving the seats along the windows to moms with toddlers, and younger women with department store bags, headed home.

Livy held her handbag tight. She grabbed the overhead rail as the car lurched forward. The driver wore blue overalls and stood in the middle of two great gears. He turned his head and half-shouted, "Next stop, Burleith. That's Burleith, next stop."

Livy found a small area of space between two much taller men, both of whom held today's paper in front of their faces. One chortled as he read the comics, while the other scanned the front section.

Behind her a shorter man, who chewed gum with the intensity of a bullfighter, smiled at her. She gripped the handbag and moved away, turning toward the center of the car.

There, over the shoulder of the man reading the funny papers, stood Yuri Kostin. He had his fedora pulled down to the bridge of his nose, but she recognized the unmistakable curve of his lips and the V-shaped chin. He lifted his head, and for a moment they made eye contact. Then he turned to the window.

He must have been following her the whole day. How else could he have gotten on the streetcar without her knowing it? How could she have missed him?

Five minutes later the streetcar came to a stop and allowed passengers to get off. Both newspaper readers left, as did a number of the women along the window seats. Livy glanced in Kostin's direction. He didn't move. His head still down.

"Ma'am." A lanky man in khakis and a blue shirt gestured for Livy to take the seat closest to him. She smiled, quickly glanced at Kostin, and took a seat with one empty space beside her. Kostin's head turned in her direction as the streetcar began to move. The last stop had thinned out the car by almost half. Perhaps the Russian felt safer to make some form of contact, because he shifted as if to take the seat.

Then a young woman and a little girl of about five hustled into the seat next to Livy. The woman had dark hair and eyes. She moved like it had been a long day, dragging her daughter behind her. The little girl, who wore a straw hat with a Woolworth's price tag attached to it, sat down first. He mother bustled her out, plopped down beside Livy, and pulled the little girl on her lap. "Here we go, honey. Sit down—sit right here."

Kostin angled away from the window, his hat still low on his face.

"Sweetie, take that off." The mom swiped the hat off the little girl's curly head and used it to fan herself. "It's way too big for you anyways." The little girl looked at her mother and turned away without a word.

"Well, I thought it was funny," the woman said, just a bit too loud. She said to Livy, "You have kids?"

"Um, no—no, I don't." She smiled at the mom, her eyes still on Kostin.

The mom raised an eyebrow. "Well, they're a pain in the beehind most of the time, but once in a while they can be good for a few laughs."

Kostin tipped his hat back and looked at Livy. The corners of his mouth turned up, almost as if he found the situation funny.

"This one is sure a handful sometimes, but her brother—just like his Daddy—never stops talking," the mom said. "Quit squirming, Maggie, that hurts Mama."

The driver boomed out, "Next stop, Oak Hill."

Livy gave the little girl a smile and tried to look away, but the mother leaned over to her. Her eyes went all mysterious, and she lowered her voice.

"Do you know that fella in the gray hat?" The mom indicated Kostin. Livy held her breath and shook her head. "Well, honey, let me tell ya, that man's got a thing for you. So, unless you do know him, you might want to be careful."

Livy's eyes widened. "What do you mean?"

"I know a little something about men. That guy right there hasn't taken his eyes off you this whole time. And, believe me, I know that look."

"I'll keep that in mind."

The mom leaned in, whispering. "I'd be careful if I was you. Man looks like trouble. 'Course, you know, some girls like that."

"Do they now? Your daughter is lovely, by the way."

"Yeah," the mom said, "and she knows it too."

The streetcar eased to another stop. The mom scooted her daughter off her lap and, grabbing her hand, made for the exit. Kostin wasted no time in taking the vacant seat as more passengers got on and filled the car back to standing room only.

Seconds later, it began to move.

They didn't speak. They couldn't. But Livy felt what the woman had said. The way Kostin looked at her, the way his arm touched hers now. This was more than just a dead drop. The Russian wanted to see her. She knew when a man was interested in her, of course. Every woman could tell that. After the war, when they'd met in London, Livy never imagined she'd see him more than a few times. She'd been right. Kostin moved on to someone else. He wasn't the type to make lasting connections, and for Livy, at that particular moment in her life, that alone was a big part of his attraction. But the sense she got from him today—the same sense the mother beside her had felt—felt very different.

The streetcar's bell rang and the last passengers took their places in the aisle. Every seat, every inch of space teemed with people headed to Georgetown.

Kostin took off his hat and looked down. He spoke quietly.

"You have something?"

"I do."

"With you?"

Livy nodded.

He fanned himself with the fedora, speaking quietly. "Not here. Tonight. I need to see you, Livy."

She heard it in his voice now. A longing. His leg touched her thigh. She felt his desire for her even in the heat of the packed streetcar. She'd felt it in the hotel room two nights ago, but in a different way. Kostin needed to be in control then. Today he seemed almost vulnerable.

He put his hat on and looked at her, smiled, nodded. "Excuse me," he said. He reached across her toward a window at her shoulder. His fingers grazed her cheek briefly. She could smell his scent, a strong dark cologne that replaced the reek of the packed car.

Kostin opened the window, withdrawing his hand. "Do you mind?" he asked.

"Not at all."

Livy looked down. The folded city section of the newspaper now lay in her lap. She put her hand over it and said, "It's bloody hot in here."

Kostin nodded and turned away.

The streetcar began to slow. Passengers shifted toward the doors. Kostin stood to join them. The microphone squawked on. "Georgetown, Dumbarton Avenue." The Russian did not look back at her as he exited the car.

Livy waited. The streetcar's bell dinged again. Her stop was next. She unfolded the city section Kostin left with her and scanned the front. A message in black ink had been written in the bottom right corner. It said, *Gayety Theatre, Ninth Street. Nine o'clock. Do not walk alone.*

Chapter Eighteen

"You sure *that's* where you wanna go, miss?"

The cab driver swung the big car around another turn. Livy looked at her watch. Almost nine. She wondered how far away it was. Would she be late?

The driver looked to be in his late fifties with steel-gray hair kept in a military buzz cut. He wore a gray button-up shirt. Through the rearview mirror, Livy could see the cab company's logo on his chest.

"I mean it's none of my business, but if you was my daughter, I wouldn't take you to this particular street at this particular time of day."

"It's really all right. I'm meeting a friend."

The cab turned right on Ninth Street. Around the corner stood Ford's Theatre, where she'd waited for the contact only the day before. But a few blocks east from the historic location, it was a very different atmosphere.

The cab turned onto a block that felt like a world unto itself. Bright flickering lights gave the darkness deep blue and red hues. Men stood on street corners, fistfuls of tickets in their hands, calling out to passers-by. An electric sign on the right flashed

"Peep Show." The cab slowed as it approached a crowd of mostly men standing in line in front of what looked like a box office. What kind of theatre exactly was this, she wondered?

The driver found a spot across the street, and Livy looked at the marquee above the line of men. The words "Gayety Theatre—Burlesque" flashed over a smaller sign, which promised "Stella Mills. The One and Only. Onstage Tonight."

Livy had been to her fair share of shady spots over the years. The Pigalle in Paris had a similar ambience, but this part of Ninth Street had the feeling of steep decline. Storefronts offering "Adult Pictures" had broken windows. A man staggered out into the street from the front doors of the Port Arthur Chinese Restaurant next door to the Gayety Burlesque. A passing car blasted its horn in anger at the drunk. The man tried kicking the car but missed and fell down in the street. No one came to help him.

The cabbie turned around. "Listen, I can wait until you see your friend, if you want."

Livy put a hand on his arm and smiled. "I can see after myself." She paid him the thirty-cent fare and an extra couple of dimes.

Stepping outside the car, she smoothed her black pencil skirt down. It felt a bit too tight, but then it needed to be tonight. Her button-up blouse and short jacket felt equally snug. She couldn't wait to be back in her room, out of these clothes, and in a hot bath. She'd purposefully dressed for Kostin. Using her body, she hoped, to strengthen their connection and deepen his trust. Still, Livy couldn't but wonder what exactly she might be getting herself into. The words of the mother on the bus rang in her ears.

Livy crossed the street to the theatre. The drunken man had pulled himself up and kept calling after her. "Hey! Hey, honey.

I said hey! I'm talking to you!" Livy ignored him, and hoped he wouldn't walk up to her. If he touched her, she'd break his windpipe. This wasn't the right time for that. There was work to be done now.

More than a few of the men in line turned as she stepped up on the sidewalk. A few leered, running their eyes over her exposed calves and tight skirt. A few others looked embarrassed, trying to see if they recognized her or, more importantly perhaps, if she recognized them.

Livy's watch put the time at five after nine. Had Kostin left? She looked south on the street, which appeared seamier still. The lights dimmer. Shadows moved in and out of doorways. She didn't see the Russian. She decided to run the gauntlet of men standing in line at the Gayety. Perhaps Kostin had gone inside. She walked quickly, trying to ignore the comments as she passed. Some more vulgar than she could have imagined. And she could imagine a helluva lot. Still, Livy couldn't afford to stop and put one of the pathetic in his place as a lesson to the rest.

As she reached the other side, near a bar called the Gayety Buffet, she heard footsteps behind her. Instinctively, her right fist stiffened. She pivoted, her hand ready to strike.

"Come with me." Kostin took her by the arm and led her into the next-door bar. He didn't speak as they pushed past tables of loud drunken men and the women for which they bought drinks. The thick cloud of smoke in the bar penetrated the back of her throat. Kostin turned past the counter, nodding at the bartender, and opened a wooden door.

They stepped into the lobby of the Gayety Burlesque Theatre. Kostin led her up a flight of stairs to the balcony. The interior of the Gayety matched the disrepair of its exterior. It looked like it had been years since the place had a coat of paint. The thick red carpet, which at one time must have seemed velvety and decadent, peeled up at the side of several steps, revealing dirty wooden floorboards underneath.

At the top of the stairs, Kostin led her down a circular hallway with several doors, all numbered. A few of the letters had cracked and hung at an angle. The Russian opened the door for number 14, ushering Livy into a private box that overlooked the stage below.

Despite its state of disrepair, Livy could tell the Gayety had once been quite the place to be. It reminded her of a few of the great theatres in London—that is, if Mae West had designed them. Everything, from the great proscenium that framed the stage to the sculpture around the three tiers of balconies, was overdone. Gaudy gold figures carved into the walls stood watch over the balcony seats. Onstage the thick red curtain with its golden frayed fringe sagged from the rafters. A drop, one Livy reckoned must have been painted in the twenties, depicted a blonde nymph wearing a sheer gown, lying provocatively in a lime-green field.

Livy understood now why Kostin had chosen to meet here. It was the sort of place no one wanted to be seen.

A tired quartet played a lazy waltz as the rest of the audience filed in. The men pushed and prodded one another, vying for the best seats closest to the stage. Livy reckoned the theatre might hold more than a thousand, but even counting the people out on the sidewalk tonight, they'd be lucky to have two hundred.

"You brought the documents?" Kostin asked as soon as they'd taken their seats on two bentwood chairs in the less than opulent box.

Livy opened her smaller dress handbag, pulled out the folded papers, and handed them over.

"In the 1920s, they say this theatre rivaled the great music halls in London and the Moulin Rouge in Paris," he said. Kostin made no attempt to conceal the documents as he pored over them. "But now it's lost its—what's the word?—shine?"

"Luster."

A wide grin split Kostin's face. "I love how you say that word. *Loostuh.* I do not know that word, but I don't care when you say it. They say presidents once came here. Now? No *loostuh.*"

"Maybe the boys just want to stay home with their families and not pay top dollar to see some bird in her knickers."

Kostin laughed. He seemed more relaxed than he had the last two meetings, although the dark circles under his eyes told a different story.

Kostin held up the documents. "You can get more of this?"

"I can try. It depends, though."

Below them the quartet ended their final number. Almost all the players remained in the same key for the last chord. A tall, thin man with a mustache, which curled unfashionably at the ends, took center stage. He wore a tuxedo that might have fit someone else but hung loose around the emcee's skeletal frame.

"Good evening, good evening, and welcome to the world-famous Gayety Burlesque Theatre!" The line begged for applause. It received only a smattering. Most of the men filing into their seats didn't even stop to listen.

"Tonight, the renowned beauty, Miss Stella Mills, concludes her run at the Gayety," the emcee continued, "but first—"

"Bring 'er out now!" someone shouted.

"I paid to see her tits!" another called, which created a wave of laughter from the back of the house that rolled all the way to the front. The emcee didn't flinch. He gave the impression of a man who'd heard it all before. Onstage, the emcee poked his head behind the curtain, gesturing wildly as the audience noise level grew.

"Why exactly did you bring me to this place?" Livy leaned forward to be heard over the din.

"I like it here," Kostin smiled. "No pretension. You understand? Besides, this is the last place anyone from my embassy would ever be seen." The Russian folded the documents and put them in his pocket. "I have to tell you, Livy, you made a bad mistake yesterday."

Onstage, the emcee gestured behind the curtain. The quartet began an off-key vamp.

Livy feigned nonchalance. "Did I now?"

"At the hotel. You embarrassed the man sent to watch you."

Livy's mind flashed back to the Gray Man at the Mayflower. Not FBI, but a Russian. Now she remembered. She'd seen him with Kostin at the National Theatre the night of *Oklahoma*. His presence at the Mayflower must mean she was still in what Keller called "the testing phase."

"Maybe he should've been less obvious. Isn't that the whole point of surveillance?"

"Okay. You can see him. Know he is there. But you went far beyond that."

"I thought we were supposed to trust each other, Yuri."

The Russian turned on her sharply. "These days no one trusts anyone."

The emcee walked downstage again to address the rowdy crowd. "Ladies and gents, please. I have just this very moment sent word back to Miss Stella Mills's dressing room and have asked her to come out now and entertain you, our fine and loyal customers."

The announcement brought a chorus of wolf whistles.

The quartet switched from vamping to a pulsing, grinding jazz number. The lights dimmed, and the whistlers renewed their call. The drop with the painting of the blond nymph slowly began to rise, revealing a woman standing center stage in a spotlight.

Despite the peeling paint and the general feeling of dissolution of the Gayety, Miss Stella Mills did not disappoint. She wore an outfit that seemed to be layer upon layer of large feathers encasing her body while still allowing her to move. Her hair was shockingly red, and the fullness of her pink lips stood out even to Livy in the upper balcony. She quieted the audience with her presence alone. Taking each step very deliberately, she sashayed downstage, scanning the audience like a tiger stalking prey. Then, with a flick of her hips so intentional it must've been felt on the back row, she turned and strutted away.

The boys went wild.

The Gayety may have fallen on hard times, but Miss Stella Mills had star quality to spare.

Of course, she took her clothes off. Livy expected nothing less. Each feather that came off had its moment. Even if it only partially revealed a shoulder, Miss Stella Mills gave it life. Each part of her costume that floated to the stage, each toss of her thick red hair, each step she took seemed like an act of defiance. She commanded the stage and battered the libidinous rabble into submission.

Livy admired the performance. At one point, Kostin leaned over and whispered in her ear. "She is from your Manchester," he said. His lips lingered ever so slightly before pulling away. His touch felt at once arousing and, frankly, repulsive. Her palms felt wet at the same time her ear lobe tingled. Livy figured this place was supposed to make her lose herself and eventually give in to Kostin. She felt his desire for her. This whole dance they'd been doing since the night at the National Theatre had been building to this. Livy wondered how much she would have to lose herself in order to succumb to him.

But like Miss Stella Mills, whose finely tuned hips kept her audience in thrall, Livy also was a performer. She knew what Yuri Kostin needed her to be tonight. Just as she knew what she needed from him.

As the act ended onstage and the quarter-full house rose as one to celebrate the burlesque queen of Manchester, Livy knew she had to have Kostin's trust to have any hope of learning what happened to Margot and who might be holding her now. Kostin kept himself in the shadows, more than most people she'd known in the secret world. But he had revealed a hint of himself on that streetcar—so clearly that even a bystander could see it. Livy knew she had to dive into this role in order to exploit Kostin's vulnerability. She needed his trust above all else. She just hoped the journey didn't take her so deep she couldn't come back.

"I need a drink," the Russian said. He stood and held out his hand to her.

She took it.

*　*　*

"Gin and tonic is a very English drink, yes?"

Livy lifted her second of the night and sipped. In a place like the Gayety Buffet, she expected the liquor to be watered down, but this tasted like top-shelf gin with a mere splash of tonic. Kostin must have pull with the bartender.

"Who knows?" Livy said. "We drink vodka in England. You drink gin. Americans drink German beer. Alcohol is the great peacemaker."

Kostin smiled and drank, but the gin burned Livy's throat. She wanted to find a loo and vomit. She wanted to drink all night. Only one of those options was open to her.

"We have given you a code name now," Kostin said.

"Well, I bloody well hope it's a cracker." The moment called for her to lay on the English charm a bit thick.

"Chaika."

"Sorry, don't speak the language, comrade."

"It means seagull."

"Ah yes. Like the Chekhov play."

Kostin shook his head. "Prerevolution. They wouldn't dare name it after such a work. Besides I prefer *The Cherry Orchard*. So tragic."

"Never seen that one. 'Course, he's no Shakespeare, but then who is?"

"Shakespeare is always the same. Kings. Fairies. Love gone bad. No, your greatest writer is Conan Doyle."

Livy nearly did a spit take. "Greatest writer? Are you joking? Sherlock Holmes is nothing but an insufferable know-it-all. That whole business where he can tell what school you went to by the dirt on your shoe—what a load of rubbish. No, no, you pull out your copy of *King Lear*—or, even better, *Hamlet*—and you'll find some real profundities there, Mister Kostin."

The Russian took her hand. It surprised her.

"I've never known a woman like you, Lee-vye."

She rolled her eyes. "Listen, luv, this is hardly the sort of place where you propose to a woman."

"Stop. No, no, you misunderstand. Listen to me. Another drink? Yes?" He lifted two fingers to the bar.

How many other girls has he brought here? she wondered.

"This—what we are doing together now—could end very, very badly. I don't want that to happen. That is why I had to warn you about the man that followed you. You must be careful. It is . . . complicated."

"The whole bloody world's complicated, Yuri. Been like that for years."

The drinks appeared at the end of the bar, and Kostin brought them back to the table. He went on. "I thought that after the war it would be changed. Peacetime, yes? We could live the life we all dreamed of during the war. But there is no peace. It's just more war. Maybe we are not killing each other in the snow. Yet. I don't know."

Livy recognized this moment. The confession. She could use this later. She tightened her grip on his hand.

"You're tired, luv. We all are."

"Sometimes I wonder if this is all we will ever really know. That the life most people live can never be ours because we are forever at war." His shoulders sagged as he spoke, as if a literal weight pushed him down, drained his voice, and aged him.

"We're both tired of it. Sometimes it feels like we fought the Nazis just so we could start fighting each other."

Kostin nodded. "Do you ever think about something different? You know maybe . . . a husband? A child? A little Livy?"

The change in tone startled her. She dropped her eyes and smiled, wondering how to play this new moment. The soft, vulnerable spot of the man Germans had called *Der Rote Teufel* in full view. She had to deflect.

"I told you already this is a rubbish spot for a marriage proposal."

"You make a joke because you know the answer but will not say it."

"All right, then Svengali, what's my answer?"

Kostin, who seemed a bit tipsy, touched his fingers to his temples and closed his eyes. "You must open your mind so I can see inside Livy Nash," he said, laying it on thicker than Bela Lugosi. Then he opened his eyes, took her hand, and gave it a long kiss.

"A woman doing what you are doing, who has done what you have done, would choke to death in a marriage." His lips caressed the fingers of her left hand. "No one will ever put a ring on this finger."

Livy scoffed and took a long pull of the gin. The liquor went down like water now, but his words burned in her stomach. The honesty of the remark mixed with the gin haze in her head smarted. Inside, Livy scolded herself. This wasn't real life. This was an act. This was burlesque for the boys. This was for Margot. *Play the part and forget the rest.*

She threw her head back and began a slow clap. "Your mind-reading act isn't bad, but I think you should look for a new one. Ever play the ukulele?"

Of course they had another round. They talked about everything except secret documents and clandestine meetings. Halfway through their fourth drinks, the one and only Miss Stella Mills walked in through the door behind the bar. A few people applauded and waved. She flitted through, waving her hand a bit, like the king on V-E day, and was helped to a waiting car outside.

Once she cleared the bar, Kostin stood and took Livy's hand, and they went back into the Gayety Theatre. The whistling men had left. The lackadaisical quartet had packed up its instruments. An usher walked through, picking up trash. A janitor lazily pushed a broom across an aisle, collecting cigarette butts and paper cups. Spilled beer made parts of the floor sticky.

Still, the grand old place had an ambience in the quiet that made it compelling. They walked up the stairs back to the balcony, and Kostin found the door with the sagging number 14.

He let Livy in. The theatre was dark except for two ghost lights on the edge of the stage. The dim light hid the peeling paint and the stained carpet. She walked to the edge of the box and stared out at the stage, illuminated by the harsh glow of two light bulbs.

It looked like a proper theatre now. A place of magic instead of a rundown burlesque theatre where women stripped down to their pasties and knickers.

She felt Kostin's breath on her neck. His hands on her hips. She'd known this would happen. She felt prepared for it. When it happened, when his lips touched her neck and her desire stirred, Livy felt an overwhelming sense of the past. It felt as if the year after the war—the year she'd spent inside a bottle—had come to reclaim her. The shame inside her wasn't loud enough. Another voice dominated. It said, *It's about the job. Use him. Get what you want. And get out.*

He slowly undid the buttons of her coat, his lips caressing her neck as he undid her blouse. She felt his fingertips on her breasts. For a moment, she gave into the sensation. Livy remembered the Russian's considerable skills as a lover. He moved slowly. Made her feel each moment.

She tried to turn off her brain. Four gin and tonics couldn't do it, though. Livy stood outside of it all, observing, analyzing, thinking steps ahead.

He turned her toward him. His left hand held her around the waist, and he brought her mouth closer with his right. She felt his breath on her lips before he kissed her. The glow of the stage made his blue eyes almost purple. Livy wondered what he saw in her eyes.

But she didn't give him time to pause or evaluate. She pulled him against her, pressing her lips to his, hands pushing his coat down, fumbling with his belt. He pushed his hips against hers, grabbing her skirt. Lifting. She was afraid she'd push him away and run back to the bar to order more and more gin. She wanted it over. All of it. Over.

She grabbed him, breathless. "Now, Yuri. Hurry."

Chapter Nineteen

～

An hour later Kostin hailed a cab for Livy to take her back to the Statler. He apologized for not sharing the ride but told her the risk was too great. They kissed before she left, and he held her in his arms. As before, the Russian said he'd be in touch.

The streets of DC felt empty at this time of night. Livy looked at her watch. Almost one. The driver whistled an old Cab Calloway song. She couldn't remember the name.

She put her head back on the canvas seat and watched the buildings pass by. On one corner she saw two women facing each other, arguing by the look of it. The older of the two punctuated whatever she said with hard jabs of her finger. The scene took Livy back to Paris and a woman she'd met during the war. Antoinette had been a member of the Resistance. She was only twenty and pretty, with curly dark hair and deep black eyes. Naturally men found her irresistible. Especially the Germans. Antoinette slept with any number of Nazis, always bringing back key information. No one ever questioned that. Still many people hated Antoinette. She would pass the lines to get into stores, and people would call her names.

Collaborateur. Putain. A whore.

The Germans she'd slept with meant nothing to the French girl, but still her own people mocked her.

Livy wondered if they would call her the same.

The thought plagued her. She smelled like sex and gin. It was all over her. The cabbie had to know. The comfort of her hotel room would settle her, she hoped. A hot bath. Then bed. That's what she needed. She could think then.

The taxi pulled up in front of The Statler. The night doorman stood outside the big glass double doors. Livy paid the driver. The uniformed greeter stepped aside as she approached. His smile felt subtle and knowing. She had to look like utter hell. Like a woman in way too deep. That's certainly how she felt.

As she walked to the door, she noticed a car parked on the corner of K Street adjacent to the hotel. Shadows obscured the car's interior, but Livy had seen the big blue Packard before.

* * *

She woke up the next morning with her first full-on hangover in two years. The taste of last night's gin combined with cigarette smoke stuck to her tongue. She resolved to spend the morning in bed, hoping the comfort of the thick sheets and the silence of the room would help her think.

Alice!

She'd scheduled a meeting with the woman from the British Embassy that morning. The full English breakfast. She scrambled around the room to find her watch. It lay under a pile of clothes she'd worn last night. Damn it all! She had thirty minutes to get to the restaurant.

Livy threw herself together in record time. She covered her unruly hair with a beret and slipped into shoes as she opened the door into the hallway.

The morning doorman gave her a reserved smile as he hailed a Diamond cab. She got in and gave the driver an address on Massachusetts. As the car pulled away from the curb, Livy spotted the familiar blue sheen of the big Packard turning onto Sixteenth Street just behind her.

*　*　*

Livy was only ten minutes late to the pub. Alice had taken a wooden table near the front so she could watch the door.

"Lancashire people—always late. They teach you lot how to tell time?" she said, with a laugh. Livy smiled even though her head pounded.

The pub, which was called O'Flaherty's, was owned by a man from Leeds named Anthony, a big man with patches of hair on the sides of his head and the puffy nose of a former drinker. Livy guessed him to be in his sixties. Anthony said he'd decided to use an Irish name for the pub because "Americans think the Irish invented drinking." She could tell he liked Alice. They flirted playfully despite the vast age difference, and then he shuffled back to the kitchen.

A few minutes later he brought them each a full English breakfast consisting of three crispy slices of bacon, two eggs done over easy, perfectly cut grilled tomato slices, mushrooms, a smattering of baked beans, toast with marmalade and strawberry jam, and a heaping cup of hot tea. He left four fried slices of black pudding on a separate plate. Livy knew many people back home who loved the dark concoction, but the thought of putting a piece in her mouth made her want to retch. The pudding, although more accurately a sausage, was made from onions, oatmeal, a few different herbs, and pig's blood. She wondered what Anthony did back in that kitchen of his.

The two women chatted about home, as well as the war, while they ate. Alice told her she'd worked at an SOE home station, receiving and translating codes from agents in the field. Livy listened and felt her heart lighten. Here, finally, was another young woman who seemed to understand her, who didn't judge Livy for the way she talked or dressed. God knows she needed a friend now more than ever. And Alice did make her laugh with her homegrown stories and sly jokes. Just like Margot. But as much as Livy wanted to trade war stories, she confessed only to driving RAF pilots to their planes at Squires Gate Airport. Nothing more.

Livy sipped the robust tea as they talked, which helped soothe her stomach a bit. She didn't dare eat everything on the plate. Her hangover was no match for grease-fried bacon and eggs.

Alice finished most of hers but decided to wrap the black pudding and take it back to the embassy. As she dropped it in her purse, she pulled out several folded pieces of paper.

"Almost forgot," she said and handed them to Livy.

Inside, paper-clipped to a copy of a War Office personnel document, was a small black and white photograph of Margot Dupont.

There she was. The photo must have been taken at SOE headquarters in Baker Street, a standard identification image for use during training. Livy allowed herself a smile at Margot's attempt to look so serious and official. Like a proper spy. She had soft eyes and dirty-blonde hair that curled slightly at her shoulders. Margot's upturned nose and girlish features belied a toughness that Livy had envied when they first met.

"Do you mind if I hold onto the photo?" she asked. "Just for reference, really."

Alice finished off her tea, and said, "That's okay then, but you can't use it for print or anything. I could get in trouble if that got out. They're persnickety about that."

It was nearly eleven when Alice left the pub to get back to work. They left a big tip for Anthony and said goodbye to each other out front. Alice strolled off down Massachusetts. Livy turned the other way, fancying a walk after always being carted around the city in public transport.

She'd not taken ten steps when a tall, hatless man in a black suit overtook her quickly. Reaching her side, he slowed, matching her step for step.

"Perfect day for a walk in the park," he said. American. Big manufactured smile. "The National Zoo. One hour."

He picked up his gait, looking like another businessman in a hurry in a city of perpetual motion. Livy watched as a car turned from a side street and pulled up to the curb alongside the hatless man. He walked around the car and hopped into the passenger seat of the blue Packard.

*　*　*

Livy decided to walk the rest of the way and arrived outside the great steel gates of the National Zoo in Rock Creek Park ten minutes before the set time. She scanned the area to make sure she'd not been followed by anyone else.

Running through the heart of the District of Columbia, in much the same way Central Park bisects New York City, Rock

Creek Park seemed to be a popular lunchtime destination. Moms with kids in tow lined up outside the zoo gates while a mix of businessmen, tourists loaded down with cameras, and couples meeting for lunch made up the bulk of the foot traffic.

So the blue Packard belonged to the FBI, and the Gray Man had been Russian. Kostin had confirmed as much. Livy doubted she'd see the bullet-headed man in gray again after he was unceremoniously escorted from the Mayflower. She took no chances, though, walking a minute, then stopping to see who might be behind her or lurking on the periphery. A few steps later, she'd stop again to see if any of the same faces remained in her vicinity.

Satisfied she hadn't been followed, Livy headed back to the entrance. This time, she saw Sam Keller sitting on a wooden bench directly opposite the zoo archway. He wore a brown suit with a pressed white shirt and no tie. He looked almost relaxed. Livy approached, and he stood up, arms out, and hugged her tight.

"It's been a while since we've seen each other." His voice shifted to a whisper as they embraced. "Old friends. And we're just going for a walk."

A great smile broke out across his broad face as his voice resumed its normal volume. "It has been so long. I didn't even know you were in town. Listen, how long you got? Time for a walk? Come on. You gotta see this place. Everything's still in bloom."

The pretense was a ruse, but Keller had undersold the lush greenery of the park. They made their way along paths framed by thick, old trees whose green leaves provided a bit of shade in the Washington heat. Other couples passed them and smiled. A

few people rode bicycles up ahead. Somewhere in the near distance, Livy heard the sound of running water. It felt as if she'd
been plucked out of her world and placed somewhere safe.

But that was an illusion. This idyllic locale merely served as
backdrop for another meeting with another man. Another
report. More orders. Her fingers traced the outline of Margot's
picture in the pocket of her skirt.

"You look rested today," she said. Keller looked like he'd had
a week off.

"Thanks. Seven hours does wonders." He looked down at
her. "I can't say the same for you."

"Such a flatterer, Mr. Keller," Livy snapped back. "The Russians are following me too, you know. You sure they're not
behind us? Maybe sitting up in one of these trees?"

"I've got a couple of boys with binoculars on us and the sur-
rounding area. We've got it covered."

"I feel so protected."

Keller shot her a look. "You were out late last night."

"Missed curfew, did I?"

"Just tone it down a notch, okay? We're on the same side."

Gravel crunched under their shoes as they reached a rock
bridge that passed over the creek Livy had heard earlier.

"You met him last night?"

"I did."

"And?"

"I gave him the new material."

"And?"

"He took it."

Keller waited.

"He took it, and we got drunk and had sex. Is that better?"

The words hung in the air between them. She wanted to go on and say, *I'm drinking again. I feel awful and wrong inside. I don't know if I can stop or if I've gone too far. I'll be damned if I leave my friend in a prison one more day than is necessary, but I'm terrified I'll lose myself and never find my way home."*

Keller reached to straighten a tie that wasn't there. "I'm assuming it was . . . mutual?"

Livy had no idea what to say. Her eyes latched onto a ray of sunshine forcing its way between two branches like a spotlight. She felt the impulse to flee into the woods. To be gone from all this. Finally, she glanced up at Keller.

"No, he didn't force me."

"Okay."

They reached the end of the bridge, and Livy stopped.

"It's best if we keep going," he said.

"He's in trouble, I think."

"And what makes you think that?"

"He said he was tired of it all. He kept saying things like 'No one trusts anyone now.'"

"Did he say more? Talk about his personal life maybe?"

Livy shook her head.

Keller looked as if he didn't know what to say. He put a hand on her elbow. She jerked it away and leaned against the bridge. Her eyes down on the creek.

The FBI man moved beside her. "I think we've reached a point now where the operation needs to be altered."

"What?"

"A change in tactic. The work you've done so far makes it possible."

Livy rubbed her eyes. "What are you talking about?"

"We have an opportunity to compromise Kostin now. You've given us that."

Livy had no idea what the man meant, but something about this sudden change, based on the two pieces of news she'd given Keller, did not exactly fill her battered heart with sunshine and daisies.

"I thought that's what we were working on."

"It is. Well, it *was*, but if we change tactics, things could move faster for both of us. It wouldn't be that difficult. We could even make it work at The Statler. I sent some people in the other day to see if cameras were possible in your current room. We can't completely control the environment, of course, but it's doable."

The realization of what Keller meant hit like a solid right to Livy's jaw. She felt dizzy and held on to the bridge as the full implication became clearer.

"A honey trap, you mean?"

Keller nodded. No change in his expression. "It moves things along quicker. Once we have the film of the two of you, then if Kostin gets Berlin, we have him. Think of that. The MGB Berlin *rezident* is in our back pocket."

"And what about the reason *I* was sent here?"

The FBI man shrugged. "Once we have Kostin, then whatever he knows we'll know."

She slammed her hand down on the rail and stepped toward Keller. He shuffled back. "Once you have him, I'll be pushed aside," she said. "I know how these things work."

"Just keep your voice down, Miss Nash. Nothing's been decided yet."

"I won't do it."

"You're tired and not thinking clearly."

"I'm thinking clearly enough to know I won't let you use a dirty film of me to get what you want. That's not why I am here. That's not the operation."

"No? How is this any different from what's already going on between the two of you? Except we get evidence that one of their top people is sleeping with a British agent."

"Who he thinks is working *for* him. This was about building trust. And that's all."

Leaves fell into the creek and floated downstream. Livy stepped back from Keller and watched a little boy pick a big maple leaf out of the water and proudly show his mother. Keller leaned against the bridge, trying to make eye contact.

"Do you know why the Germans called him the 'Red Devil'?"

"I've read the file."

"Files don't deal with reputations and how they're made. They're just about facts. In the war, Kostin was with a group called SMERSH. It's an acronym but the words mean 'Death to Spies' in Russian. One of Kostin's jobs was to interrogate Nazi deserters. This was near the end, and the Red Army was still weeks from Berlin. Kostin would squeeze these men for every piece of information they might have. He's a damn good marksman. He knew where to shoot a man to maximize pain but keep him alive long enough that he'd talk. I don't mean just kneecaps, but places where the pain is so bad they must have begged to be finished off. He even had a calling card, you might say. When he was done with them, he'd shoot both eyes out, then hang the bodies up as a warning."

Keller's little story did its job and gave her a bit of a shiver. Then she thought about Peter Scobee, another man she thought she knew. A man whose kind exterior masked something dark. This time was different, she told herself. She had no illusions about Kostin. And she had her own dark side to worry about.

"So let me ask you, Miss Nash, do you think you can establish real trust with a man like that?"

"I know what I'm doing."

Livy turned away from him. The tranquil natural scenery, combined with mums and children out for a day, looked like a Normal Rockwell painting. The only thing wrong with the picture was the two of them. The spies in the park, manipulating lives all over the world.

"What if he starts to suspect you? You think he'll show you mercy?"

"Are we done here?"

Keller leaned in. His eyes lightened and the big Midwestern face softened. "This operation has gone a lot further than I ever thought it would, Livy. That's thanks to you. But what I'm suggesting can end it. If we threaten to send that film to his embassy, then Kostin knows that the next stop for him is Moscow, to get a bullet in the back of the head. We'll have him. He'll give us what we both want."

"Mr. Keller, you're not a woman. We know men. Better than you do yourselves sometimes. Yuri is tired. He's a man searching for something. Into his life walks an old fling. Someone who understands him more than other women do. Someone who offers him precious secrets. And the promise of more. I'm his lifeline. I have more leverage over him to get what we both need than any blackmail you and your G-men can dream up."

Keller sighed and held out his hand to her. The gesture threw Livy until Keller said, "So good seeing you again. Please tell your family I miss them." She took his hand and they embraced. A friendly, platonic hug. The kind friends give each other if they've grown up together.

As he held her, he said, "Think about this. You're playing the long game right now. Doesn't have to be that way."

She pulled away, smiled, and turned to walk back to the zoo entrance. Keller started in the other direction.

Her nerves vibrated. She walked quickly. A gust of wind caught the front of her hair. She pushed it back into place and felt wetness on her cheek. She was right about what she'd told Keller. She knew Yuri Kostin. Livy was sure of it.

*   *   *

By late afternoon she was back in the palatial, air-conditioned comfort of The Statler. She tried to nap but couldn't. Reading didn't make her tired. It couldn't take her mind off the night before at the Gayety, the afternoon with Keller, and the realization that she might very well be in this dark game for weeks to come.

Livy ate dinner at a table for two in a corner of the hotel restaurant. She picked at her food and felt the same creeping anxiety she'd felt each night since this whole thing had begun. At the table next to her, a husband and wife tried to get a toddler to eat with her fork. *Keller is home right now,* she thought. With the missus and the new baby. And here she was. Alone. Pushing a piece of overcooked chicken around a fancy plate and facing the same demons she thought she'd beaten a year ago. She had the impulse to go back to her room, call Alice, and ask if she wanted dinner or a drink. But she couldn't involve more people or get too close. She was here to do a job, and the situation was just too volatile.

She wanted Margot out—but deep down she wanted herself out just as badly.

After dinner, she could no longer put off the inevitable. She wandered across the lobby into the bar of the Embassy Room and sat at a corner table. This place felt far more intimate than the one at the Mayflower. Only a few tables scattered around a long mahogany bar.

Livy ordered Scotch on the rocks. It felt wrong. This wasn't part of her role. No, this was her true self. Livy Nash. Drinking again. But dammit, she needed to relax sometime. She felt wound far too tight. There'd be a time later when she would quit again, when she wouldn't need its comfort. The first few sips seemed to help, but the tightness in her back and neck remained. She ordered another.

Two younger men in khaki trousers and navy sports coats had noticed her when she walked in. One was handsome, with stiff blond hair and the kind of smile that had given Errol Flynn a pretty decent career. They kept turning to her while she sipped the first Scotch. When she ordered the second, the blond's attention surged. Their furtive glances seemed to say, *She's alone and she's sticking around.*

Halfway through the second Scotch, Livy felt the fist that gripped her back loosen slightly. She rolled her neck from one shoulder to the other. Just that much release felt so good. When she opened her eyes, the blond stood in front of her. He must have felt confident, because he'd brought his drink with him.

He flashed the big smile and started to speak.

"Piss off."

His reaction made Livy think she'd come off a little stronger than intended. The blond and his drink pivoted and headed back to the bar. Neither he nor his friend craned their necks to look at her again.

Livy knocked back the last swallow of the drink. The tension in her neck was at almost manageable levels now. Yet somehow she didn't feel relaxed. Something gnawed at her.

She turned toward the lobby and saw him. Maybe she'd spotted him in her peripheral vision earlier, and her subconscious had held on to it, but whatever the case, the Gray Man sat in one of the upright chairs near the front desk, a newspaper folded across his lap. He made eye contact with Livy, stood, and moved toward her.

Chapter Twenty

Livy felt the precariousness of her position. She had no weapon. The nature of the job demanded her identity be authentic down to what she kept in the drawers of her room. Reporters who do stories on ladies' fashion don't carry pistols. Livy reached into her handbag and dropped twenty cents on the table for the waiter. The handbag had a bit of heft. Might do as a last resort. The far better plan was to get out. Now.

She headed toward the bar, away from the Gray Man in the lobby. There was another exit out onto K Street there. Kostin's words from last night suddenly seemed more significant.

"You embarrassed the man sent to watch you."

The Gray Man didn't look like someone who took that sort of thing lightly.

Despite his age and belly, the Gray Man seemed more than physically capable. His arms and torso bulged through his shapeless suit. Her only option would be to go to the front desk and report him if he followed her. But would that keep her safe in her room tonight? Livy scanned the hotel for anything else handheld and heavy that could be used to clout the big man.

She didn't have time to consider further options. Two younger men—also in gray suits—stood on either side of the exit from the bar.

Livy stopped ten feet away They stared at her, not advancing.

The hell with this, she thought, and said, "Excuse me."

She pushed past one of the younger men, who took her arm at the elbow. She kept a tight grip on her handbag and was about to test its effectiveness as a blunt object when she felt the other young man on her opposite side. He put something hard and metallic against her ribs.

"No talk," he said. "Walk to door." He had a thick accent and struggled with even a few words of English.

The man with the gun had a cracked front tooth, freckles across his nose, and dark hair. The young man who held her elbow looked the typical MGB type. Short blond hair, puffy dead eyes, and a mouth with all the charm of a letter slot at the Royal Mail.

As they made their way through the bar exit, Livy felt a chill when she saw the Gray Man lumbering toward them on the street. Cracked Tooth pressed the gun a little deeper into Livy's side.

"Move," he grunted, and they pushed her down the sidewalk toward a burgundy Ford sedan.

Livy considered her options. She could scream. The doorman was around the corner somewhere, but with the sheer breadth of the Statler, he was probably a full city block or more away. The thought crossed her mind that this little "kidnapping" was nothing more than Yuri Kostin's way of arranging a meeting. After all, she worked for them now, so why would the

Gray Man and his cohorts want to take her somewhere dark, shoot her in the back of the head, and leave her? The anxiety of that thought gripped her as the two Russian escorts marched her nearer the car, affecting awkward smiles that only made them look more menacing.

"I want to know where you're—" Livy said.

"No talk." Cracked Tooth pushed the gun in deeper. Puffy Eyes tightened his grip on her elbow.

Livy tried to calm herself. She'd fought like hell to avoid this exact same type of situation just a few weeks ago in Paris. Now, three MGB men led her to a waiting car.

She felt the scream deep in her gut. *This doesn't have to end badly.* There would be a way out of this. A way to explain. But she just didn't know what they wanted. That scared her more than anything.

She heard laughter and voices behind her, probably from the front of the hotel. Cracked Tooth spun around at the noise. Livy lashed out, bringing her handbag down on his gun hand. The automatic clattered on the pavement. She felt two arms encircle her midsection, so Livy pushed away and whirled around with a backhand to the face of Puffy Eyes. It connected long enough for her to turn and take one step toward the voices. But Cracked Tooth had recovered too quickly. He held the gun steady, and the look in his eyes told her she wouldn't make it another step.

"In car. Now!" the Gray Man hissed.

Puffy Eyes ran around to the driver's side of the car. Cracked Tooth opened the back seat and shoved Livy across the black leather seats to the far side. The Gray Man shifted his bulk into the passenger seat while the gunman joined Livy in the back.

Livy knew now. Wherever they were going, Yuri Kostin wasn't waiting on the other end.

The Ford's big engine growled to life, and the car jolted forward into the street. The Gray Man spoke softly in Russian to the driver. He kept the car's speed slow as they merged into the nighttime traffic in front of the hotel.

Gray Man said something over his shoulder, and Cracked Tooth ripped Livy's handbag away from her and handed it up front. The big man opened it and took each item out. Lipstick, compact, pens. With a grunt he tossed it back.

The car took a left on Nineteenth Street and slowly picked up speed. Livy noticed Cracked Tooth looking out the rear window, but he kept the black automatic aimed at her midsection. His eyes flicked back to her. Then to the window.

He spoke hesitantly to the Gray Man. The big man in front shifted the rearview mirror. The adjustment allowed Livy to see as well. The blue Packard followed them. Even three car lengths back, she recognized the long hood and angled grill.

The Gray Man barked something at the driver. Puffy Eyes nodded, slammed on his brakes, and nose-dived the Ford into the next right turn. Another command from the big man and Cracked Tooth grabbed Livy's head and shoved it down between her knees. He kept his hand on the back of her head, pressing the muzzle of the gun into her temple.

The force caused Livy to bite her bottom lip. She felt blood on her tongue. She tried to focus on the pain rather than the situation that had quickly slipped out of her control.

The Ford dove into a hard left. The car's tail slid the opposite way, tossing Livy hard into the door. The Gray Man barked at the driver, spitting out order after order in Russian.

Livy's head crashed into the front seat as the car braked again. The tires squealed, trying to hang on to the road. Her body bounced from side to side, but Cracked Tooth's hand remained on her neck, the gun against her head.

She had few options. She had enough strength to knock the man's hand off her neck. Maybe she could push the gun away in the same moment. Then, grab the door handle, push it open, and roll out into the street. Everything would need to happen in perfect order, and she'd still run the risk of being run down by another car. Maybe even the blue Packard itself. She decided to keep her head down. For now.

Potholes and broken pavement rattled the Ford's backseat, sending Livy's knees crashing into her forehead. The Gray Man continued shouting instructions at the driver. He called him Sergei, but that was all Livy could understand.

The car accelerated, braked, and spun hard. Then more bumps. The Ford shook and bounced. Another turn. The engine revved. A smoother road now, but Sergei kept his foot on the gas pedal.

The blue Packard must still be behind them.

Livy tried to focus on her breath, a trick she'd learned during SOE training. *When you can't control anything else, control your breath. It's yours. Concentrate on it.* She felt certain the trainer hadn't anticipated the technique being effective when you're captive in the back seat of a car during a high-speed chase through city streets, but it took her mind off what might happen once the car stopped.

Sirens! She heard them in the distance. They sounded streets away. The long wail of a Washington, DC, police car, maybe two, approaching.

The three men in the car heard them too. The Gray Man spat out a command. Sergei spun the wheels, and Livy's body lurched right and then left. It felt like the entire car spun around and accelerated in the opposite direction. The Gray Man shouted as the car's engine screamed. The driver braked quickly. Livy was pushed back, then forward. The front wheels hit yet another bump at speed, and Livy's body lifted off the seat. Her feet suspended above the floorboard for a second. The back wheels followed. Another lift, like a rollercoaster.

Then silence.

The car cruised slowly a minute, maybe two. Livy kept still, wondering where they might be, what could be happening. Easing to a stop, the driver put the car in park but kept the engine running. No one spoke. Livy heard someone light a cigarette. The smell spread through the car. Livy coughed. Breathing was hard enough with her head between her knees.

She heard the driver engage the clutch, and the car began to move. Again she coughed, and Cracked Tooth pulled his hand away from her neck. She sat up, pulling air into her lungs. Livy played the moment for all it was worth. She gasped, hands clutching her chest. At the same time, she took in the surroundings.

They were driving through a city parking lot filled with cars. Sergei must be a damned good driver. She saw no sign of the blue Packard. The sound of the sirens seemed to have faded in another direction.

The Gray Man took a long drag on the cigarette.

"Medlenneye," the big man said to Sergei. *"Medlenneye."*

He slowly eased back onto the side street in front of the parking lot. Now they had the road to themselves.

The Gray Man turned to Cracked Tooth and gestured at Livy.

Holding the gun still in his right hand, the Russian grabbed her neck again with his left. Livy was ready. Sensing he might have relaxed during her coughing spasm, Livy lashed out. She slapped his left hand away and brought her fist hard back across his cheek.

But she was too stiff and slow from sitting in such an awkward position for so long. Cracked Tooth pounded the heavy grip of the gun into the back of her neck. Livy felt the blow flare down her back. The Gray Man shouted. The Russian beside Livy grabbed her hair with his free hand and slammed her head hard into her knees. A spasm of pain radiated from her forehead to the bridge of her nose, causing her eyes to water. He shouted and placed the barrel of the gun to her forehead, pressing it deep into the temple.

She'd had to try something. Anything. But her chance had passed. Now, they'd be more careful. Livy listened to her breathing, focusing on something she could control. She wouldn't have much control over what would happen next.

Chapter
Twenty-One

They drove for another fifteen or twenty minutes, by Livy's estimate. No more swift turns or sudden braking. The blue Packard and the police had been left behind. She assumed they must be well outside the District, now in Virginia or Maryland probably, although Livy had no idea which direction they'd traveled. Not long after they left the parking lot, the roads got smoother, and Sergei kept the speed of the Ford consistent.

By the time the car came to a stop, Livy could barely turn her neck. When Cracked Tooth took his hand off it, at first Livy couldn't lift her head. She felt a knot where he'd smashed the gun into her neck.

She started to move slowly, but the Russian took no chance. His left hand held her arm, and his right kept the gun jammed into her side. Slowly, painfully, Livy turned her neck and shoulders to look at Cracked Tooth and see where they'd stopped. She felt some satisfaction that the Russian now had a nice bruised cheek to go along with his cracked tooth.

They'd parked behind a row of what appeared to be shops, all closed now. The building was one long brick structure with a steel door every twenty yards or so. The Gray Man heaved himself out of the car and made his way to one.

Sergei opened the car door on Livy's side and pulled her out. Her legs felt shaky and stiff. The blood made its way back to her feet as she stumbled around the rear of the Ford. Cracked Tooth met her on the other side of the car, and the two younger Russians took her forcibly toward the back door.

Once they reached the doorframe, Livy saw nothing but darkness inside the shop. After a minute a light turned on, a small flicker deep in the building.

The two men dragged her through the darkness toward the glow. Maybe this big room had been a shop some time ago. Now it was little more than a husk. Dust covered the floors. Their shoes stirred it up. Livy smelled a combination of mildew, tobacco, and cleaning fluid.

Up ahead, the Gray Man righted an overturned wooden chair and placed it next to a shadeless table lamp, which sat on top of a wooden packing crate.

The two younger Russians sat Livy down on the chair, hard. Cracked Tooth stood behind her. Livy felt the gun at the base of her neck.

No amount of focus on her breathing could take away the overwhelming feeling that this was a place where you took someone to be killed. As clear as that seemed to be, the conclusion made no sense to her. What was this all about? Kostin had said she'd embarrassed the big man in gray, but Livy couldn't fathom a bruised ego driving him to kill a potential double agent. Had Keller given her fake documents? It didn't add up. Nothing did right now.

Maybe they just wanted to scare her. More testing. She tried holding on to that thought.

The Gray Man lit another cigarette and gestured toward Sergei. The driver disappeared into the darkness. The big man ignored Livy. He stood, smoking, with one hand on his hip.

A current suddenly sizzled through the ceiling, and a single fluorescent bulb flashed right above them. The light blinked rapidly. So much so, Livy had to close her eyes. The effect was disorientating until the bulb stabilized.

The Gray Man took one last drag of his cigarette, dropped it on the floor, and rubbed it out. He barked another command at Sergei. Then he turned his focus on Livy.

The younger Russian hurried back to the entrance to close the door.

The Gray Man pulled out a nasty-looking knife from his jacket pocket. The thick blade had a dark wooden handle with an S-shaped guard. It looked worn along the blade, although the steel looked plenty sharp. He turned it in his hand, as if getting used to its feel, and then placed it down gently on the crate beside the lamp.

Livy recognized a theatrical move when she saw one. The knife represented a threat of torture, which she didn't care to contemplate just yet.

"You—Bree-tish spy." The Gray Man's English fit his mouth as well as his suit fit the rest of him. The words didn't sound like a question, but Livy answered anyway.

"Yes. That's right."

"You work Bree-tish now?"

God, what would happen if she gave the wrong answer to a question she didn't really understand? If a gun to the back of her head and the threat of a sharp Russian knife hadn't been enough, the Gray Man's limited English caught her even more off guard.

"I work for both. The British. And for you."

The answer didn't seem to satisfy the Gray Man. He glanced up at Cracked Tooth. The man with the gun stepped away from Livy. Before she could feel a sense of reprieve, the Gray Man picked up the knife. From inside his wrinkled suit, he produced a folded piece of paper that Livy immediately recognized. It was the first set of classified documents she'd handed off in front of Ford's Theatre.

The Gray Man opened the papers. He shoved them at Livy's face. "Thees—not real," he said. It wasn't a question.

"No, you're wrong. It is."

"Who geev you thees?"

"I picked it up. At the embassy. The British Embassy." She tried to think. The knot in her neck throbbed. The humid air in the empty shop was thick with dust. She was alone and wondered if she should have ever trusted anyone on this damned job.

"Where is Major Kostin? He's my contact."

The Gray Man smiled and then, Livy believed, started to laugh. The sound began in his chest and rattled—more like a cough than a laugh—then burst from his thick lips, revealing teeth brown from too many noxious cigarettes. He looked around to his two younger comrades as if to say, *Isn't she funny?* They didn't laugh.

The longer this went on, the less Livy liked it.

The Gray Man pulled a handkerchief from his trousers and wiped sweat off his face. He moved closer to Livy, the knife at his side.

"Again. Who—geev—you—thees?" He pushed the document in her face.

"I took it," Livy said, slowly enunciating each word. "From the British Embassy. I demand to see Major Kostin."

The Gray Man put the document back in his pocket. He leaned down to Livy, his face inches from hers. His breath smelled worse than the musty shop.

"I no bee-leev you, pree-tee girl." His chuckle rumbled low in his chest.

Livy understood the game now. The big Russian had added those last two words to increase the threat. To make Livy reveal her fear. He smiled, glanced at the other men, then back to her.

Fine, she thought. *The hell with it.*

She spat hard in his face. And before he could react, she did it again.

The Russian recoiled and wiped the spit with the sleeve of his jacket. As he finished, his left hand swept up and crashed hard into the right side of Livy's face. His knuckles made full contact just below her eye, nearly knocking her out of the chair. Somehow she held on and didn't make a sound. The big man's fist felt like being hit by the grill of a car. Her vision blurred. The Scotch, the disorienting drive, and now this had caught up to her, but she wouldn't give them the satisfaction of seeing her in pain.

She gave herself a quick assessment. Teeth seemed still intact. Her nose bled, but she was lucky it didn't seem to be broken. Livy waited until the vision in her right eye began to clear, then sat up and looked at the big man.

"I'm working for you, you mangy gobshite," she said.

The Russian muttered something quietly to the other two men. He started to remove his jacket. The younger ones didn't move. Livy sensed their anxiety. The Gray Man's eyes hardened, and he barked the same command. Now the two younger men, stepped back from her. She felt their reluctance.

Livy bit her tongue hard to clear her head. The blow to her cheek had numbed part of her face and fogged her brain. She knew the time for subterfuge was over. This was a fight, and she had to be ready. She needed her wits right now. Needed to think. Her life depended on it.

The Gray Man folded his coat neatly and placed it beside the lamp on the overturned crate. He leered down at her with a look he hadn't given her before.

They all heard the sound at once. Tires on gravel. Right outside the back door.

The big Russian looked toward the entrance. Listening. Like it was *The Shadow* on the radio. They heard the tires stop. An engine turned off. A moment. A car door slammed.

The Gray Man nodded at Cracked Tooth. The younger Russian, his automatic in front of him, walked slowly toward the door.

Bam! Bam! Bam!

The harsh insistence of the knocks startled them all. Three more came in succession on the metal entrance.

Cracked Tooth stopped in his tracks. The Gray Man hissed something at him.

The knocking stopped. A voice called on the other side of the door, also in Russian.

Cracked Tooth looked back to the older man, his eyes wide. The Gray Man sighed and threw up his hands in frustration. He gestured to the younger man, who hurried to the door, turned the lock, and opened it.

Livy heard the footsteps on the dusty floor before she saw him. Yuri Kostin walked slowly into the pool of light where

Livy, the Gray Man, and Sergei stood. Yuri barked something in Russian, and Cracked Tooth quickly relocked the door.

She lifted her eyes to Kostin, but he didn't return her gaze. The thought that he might have set this whole thing up filled her with more dread than she'd felt in this whole God-awful night.

Kostin's eyes drifted away from the Gray Man and finally to Livy's face. Then to the knife and the folded coat on the overturned crate. He spoke softly to the big man, but his tone gave Livy no sense of what he said.

The big Russian spat on the ground and inched closer to Kostin. His arms spread like a wrestler before a match.

So this was some sort of conflict between the two Russians. Over her? Was that it?

Gesturing at Livy and at himself, the big Russian went on a rant, all of it directed at Kostin. He grabbed his coat from the table and shoved the documents in Kostin's face. Yuri put one hand on the Gray Man's fleshy, sweating face and shoved him away.

The air went out of the room. The big man held his ground. The two Russians held eye contact like gunfighters waiting to see who'd make the first move. Of course, it was the Gray Man.

"Schas po ebalu poluchish, kozyol!" he yelled.

The knife flashed in the big man's hand. He heaved himself forward, charging. His size alone would overwhelm anyone.

The black automatic appeared in Kostin's hand as if it had always been there. He fired. The blaze from the barrel lit up the room like a firecracker in the night. Livy turned her head from the blinding flash. The big man yelled. When her eyes opened, she saw a red hole in the palm of the Gray Man's right hand. The knife on the floor.

The big man screamed, holding his bleeding hand. Again, a flash. The man yelped like a dog. Blood poured from his left hand now. Something fell at his feet. Part of an index finger. The big Russian had bullet holes in both hands. His cries crescendoed as he barked at Cracked Tooth.

Kostin advanced on him, the gun now at his side. He placed a hand on the Gray Man's chest and shoved him hard. His ruined hands useless, the Russian stumbled and fell onto his back. He cried out, guttural and wild, calling to Cracked Tooth for help. But the young Russian stood transfixed by the horror.

Kostin placed his leather wingtip on the Gray Man's windpipe. He ground his foot into the Adam's apple. The big Russian gurgled, his legs thrashing at Kostin.

This was what Keller had described. The famous Red Devil of the Eastern Front that so many German prisoners feared.

He had returned.

Speaking very slowly, Kostin gave the Gray Man what sounded like a warning. The big Russian nodded on the floor, struggling for breath.

Kostin leveled the gun and squeezed the trigger.

The moaning ended. The echo of the gunshot receded in the vacant shop, replaced by silence. Yuri Kostin stood over Livy's tormentor. Smoke curled from the barrel of his gun. The big Russian's right eye gone in the blast. His mangled hands curled like two great dead spiders.

Livy felt sick. The aftermath of violence—the burning smell, dust in the air, the dead man, the savagery of it all—filled the emptiness.

Kostin gently removed his shoe from the dead man's throat and turned to the two younger Russians. Cracked Tooth still had his gun but held it by his side. Sergei looked as if he might be ill.

After retrieving the Gray Man's knife, Kostin spoke to the others. He asked a question. The younger men shook their heads quickly. *"Nyet, nyet."*

Kostin gave another order. The younger men didn't seem to understand. He repeated himself. Slowly. With authority. The two Russians nodded. Sergei walked quickly to the back door. Cracked Tooth knelt over the body and started emptying the Gray Man's pockets.

Kostin put the gun away. He stepped over to Livy and offered his hand.

"I'm sorry," he said. "I had no idea he would take it this far."

Livy didn't accept his hand. She stood up on her own. "What the hell just happened?"

"I will explain. Later. But this is not a good place to be now. I need to get you out of here. Please." He offered her his hand. She could feel his desire to touch her.

Cracked Tooth called for Kostin. He had the classified documents the Gray Man had carried. Kostin put them in his own coat.

"Livy, please," he said.

Ignoring his hand again, she walked out of the pool of light toward the back door.

Outside, Sergei backed the Ford toward the entrance of the shop. Livy edged around the car, breathing in the night air. Even the humidity felt like a relief after being inside the dirty building. The rush of fresh air made her cough. She tasted dust and chemicals.

Kostin came up behind her, grabbing her by the elbow.

"Take your hands off me," she said, her voice quiet and assured.

"We have to go. Please just sit in the car and wait. I won't be long."

Livy followed him to a gray Dodge coupe parked a few feet away. Kostin opened the door for her. She collapsed into the passenger seat.

"One minute. No more," Kostin said. He went to close the door.

"Leave it open."

He did and hurried back into the building.

The night had finally caught up to her. Her right cheek ached. She adjusted the rearview mirror to look at herself. Even in the dim streetlight, she could see a bruise and swelling around the right orbital bone. Apart from the mark on her face, she looked somehow different. Dark creases slanted under her eyes. A corner of her mouth was swollen from the punch. The knot in her neck was hard and sore. She looked and felt like the sort of woman you don't want to meet in a dark alley.

Still, she'd been damned lucky. Kostin showing up when he did had saved her from a far worse night. That didn't put her in the mood to be grateful, though. She needed food, aspirin, and to get away from these people.

Then she thought about Margot. How many times in the last few years had men threatened her in just such a way? Was it constant? A way of life?

Livy exhaled and considered her character, the double agent. She'd play this for all it was worth. The brush with death—she'd use it to milk Kostin's sympathy and feelings for her so that she could bring this whole thing to the quickest possible conclusion.

Voices pierced the night behind her. She turned to see Kostin and the two other Russians standing behind the open trunk of the Ford sedan. She saw them discuss something; then Livy heard grunting. A great weight crashed into the trunk. The car briefly sagged in the rear. If it'd been a Marx Brothers picture, it would've been funny. The trunk slammed shut. Kostin spoke quietly to the younger men and then hurried toward his car.

He got in, wiping sweat off his forehead with a handkerchief. Finally, he looked at her.

"How bad did he hurt you?"

"I'm fine. Just sore."

"I am . . . so sorry. I did not know Gennady would ever . . ." He let the sentence trail off as the Ford took off a bit too fast, spinning its wheels as it fishtailed away from the building.

The Russian put his arm around her and leaned in. Close enough to kiss her. He didn't, though. His fingers grazed her bruised cheek. The gesture felt sincere, intimate.

"You're supposed to take care of your sources, aren't you?" she said. "Not hang them out to dry."

"Livy, I was so angry when I found out. I wouldn't have been able to live with myself if—" He stopped himself. "We have to leave here. Now. Go somewhere safe."

"What's going to happen with . . . with that man? Won't the police be coming?"

"I've handled it all, Livy. No police. Nothing for you to worry about. You're not in danger anymore."

"I want to go back to my hotel."

Kostin threw his head back and sighed. The explosion of anger and violence she'd seen inside still had a grip on him. "Yes. Yes. All right." He started the car and took off.

"Then, I need to know what the hell that was all about."

Chapter
Twenty-Two

Kostin spoke quickly as they drove. "Gennady—that was his name—has always hated me. Even during the war. Never trusted me. I don't know why. Maybe he was jealous. But he wanted to prove me wrong about you. He said I did not see clearly, yes? Because it was you. As I said, always jealous that one."

Kostin slammed his hand on the steering wheel. "I should have known he would do something like this. I never thought— I have people at the embassy loyal to me. They warned me. Said he had come for you. I knew he would take you there. We have used that place before. Tonight changes things. For us, Livy. There are those still loyal to Gennady. They will be suspicious, even though they knew what sort of man he was."

He put a hand in his hair as his shoulders sagged. Kostin looked every bit his age now. "During the war, we seemed united. As Russians. Now, we just tear each other apart. If I am to make this work, Livy, I need your help."

She kept up the injured woman act, terrified after the experience. Not exactly a tough role to play, considering. She sat back, eyes half closed, listening. "What the hell else do you want?" Her voice tired, slurred. "I've done everything you've asked."

"I know. I know. But we must be even more cautious now, yes? My position might—I do not know—might change."

"What does that mean?"

"Gennady is dead," he snapped. "To some this will look more like a fight over a woman than over an agent."

"Is that what it is?"

He stared ahead, driving slowly. Kostin didn't speak again for several minutes. Then: "Let me take you somewhere? Tonight. We have houses here."

Livy felt numb from what she'd just been through, but Kostin's words jolted her. "No, my things are at the hotel. I have work tomorrow," she said, sounding more than a little frantic. This wasn't acting now. She needed respite.

"I cannot take the risk of driving you to your hotel."

Livy knew this might be the last time she would ever see Yuri Kostin. He'd killed a colleague. A man with allies. The Russian might disappear or be shipped off to Moscow in the middle of the night. That idea cut through the fog of drink, exhaustion, and fear that still clouded her head. Her own comfort would have to wait. The job was at hand, and she'd come too damned far to allow it to get away from her.

"I need something, Yuri," she said, leaning up and turning to him. "I need something from all this. There is just as much risk with what I've done. Your friend back there might have killed me tonight. So, now I need you to help me. Do you understand? Or this ends tonight."

Kostin pulled the Dodge over to a curb in front of a used-car lot. Row after row of big automobiles lined up. American flag streamers hung at all four corners of the business. Livy guessed it to be nearly three AM. The night felt desolate and empty, like the street.

The Russian put his hand on her cheek. His eyes scanned the bruise. She wondered if he was about to kiss her, but then he pulled away.

"You need to put ice on your cheek. Tonight, yes? Then, sleep. Try to rest. Eat. Then, come to Ford's Theatre tomorrow at three. We can talk then," he said. "You are a very strong woman, Livy, but I will take care of you. Whatever you need. I know I can trust you now."

Livy smiled, and everything about it was real. She had his trust; she knew it even beyond his admission. The time would come soon when she could ask him about Margot. Soon now—she could feel it. She had him. Not long now and this job would be over, and she'd be done with all of this.

Kostin put her in a cab. She got back to The Statler around four. The night doorman took one look at the bruise on her face and looked away as he allowed her inside. She made the mistake of asking for messages at the front desk. There were three. The Fairfax Beauty Salon had called about an upcoming appointment.

Upstairs she made an impromptu ice pack with a washcloth and a pile of cubes from the vending machine. She sat in a hot bath and held it to her swollen cheek.

Livy fell asleep, still wearing the towel from the bath.

* * *

The phone rang at eight AM. The long, single bell droned on until Livy ripped the receiver up.

"Good morning." The voice sounded pleasant, spunky, female. "We are looking forward to seeing you at your appointment this morning at eleven at the Fairfax Beauty Salon. Don't be late now."

Livy grunted something and dropped the receiver back on the base. She fell back into the soft hotel pillows. Her body needed sleep, but her mind rebelled. So she lay in bed for another hour and tried to see the way ahead. Livy knew Kostin had been shaken by Gennady's impromptu abduction of her. The incident had brought them closer in his mind. She could tell by the way he looked at her. He'd been afraid, and that fear brought out a terrible anger. The Red Devil had protected his woman. Above all else.

His woman, Livy thought. That mother back on the streetcar had seen it. Kostin was smitten. Livy was not only his source but also his lover, and he'd gone to dangerous lengths to protect her. None of that mattered to her, though. Livy knew the only way to end this was to use his feelings for her to get what she wanted. She was her own woman, and no one else's.

Half an hour later, she eased out of bed. Every inch of her body hurt, some places far worse than others. She called down to room service and ordered two scrambled eggs, toast with jam, and black coffee. While she waited, she got dressed and noticed the swelling in her cheek had gone down some, but the big Russian had left her with a juicy-looking purple bruise.

A cute young man, probably eighteen or nineteen, in a smart burgundy uniform with epaulettes, wheeled in the food tray. His eyes widened upon seeing her bruised face, but Livy gave him twenty-five cents and sent him on his way with a playful wink.

She drank the coffee first while spreading the strawberry preserves over her toast. The coffee tasted strong, and the jam had just the right amount of sweetness. She decided to savor this meal. With the death of Gennady, this job had reached a crisis point. From here on out, Livy knew the only way she could finish it would be by taking care of herself first.

* * *

"Oh my goodness, it looks so little. Are you sure it works?"

Livy stood on one side of a glass display case in a Sears, Roebuck and Co. store on the outskirts of the District. A burly man with a military haircut grinned at her from the other side. So far he'd bought her American accent hook, line, and sinker. A Colt Detective .32 special lay on the counter between them.

"Yes, ma'am. It'll fit right in your purse. But if—God forbid—you have to use it, it'll get the job done."

"You're a pretty good salesman, ya know," she said, looking up just as his gaze quickly shifted from the bruise under her eye. "Oh, it's a beauty, don't you think?" she said, touching her cheek.

"I'm sorry. I didn't mean to—"

"No, no. Do you have kids?"

He shook his head.

"Well, if you ever do, be careful. Their little heads can be deadly weapons. My oldest almost broke my nose with his noggin once. Number two got me last night."

"Well, now I see why you need that gun," the salesman said.

They both started to laugh.

* * *

Livy arrived at the safe house several minutes late. She came in through the back entrance, even though she'd spent the previous half hour making certain she'd not been followed. She couldn't imagine that after the events of last night the Russians could put together another surveillance team this quickly, but it paid to be cautious.

Sam Keller stood in the hallway. He had on the same suit he'd worn to the zoo, with another crisp shirt.

"God Almighty, you had us all so damned—" He stopped, mid-sentence. "What happened to you?"

"Do you have any of that bad coffee?"

Keller just stood there, eyes on her face.

"I'm all right, but coffee would help. Two sugars, though. Make that three."

Her quips seemed to break Keller's trance. He nodded and turned to the kitchen.

Two cups later, Livy finished telling Keller the story of the confrontation between the two Russians.

The details of the meeting with Kostin this afternoon she kept to herself.

Keller listened, barely able to mask his nervousness. He drummed his fingers on the arm of the chair. Three times he lifted his cup and put it back down on the table beside him without taking a sip. He didn't speak for almost two minutes.

Finally, he said, "Okay, then. Well, we gave it our best shot."

"What?"

He looked at her with surprise. "You landed in the middle of a pissing contest between two Russians and nearly got yourself killed. That's not happening on my watch. You're done with this."

Livy bristled. She wouldn't let him place the blame for this on her perceived inexperience. "Fact is, you're overreacting, Mr. Keller. I know what I'm doing."

The FBI man scoffed. "Go find a mirror and look at your face. Clearly, you don't."

She felt like giving his face a taste of what she'd had, but this moment called for a little more restraint.

"Look, we can't afford to let Yuri Kostin just disappear on us. Then all this has been for nothing."

"If I'd known Gennady Yakupov had been the one following you, I would have pulled you out immediately. I doubt very seriously that anyone trusts Kostin at that embassy after all this. His career is more than likely finished. The Soviets sure as hell aren't going to hand Berlin over to him now. This is pointless. I'm ending this."

Livy's face and neck throbbed. She'd been nearly killed last night in some dark backroom in the middle of Washington. Enduring Keller's lecture was simply more than her battered soul could take.

The hell with this.

She stood up, looking down at Keller. "I came here to do a job, and I'm finishing it."

"Maybe you're not hearing so well today, Livy. Just calm down, all right? Have a seat and let's figure out where we go from here."

"Thank you for the coffee." She spun on her heel, moving toward the door.

"Just where the hell do you think you're going?" Keller leapt up and grabbed her elbow. She tried to shrug him off, but he had a tight grip. The next moment happened so quickly.

He grabbed her other arm, towering over her. She put a hand on his chest to move him away, which only caused him to lean into her. Using his strength to control her. His big body on hers. She felt her back collide with the wall. Keller over her, leaning down.

She'd had enough. Livy chopped at his neck with the hard edge of her right hand.

"Stay the hell away from me," she yelled.

The blow moved him back. Livy pushed away from the wall, but he came again, grabbing Livy's arm hard, wrenching her around. She spun, throwing a right punch. Keller caught it.

The sudden violence seemed to shock them both into a sort of paralysis.

Keller's breath was ragged. He regarded her differently, as if surprised by what she could and would do. But the look in his eyes indicated he had no idea what to do next. Slowly, he released her right hand and stepped back.

The confrontation gave Livy a moment of release from the stress in her body, although her muscles still felt tight. They both stood, catching their breath.

Keller spoke first. "Let's just get you back to your hotel, all right? You've been through a helluva lot." He withdrew further, straightened his coat, and pushed the front of his hair back into place.

She sensed discomfort in his body language, but Livy couldn't imagine Keller changing his mind about the assignment. He'd decided she was an amateur long ago. Well, he might not think much of her experience, but Livy knew exactly what she needed to do. She had a part to play.

Giving him her best nervous smile, she shrugged her shoulders and glanced down. "Look, I'm tired. Every single part of me aches. I've had no sleep at all. Maybe we could talk later. When I've had—"

"Of course"—his voice scratchy from the blow to his throat—"but I'm sending someone with you. You're not leaving here by yourself."

"Look, I'll take a cab straight to the hotel. I just need . . . rest." She backed away from him, the door little more than ten feet from her.

Keller shook his head. "I'll make a call. Okay? I want to make sure you're—that someone can keep an eye on you."

She pushed the hair away from her face, letting him see the bruise. Playing the role of the inexperienced girl agent, in way over her head, who needed the man's help. That's what he wanted to see, and that was the distraction Livy needed.

Livy picked up her handbag. "Fine."

He turned toward the kitchen, smiling at her. "Give me a second. Just have a seat, all right?"

Livy nodded but didn't move.

Keller turned his back and disappeared around the corner.

She waited until she heard him pick up the receiver and start dialing.

"This is Keller. Get me Hobbs. Yeah, right now."

Livy knew she was saying goodbye to her sanctuary. The next step would push her further into Kostin's hands, but if she remained with Keller, then Margot might very well be lost forever.

Keller continued to talk on the phone in the next room. She walked out of the house, leaving the door open behind her.

* * *

Livy didn't go back to the hotel. She assumed the FBI would have someone there soon to watch over her. Despite the confrontation at the safe house, she knew Keller'd do whatever it took to keep her on a leash. She spent the better part of an hour making sure he hadn't followed her after her dash out into the street.

Livy knew she had to be on her own, completely, to have a chance of finding out where Margot might be. Keller's operation might be over, but hers was far from it.

Once again she found herself walking the block near Ford's Theatre. Cloudy skies and a light breeze from the north cooled down the city.

Livy was in place at five minutes to three and felt reasonably certain she hadn't been followed. No sign of the FBI's blue Packard or any other car for that matter. She'd crossed streets so many times and stopped to look in so many shop windows that if she had a tail, it had to be the Invisible Man.

She made her way toward the wooden bench at the edge of the theatre and J.C. Harding Electrical. An old man in ballooning khakis, a tropical shirt, and cardigan took up most of the bench.

She said, "Excuse me," and took the seat beside him. He nodded as he used his right hand to fan himself.

Popping the latch on her handbag, Livy pretended to search for something. The sight of the Colt gave her added security. She glanced at the old man and wondered if he planned to perch there the whole afternoon. He showed no signs of moving.

Livy closed her bag and looked at her watch. A couple of minutes after three. She glanced up and down the street. She didn't recognize anyone. Would it be the striking young woman again? Leaning back, she allowed herself to think the worst: Kostin bundled off to Moscow and with him, her chance of ever getting a fix on Margot's location.

From there her mind flew home. She found herself thinking about the smells and particular sounds of Fleming's office on the Gray's Inn Road. Pen Baker's always-enticing perfumes, the clink of the cut-glass tumblers in Fleming's office bar, and the crisp *whoosh* of the soundproof door to his inner office.

She wondered if any other signals had been received since she left. Had Margot risked everything to send those few? Was she now on the receiving end of some sort of punishment for her transgressions? Livy's two weeks in the German prison at Fresnes during the war seemed like a holiday by comparison.

"Do you have the correct time?" she asked the old man.

"Nope," he said. More of a grunt, really. "Watch broke last month. Gotta get it fixed. Sometime."

Livy nodded and futzed with her own watch: 3:05. At that moment, a very small woman with tight gray hair, wearing one of the most colorful frocks Livy had ever seen, shuffled out of the front of the theatre toward the old man. She stood on the sidewalk and yelled, "Smithsonian," in the direction of the bench.

"How far?" the old man asked, hefting himself up and fairly stumbling in the direction of the small woman.

Livy watched them walk south, side by side. She smiled and then wondered if that might ever be her one day. Her mind went to the last man who'd truly caught her fancy. Another American, Tom Vance. But they'd not seen each other in over a year. Last she heard of the handsome Southerner he'd been transferred to Vienna. It wasn't out of the question that their paths could cross again one day, and then, who knows? Growing old with Tom Vance? The incongruity of the image almost made her laugh because at this moment that seemed to her about as possible as a trip to the moon.

The thought vanished quickly. Livy felt the contact before seeing her. The same young woman with the violin case stood behind the bench, just to Livy's left. She remembered the perfect cheekbones, the defiant jawline, and thick dark hair.

"Walk behind me," the young woman said, looking up the street. "Keep a distance."

She then moved off toward F Street in the opposite direction from the old couple. Livy let her take about ten steps and then followed slowly. She scanned the street as they walked. No longer did she feel like a helpless little woman at everyone's mercy. She had protection. The Colt made her independence from Keller and the FBI seem real. No more playing Ophelia. Medea now. A woman of decisive action.

The young woman paused at the intersection of Tenth and F along with a tightly packed crowd of pedestrians. Livy had no option but to catch up and stand beside her.

"The cab," the woman said. "Take it." And she turned and headed west on F Street, leaving Livy at the intersection. Ahead of her, the traffic signal changed, and the group surged across the street. Parked on the curb across F St, in front of Saxon's Clothiers, was a Diamond cab.

Livy noticed the car's light was solid. She ran around to the passenger side to speak to the driver, a man in his fifties with salt-and-pepper curly hair and wearing a flat cap. The driver did not look at her.

"We can take you where you are going," Yuri Kostin said from the back seat.

Chapter
Twenty-Three

The cab dashed through midday DC traffic, flying down Pennsylvania and Constitution until it turned north on Maryland Avenue. The driver kept the windows down, so the speed of the car caused wind to whip through the automobile.

Kostin only spoke twice. Once to tell Livy that she would be "safe" and the second time to say something, in Russian, to the driver. Livy reckoned it to be a joke since the driver laughed along with Kostin.

They quickly left the downtown area, and within fifteen minutes had crossed into Maryland. The surroundings changed dramatically. One moment the concrete and stacked buildings of the city; the next, walk-up houses with manicured lawns. The cab drove past a group of children playing hopscotch on the sidewalk and at least one game of pickup baseball.

At the end of a winding street, the cab turned onto a more recently paved road. There were fewer and bigger houses now. Up ahead, Livy could see a small lake with a single wooden pier. At its furthermost edge, half a dozen fishermen lazily dragged their lines through the water.

They finally turned into the circular driveway of an imposing Beaux Arts–style house. The lawn had been carefully trimmed, as had the hedges that lined the facade. Kostin gave another order in Russian, and the cab turned down a drive beside the house. Following it all the way around the building, the car stopped at a back entrance covered by a stone archway.

Kostin hopped out of the car quickly, opened Livy's door, and ushered her inside.

He flipped a light switch to reveal a spacious sunken den. Leather sofas encircled a metal stove in the center of the room. Tall, thick bookcases, stuffed with leather-bound volumes, lined the walls behind the sofas. It looked clean, modern, and very expensive.

"Exactly, where the hell are we?" Livy asked.

Kostin smirked. "This is our American *dacha*. We bring special guests here. Like you. A very special guest."

"You always bring them in through the back door?"

The Russian ignored the quip and started up a narrow, wooden staircase. Livy followed. At the top they emerged into a formal living room furnished in a style far more decorous and European. The chairs appeared to be Queen Anne. Two twin sofas looked stiff, with ornate wooden carvings on the armrests. The draperies were, of course, closed.

Kostin stood in the center of the room. "It's quite large. There are four bedrooms on the second floor," he said, pointing to a landing that overlooked the living room. "A full kitchen, of course, down here, and then the downstairs area. But you will have it all to yourself for a few days."

Livy turned to him. She hadn't expected this. "To myself? Well, it's a lovely prison, but I think I prefer freedom." This quip had more bite.

"Livy, it was dangerous for you to be at the hotel all alone," he said.

The Russian moved closer to her. The lure of sex lingered between them. It had always been there. But now it had the added whiff of desperation about it. It was all over Kostin. She saw it in the quickness of his stride, the lines under his eyes. She saw it in the way he looked at her. Sensed his desire in the way he put his hands on her shoulders. She could encourage it. Pull him further in. But she decided to make him wait.

She said, "I thought you took care of the danger last night."

Kostin stepped back, the moment broken. The memory flashed across his face. "Gennady was well liked by many people. In Moscow too. He used to brag he had watched movies with Comrade Stalin. American cowboy films. So, the situation is difficult, but we can make it work."

A part of Livy wanted to kiss him. This man—this violent man—was her touchstone now. Yet to her he was something different. The intimacy of it might calm her, she thought. Might help her stop thinking about where the liquor cabinet was in the house. Might help her think more clearly.

But then she remembered something Anka had said: *"You walk into the shadows, my dear. You can lose yourself in there."*

Livy knew exactly what she meant now. For better or worse, she had crossed over into Soviet territory. This big house and all its comforts hid a far darker purpose. She felt like she'd stepped into the International Departures Lounge, next stop Moscow.

They had her now, and she was nowhere near finding out where Margot might be.

"You were also being followed," Kostin went on. "By the Americans. Or maybe your own people. If we are to move forward, then I need to keep you close."

"Yuri, this wasn't part of our deal," she said, turning up the girl-in-over-her-head act. "I know what prison feels like. The decor here may be a bit nicer, but the result is the same."

"I have no intention of keeping you here more than a day, two at most," Kostin said. "You can be so valuable to us. We care about you. *I* care about you. I understand that our arrangement is two-way, yes? You have done so much for me, and I will help you. I promise."

Livy looked at him with soft eyes, conceding the point. "Is everything all right? After last night. I mean—with you?"

He put a finger to his lips and pointed up. The house would be bugged to the rafters.

"You must be hungry," he said, breaking into a big smile. "Have you ever tried Russian food?"

"You cook?"

His wolfish grin returned. "Some. We had a cook in my unit during the war, but he was too drunk to remember the ingredients, so everything tasted the same. But I am going to make you traditional Russian dish. *Solyanka*—sweet and sour soup. But we don't have long."

"Another special guest?"

"You could say that. The First Secretary of the embassy wants to meet you."

*　*　*

The soup, honestly, was a bit much. It's beefy taste and thick, spicy base went down hard on Livy's stomach. Still, she ate it, sipping vodka on the side. She had to admit the fatty broth and the ice-cold liquor complemented each other perfectly. If only her system had been in a more forgiving mood.

During dinner, Kostin's once jovial mood became tinged with anxiety. He rarely spoke. Instead, he ate much too quickly. Finishing first, he left the dishes in the sink and poured himself a second glass of vodka.

Just after nine o'clock, they saw the headlights of a car pulling into the circular driveway. They sat, facing each other on the stiff sofas in the front room, and listened as the house's back door opened and closed. One set of boots clamored up the wooden stairs, then a second, and finally a third pair of feet, fainter.

The downstairs door opened, and the man Livy knew as Cracked Tooth came through first. He stood aside and allowed another man—smaller and somewhat older—into the room. Livy recognized the last person of the trio. The young woman, the violinist who'd been her contact outside Ford's Theatre twice, entered, closing the door behind her. The ever-present instrument case was at her side.

Kostin shot to his feet as the older man ambled over. The newcomer ignored Kostin's gesture, giving all his attention to Livy.

"Miss Nash, I believe?" he said. His accent was heavier than Kostin's, but he spoke English well.

Livy stood and sized up the man who was clearly the boss. He had a round face and round glasses. His dark hair receded at the temples but grew thick on top and the sides. Despite the

Washington humidity, he wore a dark wool suit and showed no signs of being uncomfortable. Livy thought he looked like the most ruthless accountant she'd ever met.

Kostin stepped in between them. "This is our First Secretary, Georgi Borisovich Sokolov."

Livy knew that First Secretary meant the MGB *rezident*, or station chief, here in DC. More than likely it also meant Sokolov was the top man Soviet Intelligence had in the States.

The Russian bowed in mock humility on being introduced, and asked Livy to sit down. Sokolov took one of the Queen Anne chairs next to her.

"Yuri Mikhailovich, do we have tea here? I think we could all do with a cup."

Kostin hesitated. He looked unsure how to answer. He said, "I believe so, comrade."

"Good. Would you be so kind?"

Livy understood. Sokolov could have ordered the other two Russians. Instead, he asked their superior. Kostin nodded and went off into the kitchen without a word.

Sokolov unbuttoned his coat and crossed his legs. He didn't smile. The meeting felt like business, and nothing more.

"Miss Nash, I hope you understand it is quite rare for me to speak with someone in your position," he said. "We all must take precautions. I am being watched wherever I go in this city. But given the circumstances—the unfortunate incident last night—I very much wanted to meet you."

"I'm flattered . . . sir." Livy glanced around at the two others in the room. She still had a bump on the back of her neck to remember Cracked Tooth by, and the unsmiling young woman somehow seemed more menacing at night. The three of them looked like they could form a firing squad pretty quickly if someone handed them rifles.

"Yuri Mikhailovich tells me you served during the war," Sokolov said casually, as if he hadn't looked through every file about Olivia Nash he could put his neat, little thin fingers on.

"I did. I was in France for just over a year."

"And yet when you returned home there was nothing for you." Sokolov didn't phrase it as a question. "Many of your countrymen—many of mine for that matter—just wanted to be away from the fighting. To marry and have a family. But not you."

"Is it wrong to want to do what you're good at? I gave them everything in the war and lost more than I can tell you, Mr. Sokolov."

"We all lost someone. Some lost everything. Miss Nash, I understand this work appeals to you. What I do not understand is why you would choose to betray your country. You do not seem to want money. So, I wonder, what is it you want?"

"Purpose. I had that once. I want it again."

Sokolov smiled. "You do not strike me as an ideologue. So, I take it, your motive is revenge?"

"You may take it however you like. I don't think it's naive of me to assume that if I provide a service, then I can expect compensation of some sort from those who've benefited from my help."

"Indeed."

Kostin came back into the room with a tray holding a teapot and three cups. Livy found the sight of the formidable Red Devil playing parlor maid disturbing. Especially since he stood between her and another trip to that abandoned shop outside town. He placed the tray in front of Livy and sat down on the sofa opposite her.

Sokolov poured tea into his cup and held the saucer on his lap as it cooled. "You do not work for MI6 directly then?"

"No."

"You are a journalist, but they ask you to do things for them when you are abroad?"

"That's about right."

"Who are your contacts at MI6?"

Kostin poured tea for her. She took the cup. The warmth of the mug felt out of place in the midst of this chilly interrogation.

"I don't report to anyone there specifically. Usually I turn over my notes to a secretary. Different folks on different days."

Sokolov put one lump of sugar in his tea and stirred slowly. "How long have you known Ian Fleming?"

The question caught Livy off guard. Of course he'd ask about Fleming , but she worried where this might be going? What did he know? Livy took a sip of the strong drink. She hoped it might cover the twitch she felt in her eye. "Just over a year now."

"He is your editor?"

"He's an arrogant, self-centered Romeo who's past his prime. And, on occasion, he's my editor."

Sokolov studied Livy with a smile that he probably thought expressed kindness. It didn't.

"We have given you the code name Chaika," he went on. "Yuri Mikhailovich tells me you're familiar with Russian literature."

"I know Chekov's plays. I grew up in a theatre—of a sort."

"I think art helps us understand one another, don't you? I'm told Comrade Stalin even reads the American poet Walt Whitman. It's a good example for all of us."

"Mr. Sokolov, I didn't offer to slip your lot the occasional classified document because I have a copy of Marx by my bedside. No offense. I did it out of anger and frustration. Mr. Fleming may be my boss and all, but he thinks he can treat me how he likes simply because of where he was born and went to school. That's about as far as I go with the worker's struggle, if you take my meaning. I'm willing to help you, and one of the reasons is that I trust this man," she said and shifted her gaze to Kostin.

Sokolov didn't quite know how to react to this unexpected endorsement. He sipped his tea. His face betrayed no response.

Livy had always been taught that honesty in an interrogation worked best. She did believe most of what she'd said. Her description of Fleming may have been exaggerated, but she'd bet more than one woman might very well describe him that way. A man like Sokolov was more likely to believe her motivation if it was messy and complex.

Sokolov put down his teacup, cut his eyes at Kostin, then turned to Livy. "Miss Nash, we believe you could be more effective for us in England."

Livy's palms began to sweat. What the hell did he mean? She took a deep breath. Exhaustion swept over her again. Her mind raced through scenarios where she would never be out of the clutch of this damned assignment and these people. She lowered a hand to her waist and felt her breath.

"I have work to finish in the States."

"Of course, of course. Once you are back home, we will arrange for you to have a new contact. I believe you met him once. Grimov, yes? Yuri Mikhailovich will assist in the transition."

Sokolov put his cup down and stood, prompting Kostin to stand as well.

"Thank you for your time, Miss Nash," Sokolov said, extending his hand to her. Livy took it. "It was a pleasure meeting you." Again, the smile that looked right out of some Soviet charm school. He gestured to Kostin, and the two Russians walked downstairs, followed by Cracked Tooth.

The young violinist remained in the room.

"I will sleep in the suite at the end of the hall," she said. "You may have any of the other rooms upstairs."

"You're staying with me?"

"Of course." Despite her beauty and youth, the young woman's voice and demeanor seemed hard as a piece of flint.

So be it then, Livy thought. Locked in a velvet prison with the Beast who just happened to be disguised as Beauty.

* * *

Half an hour later, Livy heard a car drive away from the back lot. Kostin came slowly up the stairs into the living room. He didn't say a word, but went straight to the kitchen and came back with a bottle of vodka and two glasses. Condensation hung on the carafe.

He took a seat near her on the sofa and poured for them both.

"Yuri, I still have responsibilities in town. I can't be away long."

"Someone will bring you back to the hotel in a day or two." He took a long pull on the vodka.

"Someone?"

"You've met Nadia, yes? She will make sure you have what you need." Kostin seemed even more distant than when they'd first met after watching the play. He stared at the closed curtains as if he could see through them. Sokolov had been dismissive of him, forced him to get tea. Was that a sign of Kostin's loss of position at the embassy? Keller would be pleased that the dreaded Red Devil had been taken down a notch, but Livy needed him to feel closer to her.

She remembered what the woman on the streetcar had said to her. She'd seen something in Kostin's eyes. Love? Is that how the Russian really felt about her? It seemed insane, but Livy knew of no other explanation for his behavior. He'd protected her from his own countryman and colleague. He'd murdered the man. Brutally. All in defense of her. Livy knew she was playing with fire, but to finish the job she had to rekindle that intimacy again. Truth be told, she couldn't imagine a more precarious situation than this.

"And you?" Livy asked softly. "Where will you be?"

"Wherever they tell me to be," he said, finishing his drink. He poured another. "You don't want?" He indicated her untouched glass.

Livy picked it up. If Kostin was about to be replaced even before they sent her back to England, then the job was over. Livy knew she had to be decisive. She had to give Kostin a reason to want to stay.

She took his hand in her own.

"Thank you for all you've done for me," she said, clinking glasses. Kostin nodded and they drank. "I will see you again, won't I?"

Livy caressed his palm. Kostin didn't meet her gaze. "I don't know. It's not my decision."

"Yuri," she said, her voice almost a whisper, "I have to see you again. Please."

Kostin glanced at her, his hooded eyes so difficult to penetrate. "Nadia will go to the store tomorrow sometime. I will check on you then." His voice was flat, expressionless. Their every word would be on a tape that would end up at the Soviet Embassy. Livy assumed the embassy was the "store" where Nadia would be going.

He kissed her hand and his lips lingered there. He kept her hand tight in his. "You need rest."

She finished the vodka, put the glass down. She lifted his hand, placing it on her right breast as she put a finger to her lips. Livy saw the moment land on Kostin's face. His fingertips caressed her while his eyes darted toward the second floor for any sign of Nadia, the chaperone.

It felt a bit like being back in school.

Except this was business for Livy. She kept his hand there, hers on top of his. Kostin's palm cradled her breast. The carnal look in his eyes gave way to vulnerability. She could see he needed this.

His touch aroused something in her. She couldn't deny it. But a part of her felt disconnected. She heard the taunting voices of those women from the war. Pointing fingers. Whispering.

Putain.

Livy accepted their disgust and tried to focus on the source of their taunts. The collaborators. Their motives. Women like

Anka. How far did she have to go to serve her country? She kept the image in her mind to maintain distance. This was a job. She was acting a part.

A door opened on the second floor, and they heard Nadia's footfall. Kostin withdrew his hand, giving Livy a quick kiss on the lips. He stepped away to talk to the Russian woman.

Livy poured herself another vodka.

Chapter
Twenty-Four

～

Once Kostin left, Livy chose the bedroom on the second floor landing nearest the stairs. Nadia showed her in and, since it was late, retired to her own room. Livy got to work.

The problem was the gun.

The photograph of Margot as well, but mostly the gun. If she was to be stuck in this damned house for however long, she might have to account for both of them. Livy could explain the presence of the small picture much more easily than she could a loaded Colt .32. But she didn't plan to do either. First, she pulled a pencil from her handbag and pried loose a few threads around the waistband of her skirt over the left hip. She took Margot's photo and slid it carefully into the lining where the threads had been dislodged. She folded the seam back down, ensuring the photo wouldn't fall out.

Once that was done, she walked around the room, making mental notes about where everything was positioned. Of course, the room was bugged. She assumed at least one listening device in the bedroom and another in the bath. She took note of the position of the lamp on the dresser, and its proximity to the wall. She did the same with her bedside table, placing her reporter's notebook an inch or so from the edge of the nightstand.

Livy wasn't in control of her space, but if she kept her belongings in very specific positions, then she'd have no problem knowing whether the room had been searched.

After a careful reconnaissance, Livy went to the big bath and turned on the water in the tub. She needed the sound of the running water to cover what she was about to do.

Bringing her handbag into the bathroom, Livy pulled out the Colt. She popped open the chamber, dropped the cartridges into her hand and placed them on the sink. She checked the spring of the trigger and pulled the hammer back. The mechanism cracked quietly. No hesitation. She carefully reloaded the gun and popped the chamber back into place.

Livy turned off the water in the tub and undressed for bed. She decided the safest place for the gun would be for it to stay with her as much as possible. Half an hour later, she fell asleep, her hand curled around the Colt's handle under her pillow.

*   *   *

Livy woke the next morning to the sound of classical music. It took a moment for her to register the melody—Tchaikovsky—and the instrument—the violin, of course. Nadia was awake.

She slowly rolled out of bed and assessed the aches and pains throughout her body. The now familiar vodka headache would have been enough. Her cheek felt every bit as sore to the touch as it had yesterday. The purple bruise under her eye looked smaller, but no less violet. The back of her neck ached whenever she looked down, which she resolved to avoid doing for the rest of the day.

Her bedroom at the "American dacha" was twice as big as her room at The Statler. Someone, perhaps Nadia, must have stocked the large closet with women's clothing. The chest of drawers had an especially extensive collection of undergarments. Livy was impressed to find her size among them. Still, she opted for her own clothes—and her own knickers.

After a long bath, she dressed. She felt the outline of Margot's picture still in her waistband. Livy then pulled the Colt from under the pillows and slipped it into the right pocket of her skirt. The gun was small, just about six inches long. She'd have to be careful, but with her hand in the pocket, the outline of the Colt couldn't be seen. She stepped into the hallway and closed the bedroom door. As she did, she plucked one hair from her head, moistened it with the tip of her tongue and gently placed it across the doorjamb.

The classic smells of breakfast floated up from the kitchen off the main room. Livy walked downstairs to find the dining table set for two, complete with what appeared to be freshly squeezed orange juice and a steaming cup of tea. As she sat down and took a sip of the pulpy drink, Nadia emerged from the kitchen, carrying a plate with eggs, two slices of warm white toast, bacon, jam, and sliced tomatoes. She placed it in front of Livy, without a word, and went back to the kitchen.

Full English breakfast, juice, and tea. Livy wondered if this was some sort of last meal.

Nadia joined her a few minutes later. The slender Russian beauty ate with gusto but didn't speak. The food proved to be as good as it smelled. Livy ate almost everything. The eggs were cooked to perfection, and the tomatoes tasted as if they'd just been pulled off the vine that morning.

Either they intended to execute her that afternoon or Sokolov did indeed have big plans for his new English double agent. She hoped it was the latter.

Of course, she had no intention of taking this show on the road. Livy sensed the final act about to begin. The lead actress felt ready, if a bit battered, after a robust opening. Now was the time to make the dash toward the grand climax and hope she was still around to take a much-deserved curtain call.

Neither woman spoke during the meal. The sounds of silverware on plates and the Russian woman's loud chewing would have been comical had it not made Livy want to scream. After a few minutes of this, Nadia wiped her mouth with the thick cloth napkin and looked at her.

"Gennady was a good man." The Russian flung the words like a challenge.

Livy looked up, finished chewing, and put down her fork. "Perhaps we should agree to disagree."

"You did not know him like I did."

"No, but then he didn't try to kill you, did he?"

Nadia still held her carving knife, and with intent. "If he thought you were lying, he had reason."

"Pity we can't ask him now."

Nadia's lovely upper lip curled. That remark had riled her but good. Nothing in the double-agent rulebook said Livy needed to cozy up to the hired help, even if she was holding a knife.

And Nadia had not relinquished her grip on it one bit.

Livy pushed away from the table and stood. She slipped her hand inside the skirt and found the Colt's warm grip.

"If you have any concerns, perhaps you should take them up with Major Kostin," Livy said. "The breakfast was very good. The company even more so."

With that Livy turned and headed upstairs to her room. At the top of the landing she looked down. Nadia hadn't moved.

*   *   *

After spending most of the morning going over and over a Tchaikovsky piece from the confines of her bedroom, Nadia banged on Livy's bedroom door. Her anger from breakfast didn't seem to have dissipated one bit as she glared at Livy and announced she'd be going to the store.

"Do not leave the house for any reason," Nadia said. "You must stay in either the living room or your bedroom. Do not go anywhere else."

Livy felt a bit like Jonathan Harker at Castle Dracula.

Shortly before two, a car pulled up in the front circular driveway, and Nadia, tying a scarf over her hair, left in it.

Minutes later, Livy heard the sound of another automobile. A Dodge coupe sped down the hill outside and parked in the back. Livy hurried upstairs to her bedroom and put the Colt deep under the pile of pillows on her bed. Then she walked over to the large mirror in the bathroom. Fine—she was wearing the same clothes as the day before, but the skirt hadn't wrinkled and the blouse had kept its shape. Livy smoothed a few spots in her skirt, pushed her hair to and fro. It would have to do.

Yuri Kostin looked like a man who'd been up all night. His usual catlike saunter had slowed down over the past week.

He went into the kitchen and poured them both a cup of tea. They sat at the square wooden kitchen table.

"I did not know they wanted to send you to England," he said. "I wanted to keep you here, but this was not my decision."

"We'll make it work."

"You do not understand, Livy," he blurted out—and then stopped himself. He took a sip of tea, smoothed his tie, and began again. "Comrade Sokolov wants you in London, because he believes we can get more immediate intelligence there. We need to know as much as possible, as quickly as possible, about the British involvement in Truman's plans.

"This man Fleming, your editor. He was in your Naval Intelligence in the war. They say he was a planner. Very creative, but he was never in the field. A man behind a desk, yes? He is nothing to us, but he knows people. Comrade Sokolov wants you to . . . get closer to him. He said you can use Fleming to get to the people he knows at MI6."

Livy feigned a look of hurt for the Russian's benefit, but inside she felt ill. Both sides wanted her to be their whore. As he continued, she listened, nodding, drinking tea, telling herself that one way or another this would be long over before it ever went that far. But she would remember this particular request. When the time came, she wouldn't forget how the Russians too planned to use her.

"Will you be there? In London?" she asked.

Kostin started to respond but shrugged instead.

Livy went to the kitchen counter. She opened a drawer, found a stenographer's pad inside and a pencil. She scribbled on a piece of paper, quietly tore it from the notebook, and replaced pad and pencil in the drawer.

She handed the note to Kostin. It read, *Is there anywhere private?*

He folded the note, pulled a silver cigarette lighter from his coat pocket, and lit the paper. He dropped the ashes into a trashcan and walked out of the room. Taking her hand, Kostin led Livy upstairs and down the landing to Nadia's bedroom at the end of the hall. He tried the doorknob, but it was locked. Kostin opened it with keys from his pocket. The room was even bigger than Livy's and very pristine. Vaulted ceilings. Carpet in the bedroom. A four-poster bed. Italian marble floors in the bath. A worker's paradise.

Kostin closed the door quietly. He led her to the large closet beside the bed, similar in design to the layout in Livy's room, but there the resemblance ended. Kostin slid the doors open, pushed aside several dresses and coats to reveal a half-size door. He flicked through the keys on his ring, found the smallest one, inserted it, and turned the lock.

Putting a finger to his lips, he stood aside and let Livy enter first. She ducked her head into a completely dark room. A whirring sound, almost like bees in a hive, surrounded her. Kostin pushed in behind, closing the door. A soft overhead light flickered to life.

They had stepped into a concealed listening room hidden within the master suite. The room itself felt about half the size of the bedroom on the other side of the door. One wall consisted of a bank of audio surveillance equipment. A large reel-to-reel machine dominated the center of the console, flanked by controls, nobs, and wires plugged into various outlets. Smaller reel-to-reel machines were mounted at three other spots along the control panel. All the labels were in Russian, but Livy had to assume that each room must have microphones that fed into these tape machines. Three rolling chairs lined the console, with three sets of headphones on a desk alongside a trio of notebooks. Livy wondered how often the "American dacha" had been used to blackmail its "special guests."

Despite that sobering thought, Livy realized she was in the one room in the house where they wouldn't be under surveillance. She'd never have an opportunity like this again. This was her only chance. Her cheeks felt warm and her breath came in spurts. The Russian would of course interpret these outward signs as something entirely different. Kostin had not brought Livy here for the grand tour. He had another purpose in mind.

The Russian closed the door behind them and pressed his body against hers, pushing her into the door. His hands on her hips, Kostin kissed Livy hard. She tasted vodka and tobacco on his breath. Livy knew he needed this. She sensed his desire every time they were together in the same room. She pushed her mind away from the moment, critiquing her performance. Did she seem aroused enough? Too much moaning? Inside she felt nothing, but that was the advantage of being a woman at a time like this. It was all about the show.

Livy's mind raced ahead even as his hands unbuttoned her blouse. His lips dug into her neck.

There would never be a perfect time for what she needed to ask. Best catch him off guard, when his mind, and hands, were otherwise engaged.

"Yuri," she said, her voice appropriately breathy. "I have to tell you something. Something I couldn't say out there. Please."

He lifted his head, his hands still on her breasts. Another kiss on the lips and he pulled back. "Yes?"

"I told you there was something I needed from you."

"Livy, we will take care of you, of course. There will be money every month, and eventually—"

"That's not what I meant. I need a favor. From you. Something that's personal to me."

He pulled back, his brow furrowed. Curious.

"It's—it's about this friend of mine who went missing after the war. She was with SOE too. Afterward I went to meet her family."

He put his hand in her hair and held her close. "All right. You do not need to be nervous. Just tell me."

"They've never known—you know—what happened to her. She's still listed as missing, presumed dead. They're such a sweet couple—in their sixties, I think—but there is this great sadness about them."

Kostin listened, but she could see the clock ticking in his head. His fingertips gently traced her cleavage. He was a man with more than one purpose.

"Livy, I don't understand, what could I possibly do?"

"Margot—that's her name—she was at Ravensbrück. Margot Dupont. The Red Army liberated that camp, didn't they? She wasn't on the list of the dead. As far as her folks know she was still alive then. You were there, weren't you?"

Kostin sighed. "I was with some of those troops, yes, but I still don't understand what you want from me."

"When I go back to England, Yuri, I want to be able to tell them something about their daughter. Something that will give them a sense of peace. You must know Russian families who feel the same. It's killing Margot's mum and dad. If they could just have some idea of what might have happened to her."

He kissed her lips gently. "Darling, I don't know what to tell you. There were prisoners who scattered when the camps were opened. It was chaotic. People everywhere. Some were rounded up, you see. No one knew who was a German and who wasn't. No one had proper papers. Some prisoners just wandered away. A woman, though. I don't know. It is possible she was taken—somewhere."

"What do you mean?"

Kostin pulled away from her. "There are places she could be. We have camps in our sector. They are—what is the word?—temporary. There's one just north of Berlin, not far from Ravensbrück. At Sachsenhausen. There are others. I don't know, but it is possible she was rounded up with others by a Red Army patrol." He put his hands on the side of her face. His blue eyes searched hers. "This is important to you, isn't it?"

Livy nodded. "I just want to help them. If she's gone, they need to know that. Just find out for me if you can. It's all I'm asking for."

"Of course. There is a man at the embassy—Nikolai. He was with the division at Ravensbrück. That place, Livy." He shook his head. "If she survived that place, then she is a very lucky girl. But I will ask Nikolai. See what he can tell me. That's all I can do"

Livy didn't know if she should feel hopeful or angry. She'd said it. He hadn't lashed out or closed himself off. No. Instead, he leaned in and kissed her. And she kissed him back. She sensed desperation in his touch, and she imagined he sensed hers. The line had been cast, and now she had to wait to see what it might catch. But Livy could feel the beginning of the end game, and it lifted her heart.

Kostin seemed to sense the change in her as well. The intensity of his kisses became more aggressive. He lifted her onto the desk in front of the listening console. His hands gripping her hips as they kissed. She let him take over. Above all else, Livy wanted him to believe her. If he did, then she might be able to end all this and find the friend who sent those wireless cries for help.

Chapter Twenty Five

An hour later, Kostin hurried to leave the house before Nadia returned.

"I need to get back to my room and my things, Yuri," Livy pleaded with him. "Everything here has to be finalized with my office before I leave. I can't just disappear."

He assured Livy she could go back to the hotel as soon as it was safe. His ambiguity alarmed her. She wondered how the Russians might define "safe" for their prized English spy.

Nadia brought back a sack full of groceries, although Livy felt certain the real reason for her long absence had more to do with taking the surveillance audio to the embassy for review. She wondered how thick the walls of the listening room might be, and if any sounds from her afternoon with Kostin would be picked up on tomorrow's tapes.

While Nadia unpacked the groceries, Livy returned to her room. She pocketed the Colt first and then checked to see if anything had been shifted. The room looked clean. She then thought over everything Kostin had told her about the Russian camps in the east. Sachsenhausen. House of the Saxons.

She'd heard rumors for two years now that the Russians were still keeping POWs in prison camps once used by the Germans. Now she had to find out if Kostin's explanation was plausible. If Soviet troops had picked up Margot among the prisoners freed from Ravensbrück then it seemed likely that they'd relocate her.

Poor Margot. Livy couldn't comprehend a life of unending imprisonment. Moving from one foreign enemy to another.

Downstairs she heard chords being plucked. Nadia tuning her violin again. She'd already tuned the damned thing twice today.

Livy left her room and walked downstairs. She remembered seeing several bookcases in the sunken den on the ground floor when Kostin had brought her in. Hoping to find a book that might lend Kostin's story more veracity, she interrupted Nadia with her request to go downstairs.

"What is it you want down there?"

"A book. I can't exactly sit here all day staring at the walls."

"I will ask permission first, and let you know," she said, turning her focus back to the violin.

"You're going to ask a busy man like Major Kostin if I'm allowed to read?"

Nadia didn't so much as look up. "You have five minutes. No more." She looked down at the slim, elegant watch on her wrist and back up to Livy.

She thanked Nadia and headed downstairs, as the incessant plucking began again.

The ground floor felt damp and cold. Even though it was a sunny day, thick curtains hung over the two windows facing the back of the house. The black leather sofas and the deep slate gray walls gave the room a pall. Two oak bookshelves stood on either side of the room. Each unit rose to well over six feet and looked almost as wide. She'd have to go through hundreds of books in order to find one with a detailed map of Germany. And she had only five minutes. Livy also couldn't run the risk of being caught either. Even two years after the war, the country remained the most hotly contested piece of land on Earth. Nadia would be immediately suspicious.

Livy's eyes skimmed the bindings of the thick leather tomes that lined each bookshelf. Most had titles in Russian, but she recognized a few words and names. The first shelf seemed to be primarily fiction. The second contained histories dating from Ancient Rome right up to what the Russians referred to as "The Great Patriotic War." She figured one or more of those books might include maps of Germany, but as she glanced at the third shelf, she saw taller, thinner books that seemed more likely suspects. More titles in Russian hindered her quick perusal. Eventually she spotted a word in one title that gave her hope. The authorship had been attributed to the *Deutsche Gesellschaft für Kartographie*. Cartography.

She ripped the book down, kneeling in front of the shelf. A book of maps. Perfect! The early pages only included Rome and Saxony. She skipped to the back of the book and found a map labeled 1928. Before the war.

But something had changed. Like the room itself. What was it? The tuning upstairs had stopped.

Livy quickly scanned the back pages. She prayed Hitler hadn't changed the names of too many towns.

The door upstairs opened.

"You need to come upstairs now," Nadia said. Her voice as cold as the vodka in the freezer.

"Yes, of course. Let me just put this book away."

Livy used her finger, found Berlin easily enough and then traced north. It took her a few moments to spot it, but there it was. Sachsenhausen, a district in the town of Oranienburg, perhaps twenty miles northwest.

Nadia closed the door and started downstairs. The tap-tap of her hard shoes on the wooden stairs sounded like a ticking clock getting louder with each second.

The typeface of the smaller towns was written in a minuscule old European style.

Nadia had to be halfway down by now.

There! Ravensbrück. A small village almost due north of Sachsenhausen. Livy compared the distance between Berlin and the two smaller towns. Maybe thirty-five kilometers. Livy closed the book, slid it into the open slot on the shelf as Nadia turned the corner.

The young Russian started at her. "How can you read? You know Russian?" As always her tone sounded accusing.

"'Course not. Just looking at the pictures." Livy smiled. "Tea ready?" She stood and walked upstairs past the young woman.

After all this time, she had a good idea of where Margot Dupont might be.

* * *

A few hours later, Livy made herself a cup of tea and sat on one of the stiff sofas in the front room. She sat in the quiet for more than an hour, thinking. The information she'd found in the map confirmed Kostin's theory of Margot's whereabouts.

The job wasn't over, though. The final confirmation would come once the Russian asked his sources back at the embassy. So Livy waited. Upstairs Nadia played the violin. The same piece again.

She checked her watch. Nearly three PM. No more waiting.

Livy went upstairs. The lock of hair across her doorway was gone. Instinctively, she put her hand on the Colt in her skirt. Then she stepped inside. Everything looked the same, but there had been slight disturbances. She found her reporter's notebook and began to write furiously.

Minutes later, she walked into the kitchen. Nadia looked at her over the fret of the violin.

"I need to call my editor," Livy said. "It's been two days since we've talked. I need to give him something so he doesn't think I've been kidnapped."

"No calls."

"Look, if I don't at least check in today then he's going to get worried. He might even pop 'round to my hotel and ask after me. Can't imagine Major Kostin would want that."

Nadia dropped the bow to her side. "You call tomorrow."

"Newspaper stories don't wait. We have deadlines. It's one call." Livy's voice became more than a little testy.

"Call tomorrow. Maybe." Nadia's bow sliced across the strings.

Tomorrow, Livy thought, this may all be over.

Chapter
Twenty-Six

❧

London
The same night

Geoffrey Collins had been waiting for the signal again for weeks.
Every day he'd come to work wondering if this would be the day
he'd hear it again. Today he'd agreed to change shifts with Reg
Hopkins, who had a date with a woman he'd met three years ago
in France. She'd finally made it to London, and they had two
nights before she was due back. Collins was happy to help a friend.

Of course, that night, the signal came again. It began with
the signature fist. *N-i-g-h-t-s-h-a-d-e.* The call repeated twice.
Collins grabbed his log and recorded it. His heart racing as a
wave of disbelief and joy swept over him. He thought he'd never
hear the signal again. In the intervening weeks, he'd even rationalized the first instance as his own error. He convinced himself
it had all been a mistake. Written down wrong. Who knows?
But now, it had returned.

Then, something different.

A very clear, steady Morse code. *S-O-S.* He stopped writing
and listened. *S-O-S. S-O-S.* It repeated three more times and

stopped. Collins's breath seemed caught in his chest as the silence lingered. He waited. The signal, so brief and so clear, didn't repeat.

This time Collins didn't wait until the end of his shift. He picked up the single phone on the wall near the door of room 118 and asked the operator to be connected immediately to his supervisor, Alfie Bromfield. He had to assure the telephone girl that the information he had was tantamount to national security before being put through to the boss's home line.

* * *

The phone in the Kemsley News offices rang just after eight AM the next morning. Pen Baker rarely came in before nine. Fleming himself picked up on the second ring.

"Yes? Speaking," he said, his voice clear and alert. "Right. Yes. What time then? I can make it earlier if he would like. Very well. Thank you."

Fleming replaced the receiver and ran a hand through his thick, wavy hair. His heart sank a bit when the call came in from Dunbar. He figured the only reason MI6 might reach out to him at this point was to let him know the job was either done, or that something had happened to Livy. He walked back into his office still wearing yesterday's trousers and a white undershirt, both heavily wrinkled after last night.

Since Livy left for the States, Fleming had slept most nights in his office, waiting for just such a phone call from Henry Dunbar. Or anyone who might know something about Livy Nash. During the day he'd pop around to his flat for clean clothes, then wake well before Pen arrived, bathe and dress in the men's washroom down the hall, and look his normal self by the time the business day began.

Of course, Pen had commented on the dark circles under his eyes as well as his general irritability, but she attributed it to turbulence in his mysterious private life. Fleming trusted and admired Pen both for her resourcefulness and icy efficiency. He never discussed personal matters with her. Nor had he addressed the night at The Ivy restaurant where Pen had watched her boss make a drunken pass at Livy. She'd been a bit brusque with him since that dinner. He missed their repartee and, at times, Fleming had wished he could confess all to his secretary. This, however, was a case where Fleming's reputation as a cad worked for him in the service of the operation.

Dunbar wanted to meet Fleming at ten that morning on the Tin and Stone Bridge in St. James's Park. The day, rainy with persistent clouds, fit Fleming's mood.

He'd known the risks sending Livy into this situation. He hoped she'd understood them as well after meeting Anka. There had been more than several occasions over the last two weeks when Fleming had wished the Austrian woman had frightened Livy off the job. Many nights he reassured himself the decision had been hers and hers alone. *I gave her every possible out.* He also knew that if he had denied Dunbar's request to go after Kostin, then his own tangential relationship to the Intelligence Services might have been severed.

The memory of the grisly photograph of Livy's double agent in Paris also haunted him. Fleming craved excitement, but he knew that if something happened to Livy, he would forever blame himself.

The two men had planned to meet at the spot where the bridge afforded a view of Buckingham Palace and the Queen

Victoria statue. The rain had stopped. The cloud cover foretold the prospect of a continuance, so Fleming rolled his umbrella and strolled along the walkway.

The weather had kept most people inside today, save for the occasional mother pushing a pram, or businessmen in raincoats and hats, out for a morning constitutional.

Dunbar was already there. Dressed in his usual hound-stooth, pipe clenched between his teeth. Fleming thought he looked like an older, tired Richard Hannay. Neither man spoke at first. Two couples, both arm in arm, stopped between them to admire the view. After a minute or two, they walked away. Dunbar removed the pipe from his mouth and looked at Fleming.

"You look awful, Ian."

"Lovely to see you too, Henry."

"Let's take a walk."

They strolled north in the direction of Westminster and Big Ben. Fleming waited for Dunbar to break the silence.

"What have you heard from that girl of yours?"

"Nothing at all. She apparently contributed to an article written by my man in Washington, but that was several days ago."

"Pity."

Fleming frowned. "Is it now? You know, you could've sent a courier if that's all you wanted. But I suspect there's more, so why don't you tell me what you know, Henry?"

Dunbar kept walking, eyes front. "Eastcote had another wireless signal last night. Same fist. Same everything as the first contact. Only this one was different. After the identification signature, the operator sent an SOS. Three times. I thought perhaps—I don't know—something your girl did might have prompted it."

Fleming stopped, pulled his silver cigarette case out of his pocket, fit the distinctive cigarette with three bands into his holder, and lit it.

"Forgive my confusion," Fleming said after taking a thoughtful draw of his cigarette. He'd been smoking and drinking too much the last two weeks. His doctor wouldn't approve. "How exactly would Olivia be able to influence a poor woman ostensibly being held in a Soviet prison in Germany, when she is in the United States?"

Dunbar bristled. "It was a question. Don't read too much into it, old man."

"Well, then, as I said, I've not heard one word from her since she left two weeks ago. Surely your man at the FBI has given you some sort of status report."

"It's all been too bloody quiet over there for several days. Something's going on. Now this signal last night. It's got to be connected."

The two men walked and smoked along the misty bridge. Fleming felt the tapping of raindrops on his navy mackintosh, so he unrolled his umbrella.

"Well, as delightful as your company is, Henry, I do still have work to do."

Dunbar grabbed his arm. Raindrops pelted down on the MI6 man's shoulders. His eyes scanned the bridge in both directions. His quiet voice carried even over the patter of the rain.

"You need to know—I've not been completely forthcoming about Margo Dupont."

Chapter
Twenty-Seven

❧

Washington, D.C.
The same morning

Like the day before, Livy woke up in considerable discomfort. Her cheek was less sensitive, but her neck still felt stiff and sore. Sitting on the edge of the bed she tried rolling it out. Even slow stretching sent shooting pain through her neck and shoulders.

She walked to the bathroom, turned on the tap, and retrieved her blouse and skirt from the closet. The last thing she felt like doing was wearing anything supplied by her Russian captors. She hung her wrinkled clothes in the bath, turned on the water, closed the door, and let the steam smooth them out.

Breakfast was ready as usual, but this time Nadia had only prepared toast and tea. A significant step down after yesterday's plateful. The young woman didn't sit with Livy while she ate, opting for the living room in one of the Queen Anne–style chairs, where she pored over an issue of *Life* magazine.

Livy had very little appetite. She had a piece of toast, drank half a cup of tea, and joined Nadia in the front room.

"I'll be going back to the hotel today, then? Isn't that the plan?"

The Russian woman ignored her. Engrossed in her reading.

"If I'm not going back to my hotel, then I've got to at least phone my editor," Livy said. The anxiety in her voice was not an act. She'd heard nothing from Kostin since the day in the control room. What had happened to him? She couldn't stand another moment in the house with this cold, bitter young woman. Again, no response.

"Did you hear me?"

Nadia flipped a page. "I hear."

"Well, how about a bloody answer then, luv?" Livy lashed out.

Nadia stood. "No answer to give." She brushed past Livy into the kitchen.

Livy thought about charging past her, grabbing the vodka from the icebox, and finishing it in her room. Instead, she took a deep breath and tried to sound several degrees calmer.

"I'll be upstairs. Organizing my notes. All right?" No reply came, so she turned. Her neck twisted, sending pain up into her skull and down her back. Livy cursed under her breath. She put a hand on her shoulder and massaged the muscle. Her body seemed to be rebelling now. She hated waiting, and right now that was her only choice.

*   *   *

A hot cloth pressed against her neck, Livy sat on the edge of the bed, going over what she'd just written in her notebook. No shorthand this time, but she knew Nadia wouldn't be able to decipher the old code she'd decided to use for this particular missive.

Livy'd spent the better part of an hour going over her notes without a sound from the young violinist. No practice today yet. Nor had the Russian checked on her, as was the routine.

After reading through what she'd written a final time, Livy carefully tore the pages out of the notebook and rolled them into the thinnest tube she could manage.

Downstairs, she heard a car pull into the back drive and a door open and close. Nadia's ride to the Soviet Embassy must have arrived.

Livy reached into the waistband of her skirt, where she kept the photo of Margot. She withdrew the small picture and slid it between the notes. Then, wrapping them carefully, she slipped the paper along the seam of her skirt and folded it over.

She heard the door to the downstairs open and close. Whispers in Russian and then the sound of heavy footsteps coming upstairs. Livy turned to her door as it was flung open.

Yuri Kostin stood in the doorway. He hadn't waited until Nadia left. Livy could smell vodka on his breath from ten feet away. The Russian hadn't shaved or slept, from the look of him. He slammed the door shut.

"Yuri, are you—?"

Kostin held up a hand to silence her. He stalked across the room to a somewhat abstract painting that looked like a meadow, painted by Picasso's less talented brother. He took the painting off the wall and tore into the paper backing of the frame. At once she saw a very fine black wire snaking out of the back of the picture into a pin-sized hole in the wall.

Kostin reached through the paper and wrenched out a piece of metal about the size of a half crown. He then pulled on the wire once, twice, then a third time before the black line snapped.

He threw the bug and its wire on the dresser, leaving the painting lying on the floor.

He came at Livy fast, so quickly she didn't have time to react. Kostin grabbed her upper arms and held her close. At first, she thought he might kiss her, his previous passion hard to distinguish from whatever this was.

"Margot Dupont," he said. "How do you know her?"

"I told you. She and I trained together."

Kostin scoffed and shook his head. He pulled her closer, their hips touching.

"Listen to me," he said. "Tell me the truth, Livy. I need you to tell me the truth."

What did he know? What had happened since yesterday? She felt the immediacy of the moment in every nerve ending and every bone. Adrenalin and fear healed her physical pain for the time being. *This is how it happens,* she thought. *People get weak at times like this. They spill their guts in exchange for some sort of mercy.* She couldn't give in. Not with this man. Not right now when she felt so close to finishing the job.

She put her hand on his face. Her eyes locked on his. "I don't know what's happened or why you're asking me this, but I am telling you the truth. Margot and I became friends during training. I've gotten to know her family since the war. What happened? Did you find out something about her?"

Kostin listened, but as she spoke, a cloud darkened his eyes, the energy he'd walked into the room with, gone. He dropped his head, loosened his grip on her shoulders, and turned away.

"Yuri?"

He stood facing the closed door. Livy was good at reading people, but she couldn't keep up with his changing moods.

"I told them I believed you," he said. His back to her. Voice soft. "I told them I was certain. I told myself that as well." Kostin turned to her, his hooded eyes half closed. The wide mouth turned down.

"I need the truth, Livy. Please."

She had two seconds to think it through: change the story or stick to the closest she could come to the truth. No choice really.

"I'm telling you the truth." Her voice even, calm.

She didn't see his hand until it was too late. The right whipped across his body and slammed into her face. The ferocity of the blow surprised her. Her cheekbone and jaw took it all. It spun her around and dropped her hard on the bed.

She felt hands on her back, turning her over to face him. The punch disoriented her, landing in the same painful spot where Gennady had hit her. She couldn't get her bearings. Kostin was on top of her now. Pinning her shoulders to the bed.

"You knew her family? You just wanted the truth for them? To comfort them?"

"Yes, of course. It's been years. What are you—?"

"Margot Dupont is working for us." He spat the words at her. Teeth bared.

The fear of this terrible moment drained away as her heart shriveled inside her chest.

"Since the end of the war, your friend has been a double agent. Giving us information about the British. Do you hear me?"

The words rained down on Livy like another blow to the jaw. She tried to make sense of what he'd said. Rationalize it somehow. She couldn't.

"I didn't know. I had no—how could I know, Yuri?"

"Lies!" he screamed at her. "You want me to believe it was accident? You appear out of nowhere, and all you want is to find one of your people working for us? So, now you know. Go back and tell her family that their Margot is fucking the commandant at Sachsenhausen. *Ona—blyad!* Just like you. *Portovaya blyad.* Whore."

Livy had no time to consider the veracity of what she'd just heard. With each denouncement, Kostin's temper flared.

She'd seen him like this once before. The anger and stark violence in his eyes when he'd found the big Russian Gennady over her. Now here it was again. Directed at her this time. *Der Rote Teufel.*

"You lied to me. All of it lies. Wasn't it?" He chewed the words. Flung them at her. Saliva hit her face. His hands pressed her body into the bed.

"Yuri, you're hurting me. Please. I had no idea about any of that. I've not seen her for years."

Kostin grabbed her jaw, sending a shockwave of pain through her cheek and into her skull. For a moment Livy thought she might black out. She bit her lip hard. It brought her back. Kept her there.

"You did it so well. Yes, you were very good, my love. *My darling.*" He snarled the endearments. "You thought you could give me your body, and I would be blind, yes?"

"Yuri, no, that's not—"

He squeezed her jaw hard. *God, that hurts.*

The Russian lowered his face to hers. His breath foul. Eyes dark and burning. His body felt hot, feverish even, on tops of hers.

Kostin leaned to her ear. He whispered, "I believed you. Do you hear? Shh, shh, don't try to move, *moya lyubov.* You won.

You made me . . . love you." His lips grazed her ear. He kissed it, softly along the ridge. Down to the lobe. "My love," he said again. So soft. His lips tender on her skin. One hand still pressing her head into the mattress, the other kept a vise grip on her shoulder.

"I'm sorry," he whispered. The intention in his voice sent a jolt through her.

It was fight or die.

Her body pulsed against his, pushing up. Too heavy to move. She tried to lift her right knee into his groin, but his legs, anticipating the blow, squeezed hers tighter. Livy flailed and squirmed and kicked. Her whole body electrified. But nothing moved him. Maybe an inch or two. No more. He had her.

She couldn't escape. Couldn't move.

His right hand released her jaw and moved down to her throat. His thumb pressing along her Adam's apple. Gently. He squeezed. She felt her throat constrict. Her breath struggled to clear the windpipe. She slammed the edge of her right hand hard into his throat. Again. Again. She may as well have hit a brick wall. Kostin barely flinched.

He brought his left hand to her neck. Two hands now crushed her throat. She arched her back, her hips and legs thrashing under him.

Livy knew she had a minute. Maybe less. She fought to keep her eyes open. Blacking out would mean it was over.

She pounded him with both hands, trying to reach his face. Kostin's teeth were bared, but the anger had left his brow. Tears ran down his cheeks. The wetness dripping down as he set about trying to finish her. Livy grabbed for his eyes. The fingernails of her left hand dug into his cheek. They clung there, raking. She broke the skin, felt his blood run down her fingers. But he didn't stop. Kostin wrenched her fingers away. Her hand hit the pillows.

And something hard.

On the verge of going dark, the nerves in Livy's body jolted. She knew what she'd touched. Her fingers scraped the bed.

Let it be there. Please.

One finger in the trigger guard, another along the barrel. Her left hand gripped the Colt. Livy ripped it out from under the pillow and into Kostin's bleeding face.

Not enough power. She had so little strength. Her throat. *God.* The bones and muscle felt on the point of collapse. She tried to hit him but couldn't lift her arm. Seconds now. She was fading. So quickly.

His stomach pushed against hers. She felt his skin for a moment. Somehow she knew. Just enough consciousness. To put the barrel on his skin. She felt the contact. Somewhere, deep in her brain, a final scream of survival.

Squeeze, it said. *Goddamn it! Now!*

She pulled the trigger.

The relief was immediate. His grip slackened. One hand to his ribs. She saw blood. He reached again for her throat. She gasped and coughed. Her lungs screamed. *Air! Life! Make it stop!*

She pulled the trigger over and over. Even after she heard the metallic clack. *Clack! Clack! Clack! Clack! Clack!*

Then, nothing. She could move, though; the pressure gone now.

Livy tried to sit up. Her throat still felt his hands. The force of Kostin's grip. Her lungs trying to reacclimate. She willed herself to sit up. Her eyes refocused. She was alive. The pain assured her of that.

Blood was everywhere. It pooled thick on her blouse, sticking to her stomach. There was even more of it on the carpet. So much more.

Her vision sharper now, she looked down. Kostin lay on his back, his arms at either side. Head at an angle. His mouth open. Red soaked his shirt and jacket. The holes in his body still bled.

Livy steadied herself against the bed. The gun in her hand. Kostin's face was frozen in what looked like shock, his eyes open and wide. She felt the urge to reach down and close them.

The sound of footsteps clattered up the stairs. Running.

Nadia in the doorway. The Russian woman gasped and covered her mouth. She looked at Kostin's body as if trying to verify what she saw.

They made eye contact. Livy leveled the gun at Nadia's head. "Don't you fucking move."

The words came out rough, guttural. Unclear. Livy said it again.

Nadia stood still. Her eyes held a mix of fear and hate.

Livy wondered if she knew the gun was empty. She stood, stepped over Kostin's body.

Nadia rushed her. One hand clawed at Livy's face, the other went for the gun. The attack threw Livy. She could barely put up a fight now. Nadia screamed as her hand ripped at Livy's face and battered throat. Livy staggered back, on the defensive, and her heels crashed into something hard. She turned. It was Kostin's body. Livy never thought it would end like this. But it had and she still had a job to do. Only Nadia stood in her way of getting out now. Livy whipped her hand out of the Russian's grip and smashed the gun against the side of Nadia's face, sending the younger woman staggering back into the doorway. Livy moved quickly. She slammed the butt of the revolver down on the back of Nadia's head. It was the hardest blow she could manage, and it was enough. The Russian woman crumbled forward. She lay in the doorway, moaning.

Livy wanted to hit her again. And again. But her body wasn't ready for more. She had to get out.

With deliberate calm, she knelt beside Kostin and dug into his coat pocket for the keys to the Dodge. Keys in hand, she stepped over the expanding pool of red and picked up her handbag from the nightstand. Throwing open the closet, she searched for something that might cover the blood on her blouse. A navy jumper would do.

A coughing spasm convulsed her lungs and chest. She stopped in the doorway on her way out. No time to reflect. The end of the job was in sight. She stepped over Nadia and ran downstairs, leaving the room and her captors behind.

Chapter
Twenty-Eight

～

Livy plugged the key into the ignition and started the car. She spun the Dodge around and turned left out of the drive, away from the house. It took her about hundred yards to realize she was driving in the left lane. She swerved into the right.

She was a foreign woman driving a car in a foreign country—for the first time— and she had no idea where the hell she was going.

Livy took it slow despite the urgency she felt to get away from the house and all the death. Her body needed time to heal, but she didn't have that luxury. The clutch popped a few times. She found the brakes spongy and almost slammed into a DeSoto at a stop sign.

Afterward, she glanced in the rearview mirror to assess the damage. The right side of her face looked like it had gone ten rounds with a wall. Purple splotches bloomed across her throat.

The sharp scream of a car horn from behind brought her back to the moment. She ground the gear and lurched the car forward.

Livy had no idea how to get where she was going. The roads all looked the same. Houses. Pavement. Big cars everywhere.

She drove on, assuming that when the traffic picked up, the city would be near.

But a few wrong turns took her deeper into tree-lined streets with well-kept gardens. She tried another direction, keeping the speed of the car slow enough not to attract the attention of the police.

She considered stopping for petrol and asking for directions but figured her appearance might cause more concern and create questions she had no time to answer.

The car smelled like Kostin. The scent of his cologne, as well as the vodka he must have drunk this morning, seemed to have fused with the leather seats. As her breathing began to normalize and the pain in her throat eased the slightest bit, the drive lent the morning a transcendent feeling of normalcy, but then the car would hit a pothole, and the hurt and urgency of the moment returned in a flash.

Nadia would be making calls by now. She'd tell the Soviet Embassy what had happened. She'd report the car. Soon, they'd be looking for her. If the police or the FBI found her first, that would be one thing. If the Russians found her, she'd be dead.

It took almost an hour, but eventually she found herself driving along a road near a busy highway.

Up ahead she saw a plain, brick building with ten or more floors. It looked like so many of the office towers Livy'd seen across the district. Across the street, cabs dropped businessmen off in front of a large restaurant. The normal world was going about life and it was lunchtime.

Livy pulled the car into the flat parking lot that sprawled across the front of the building. Turning into the drive, she spotted a guardhouse up ahead, hidden under a copse of pine trees.

A guard in a crisp gray uniform stepped out, a smile on his face. Livy cleared her throat, hoping she had a voice. She slowed down as the guard came up to her window.

His expression told her all she needed to know about how she looked.

"Can I . . . are you all right, ma'am?"

Livy lurched forward and rested her head against the wheel for a moment. "I had an accident at home," she said slowly. She didn't know what else to say.

"I can call the police if you gimme a—"

"No! No, look, I'm just here to see my husband. He's having lunch across the street. He'll know what to do. About everything."

The guard looked skeptical but seemed uneasy about inserting himself between a husband and wife.

"Let me just get you a day pass then," he said, turning away.

Livy sighed and shifted her eyes to the rearview. God, proper Bride of Frankenstein material, that's what she was.

The gun! Dammit! Sloppy. Livy scanned the seat for the Colt .32. She pushed aside her handbag. Nothing. Had she thrown it in the back seat? She looked up. The guard, paper in hand, headed back to the Dodge. *There!* In the passenger floorboard. She leaned down, pushed it under the seat, and sat back up.

"Just put that on your dashboard," the guard said, handing her the pass. "You take care of yourself now, ma'am."

Livy thanked him and eased the car into the lot. She found a space as far away from the other cars as possible. She parked and grabbed a pencil out of her purse. Reaching into the waistband of her skirt, she retrieved the folded piece of notepaper. She placed it against the steering wheel and wrote more. When finished, she looked it over. The code was strictly old Firm. She didn't know any others. Livy just needed time to get it into the right hands.

She refolded the paper, with Margot's picture inside, and replaced it in her skirt. The gun was a problem. The car as well. She had no idea of the protocol for the murder of a spy in a foreign country, but it was quite possible Nadia might call the police. The neighbors might have even heard the shots. All six of them. They might have seen her peeling out of the driveway. Honestly, being arrested for murder was one of her least concerns at this point. The investigation—if there was one—would take days. She decided to take the pistol.

Livy felt oddly vulnerable as she walked across the street to the Capital Steakhouse. The jumper covered the stain on her blouse well enough, but the marks on her face would bring unwanted attention.

It took her about five minutes—and enduring the stares of a couple of businessmen on their way to lunch—to hail a cab in front of the restaurant. Fortunately the cabbie, a young man wearing a shirt decorated with palm trees, didn't seem to notice.

She gave him the address of the British Embassy on Massachusetts. As the car moved away from the curb, Livy allowed herself a deep sigh.

The moment gave her time to think about what Kostin had told her. Could Margot actually be a Russian spy? A double agent for the Soviets? She tried to align that thought with her memories of her friend during training. They'd both been so young and naive then. The war changed people. For some, it was a complete metamorphosis. God knows it had changed Livy. Still, Margot didn't seem the type to betray her country, but who did? It'd been four years since they'd seen each other, and so much had happened in the intervening years.

Livy's heart felt heavy. Emotion threatened to steam over like an unwatched kettle. She wiped a tear from one eye.

Truth be told, Livy'd never had many friends. People often disappointed her. She found the day-to-day pursuits of most women her age silly and pointless. Maybe she just didn't fit in.

But Margot had felt like a kindred spirit. They shared so much, from their sense of humor to their bilingual upbringing. That's why Livy had come this far and sacrificed so much because no matter how many years it had been, Margot Dupont was still that very rare commodity in the life of Livy Nash: a friend.

But people change. The phrase ticker-taped again through her mind. It didn't make sense though. Why the wireless signals now if she was a Russian spy? After all this time?

The cab made several quick turns, and Livy began to recognize the distinctive architecture of the district. Soon, they would be on Massachusetts Avenue. She slipped the paper from the lining of her skirt.

She looked out the back window. Cars littered the street behind them. *They could be back there,* she thought. The American, the Russians, the police.

Soon, it would be out of her hands. The decisions left to someone in London.

Up ahead Livy could see the distinctive brick facade of the British Embassy compound.

"Can you stop just in front there?" she said to the driver. "I have to drop something off, and then I'll come back."

Livy looked both ways on the sidewalk before opening the cab door. Foot traffic felt about right for this time of day. No one stood out. But then, they wouldn't.

She had about twenty-five yards to cover to get to the uniformed man who stood guard outside the brick and iron enclosure that ran around the perimeter of the building. Livy shut the door, walking slowly. She braced herself for whatever might come. Had the Russians had enough time to track her down? Would she be grabbed from behind?

Closer to the guard now, she recognized the uniform. He wore the navy coat and peaked hat that marked him as an officer of the DC Police. A leather strap across his chest connected to the holster around his waist.

She reached into her purse and removed her passport. Her hand perspired around the rolled notes.

Twenty feet to go.

Up ahead two men in dark suits, both wearing fedoras tilted back on their heads, moved toward her. Both looked to be in their mid-thirties, with military-style haircuts. Black suits on another humid summer day.

She calculated the distance between her and the guard against the speed of the two approaching men. They'd arrive at just about the same time. Her breath quickened. She had to force herself not to run. The two men were just feet away from the guard. She looked at her passport. The notes, the picture of Margot flat between the pages.

Five feet now. She put her head down, wishing she'd thought to look for a hat in the closet before she left the Russian safe house.

The two men moved with purpose. No smiles. No small talk.

She reached the guard, put her hand on his shoulder as the two other men arrived.

"Excuse us," the taller of the two men said, his eyes on Livy. Then, to the guard, "There a burger joint around here?"

The guard pointed in the opposite direction. "Left on Florida, near the Colombian Embassy. It's a walk, but worth it."

The tall man thanked the guard and tipped his hat to Livy. He and his companion headed back the way they'd come.

No more time to waste.

"I found this," she said, pushing the passport into the guard's hand. "Someone must have lost it. There's a young woman who works here. Alice. Alice Dawson. You probably know her. Would you make sure she gets this? If someone lost their passport, they'll be very worried."

"Sure," the guard said. "You could take it in yourself, you know."

But Livy had already turned, heading back to the cab. She collapsed into the back seat. Sweat mixed with the bloodstain on her blouse. She wanted to sleep for a week. Maybe the chance would present itself soon. No matter though—her job was done for now.

"Statler Hotel, please," she said. "I'll give you a dollar if you can make it in ten minutes."

* * *

Nine minutes later, the cab pulled up in front of the big hotel on Sixteenth. Livy felt as if she'd arrived at mecca. She fished around in her handbag for a moment, to find enough change to pay the driver a full dollar for the ride. The young man nodded, eyes wide. She must look like hell. She certainly felt like it.

Smelling of blood and three-day-old clothes, Livy allowed herself to think about the bath in her room, the welcoming respite of the mattress, the softness of the sheets. She tried to remember the room service menu as she walked slowly to the front doors. They had ice cream—not as many flavors as Howard Johnson's, but the thought of the cold dessert sliding down her damaged throat lifted her spirits for a moment.

She stepped up on the curb. The doorman gaped. Livy gave a little mock bow. The air-conditioned lobby felt like an oasis. The bath, the bed, a sumptuous meal with ice cream, and uninterrupted sleep all part of the fantasy she allowed herself to create. Livy knew it was a mirage, but she didn't care.

Three men stood at the front desk. Gray suits, not black. Laurel and Hardy—the two FBI men who'd greeted her on her arrival—stood beside a DC police officer. Just more men coming to get her. They all looked the same by now.

"Miss Nash," Laurel said. He flashed a black wallet. "You'll need to come with us, ma'am."

She managed a grin. "What took you so bloody long?"

Chapter
Twenty-Nine

~

The interrogator sat down and placed the cigarettes on the square metal table. He pried open the cellophane film with a discolored thumbnail, and rapped the pack against his right hand several times until three of the smokes poked out the top. Placing one between his lips, he slowly drew it out. The routine, which seemed choreographed, ended with the flick of a silver Ronson lighter. Flame ignited the tobacco, and he drew the smoke into his lungs.

This American was the second one to question Livy since they'd brought her to this nondescript, flat gray building on the outskirts of the city. Two women had gotten her "checked in." After taking all her things and issuing a pressed white blouse and cotton skirt, they'd dumped her in this small interview room with a table, two chairs, and overhead fluorescent lights that hummed and compounded the massive headache she'd been nursing.

Then came the man with the horn-rimmed glasses and the pack of Camels.

As Americans went, this one was a lot like the GIs Livy had met in France. Square head, haircut like a freshly trimmed garden, and no sense of humor. He wore a white short-sleeved shirt and a black tie that was knotted tight against his thick Adam's apple. For a moment Livy felt pity for the man. The furrowed expression on his brow gave her the impression he was as uncomfortable in his skin as he appeared to be in his clothes.

Putting the pack down on the table, the interrogator pushed it toward Livy.

"Help yourself."

"No, thank you," she said. "I don't partake."

The choice of words must have piqued the interrogator's interest. He studied her through the smoke. His thick lips held the cigarette tight, and his brown eyes narrowed, as if seeing her for the first time. Livy assumed this squinty chap must be another step up, an escalation in the severity of the conversations that took place in this white room with no windows.

Livy glanced around, wondering where the listening devices would be. Crack in the floor? Too obvious even for the FBI. Those bloody buzzing lights? No, the interrogator must've brought it in.

"You don't sound like a regular Brit," he said, dusting his ashes in a glass tray. Microphone blown into the glass, perhaps? She definitely needed sleep.

"Shall I start quoting Shakespeare, then? That make you more comfortable?" Livy waved the smoke out of her face.

He grunted and opened the black file lying perfectly aligned beside his notebook. "I have a few questions. If you answer them, this will go quickly. Understand? Let's start with your war record, Miss Nash. In 1940, you joined the—First Aid Nursing Yeomanry?" The words sounded thick on his tongue.

"I told the others all this. Didn't they take good notes?"

The interrogator punched out his cigarette and removed his glasses.

Here comes the scolding bit.

"Let me be clear. Your situation could not be more serious," he said. "Treason. Murder. Assaulting a federal officer. So I'm not inclined to laugh at your jokes."

"Hold on. Assaulting a what?"

"A federal officer. Special Agent Keller."

Livy would have laughed if her head didn't feel as if it might split open.

"Tender sort, our Agent Keller, isn't he? Suit yourself."

"I want to begin with your service in the war." The interrogator checked his notes. "Why do you think you were recruited? You'd done nothing really worthy of their attention. Was it luck?"

Livy smiled. "Better. New tactic. Make me defend myself. Keep going."

The cigarette smoke in the gray room had dissipated. The air between the two sides of the table felt clearer.

"Whatever the reason, they took you anyway. Maybe it was your language skills. Maybe because you were an orphan. No one to really worry if something happened to you in France." He checked his notes. "The Special Operations Executive. You must've served alongside quite a few genuine heroes. Did you want to be a hero, Miss Nash?"

Livy's head throbbed. She read his every move, and yet the bastard got to her. She'd murder a bottle of vodka now, given half a chance.

"Go on then," she said. "You're quite the storyteller."

"This is your story, ma'am. Let's see now. You're captured. Rescued by an Allied patrol from a Gestapo prison. But after the war there's nothing out there for you. Is there? MI6 won't have you. It's back to—what? Regular life? Did you feel that your country had used and then discarded you?

Livy looked away. The cover Fleming cooked up for her was sticking, but good. What would the critics say. "She played the part so well you'd almost believe she's not acting."

"Your life after the war must have seemed pretty dull by comparison. Did you come back feeling that your country owed you something?"

"Well, a Christmas card would've been nice."

The interrogator's expression was as blank as the white walls. "Funny. I hope you realize, though, the only way you're getting out of this room is by giving me some answers."

Livy leaned back in her metal chair, which was about as comfortable as the iron maiden, and considered her position. She'd left one prison for an entirely new one. What would they do with her here? God knows, Keller could clear this whole thing up with one sentence. Unless he figured that Kostin really had his hooks into her, and that's why Livy got violent and then fled the safe house. It made sense in a way. Keller had never taken her seriously as an agent. It wasn't out of the question that he would interpret her actions as those of a real traitor.

What a mess she'd landed in.

At least she'd made the delivery to the embassy, and with any luck Alice would be deciphering her code, and Margot's whereabouts would be on its way to London. Livy tried to see a day in the future when she and Margot might even be able to have a laugh about all they'd been through. That day still seemed far way.

"Fine. I'll answer," she said finally. "Fire away."

"You were having a sexual relationship with Yuri Kostin, isn't that right?"

Livy rolled her eyes. "Wouldn't call it a relationship. I'd call it my job."

"You previously had a sexual relationship with Kostin in—1945 in London?"

"Been doing your homework, haven't you?"

The interrogator scribbled something on the pad in front of him.

"You were directed by Agent Keller to cease this operation after the death of Gennady Yakupov. Is that the way you remember it?"

She didn't answer.

"When you were instructed to end the operation, you then had a physical confrontation with an agent of the Bureau?"

Livy looked away.

"Miss Nash?"

"Where is he anyway? Keller?"

"I'd like you to answer the question."

"I know you would. So why don't we make a deal? I'll answer yours, you answer mine."

He didn't flinch. Livy wasn't sure he was capable. "You're not really in a position to make demands right now, Miss Nash. If you'd like to move this forward and get out of this room at some point, I suggest you answer."

"Right, heard you the first time. But what you're missing is, I had a job too. From my people."

The interrogator looked up from writing. "Then you disappeared for two days after the cease and desist. Your story is that the Soviets kept you at a house in Maryland?"

"Well, it looked like Maryland."

"Did you continue your sexual relationship with Kostin there?"

Livy saw where all this was going. The interrogator was building his case against her. Seduced by the big bad Russian, she'd joined their team. Then, she'd killed him in a fit of passion. It would make a great spy novel.

"Sam Keller. Ask *him* these questions. He knows what I was doing, why I came here in the first place. I'm done talking to you."

The interrogator took off his glasses and rubbed his eyes. He looked tired too. "Miss Nash, I have to say that would be very unwise."

"Get Keller in here, and we'll all have a chat. How's that?"

"He is being questioned in a separate facility."

Livy had to laugh. It just got more absurd. "Questioned? About what?"

The interrogator put on his glasses.

"Did you continue your sexual relationship with Yuri Kostin at the Soviet compound in Maryland?"

She closed her eyes. The overhead light burned right through to the back of her skull. "I'm a British citizen," she said through clenched teeth. "I want to see someone from my embassy. I will have no further answers for you—sir—until I speak to a representative from the Embassy of the United Kingdom."

The interrogator put down his pencil, placed his pack of Camels on top of his notebook, and walked away from the table. At the door he turned to her.

"These fluorescent lights are hell if you have a headache, aren't they?"

He left, closing the door hard. The sound reverberated in Livy's head and all the way down her spine.

Chapter Thirty

~

Washington
British Embassy

It had been twenty-eight hours since Eric Dalby had slept. His job as head of station for MI6 in Washington was never relaxing, but since taking the position at the end of the war, life had settled into a certain predictability. He'd made a home in the States, even married an American woman. Their first child would turn two next month.

Then, a folded note in a passport had arrived at the front gate of the embassy. The desk girl, Alice, took it to her boss, and he in turn brought it to Dalby. He didn't know the code. Nor did he recognize the girl in the picture. Margot Dupont. The code turned out to be a cipher from the war based on a specific page in a specific book. They'd been lucky that Alice had worked codes a few years back. Once she had decoded the writing, Dalby set about verifying the information in it. That prompted the long daily call to headquarters in London.

At the moment, he had sent two of his officers to try to verify the note. One had begun to liaise with the FBI while the other sought to find out what he could on the alleged death of the MGB officer Kostin. Dalby knew if everything in the note was accurate, then his somewhat routine job might very well blow up in his face.

He picked up a spoon and stirred the milk in his third cup of tea before two o'clock. He had two phones on his desk. The black phone for local calls and a green one, which was the new transatlantic line that could be used to scramble to London. They'd made the call to London at noon. No response yet. On his desk lay a copy of the note, its translation, and a passport in the name of Olivia Katherine Nash, as well as the station's file on Kostin. He studied the Russian's picture. Handsome. Looked intelligent, but the man had been a holy terror during the war and was set to be head of the MGB Berlin station.

Not a bad one to be rid of.

The green phone rang.

Dalby picked up.

"Connecting you to London, sir. Please wait," the switchboard operator said. He heard two loud clicks, and the line went silent. The phone had been installed just six months ago and used only once as a test.

Twenty seconds later he heard the voice of Henry Dunbar, faint and muffled, but clear enough. Dalby listened.

"Yes, sir. Yes, we're trying to verify it all now, sir . . . I do understand the severity, yes . . . yes . . . Sir, if I may, she *is* a British citizen. We have her passport . . . right . . . yes, sir. I understand. Very good, sir."

The call ended.

Dalby looked across his desk at a picture of his wife on their wedding day. Next to it, a photo of her and their little boy, taken on his first birthday. He could never tell them what he was about to do. If he did, they'd be so ashamed.

*   *   *

They'd let Livy sleep in what looked like a converted office with two rollaway beds on either side of the room. A couple of metal desks had been pushed together in the center to give the cots some separation. The dark paneling of the walls and the shades pulled down over the windows gave the room a feel of perpetual night. One of the stern secretaries, whom Livy had taken to calling Glasses on account of the thick black spectacles she wore, slept in the other cot while a US Army guard sat on a chair outside the door all night. Livy couldn't rest. She found it impossible to get comfortable. Her entire body ached.

Dreams plagued her as well. Not the garden variety—"Oh, I was almost killed today"—or visions of Kostin's body looking like Julius Caesar's, with so many gaping wounds. No, she dreamed of Fresnes, the Nazi prison where she had been held near the end of the war.

It began with Livy alone walking down a long hallway with many doors on both sides. She heard the screams of women being tortured and killed behind every door. Except the last one. Livy opened it. Two bodies together as one. Margot stood in a clinch with Yuri Kostin. They did not see her, their intimacy unchanged by Livy's presence. The Russian undressed Margot, his hands moving slowly over her body. Margot was passive to his actions. As her dress slipped to the floor, Margot turned. She held Livy's gaze for a second. The look betrayed no meaning. They simply saw each other, and then Livy woke up.

After that she lay awake on the cot until Glasses told her to get up. Another day, another prison. Livy obeyed, though her body felt as if a giant had sat on her all night. At Fresnes she'd been beaten. This didn't feel very different.

The day progressed on a predictable routine. Breakfast. Another round of questioning with the male interrogator and his Camels. Lunch. More questioning. After the last round, they kept her in the interrogation room alone. The fluorescents buzzed. Livy put her head down on the wooden table. They were slowly breaking her with white walls and boredom.

After about half an hour, the door opened, and a man she'd not seen before walked in. He looked about ten years older than Livy. Pointed nose, green eyes, blondish hair receding. Blue suit. School tie.

"Miss Nash, I'm Eric Dalby from the embassy." His accent sounded Oxbridge, like Fleming's.

Livy raised her head and sat back in the metal chair. Dalby blanched on seeing the bruising around her neck.

"You should see the other fella," she said.

"What? Oh yes. As I said I'm the Foreign Office liaison here."

Meaning MI6, Livy thought.

"I'm here to make sure you are being taken care of."

"Oh, I am that, Mr. Dalby."

He steepled his fingers and sighed. "I'm sure the conditions here are less than ideal. The good news is the Americans have made no charges against you as of yet. However, I have to tell you, the circumstances are quite serious."

"That much has been made very clear to me. But what hasn't been is why they are keeping me here when I was working *with* them and *for* you."

"Sorry? For me?"

"Our government."

Dalby put his hands on the table, almost as if steadying himself. "I'm afraid I don't know what you're talking about."

Livy felt the scream deep in her gut. They bloody well wouldn't do this to her after all she'd been through. She shook her head and pounded her hand against the table.

"Would you like me to spell it out, then? In this room?"

Dalby straightened his tie, cleared his throat. "Miss Nash, what you did—or did not do for that matter—was not authorized by His Majesty's Government in any way."

"Is it ever?"

"As far as I know, you're a journalist and nothing more."

Livy slumped in the chair. *This is it.* It was a cock-up and her own people were going to let her take the fall. All nice and deniable on their end. She wished she'd thought to ask Anka how to get out when they keep piling it on your head, deeper and deeper.

"Who told you to say that?" she said.

"Miss Nash—"

"Henry Dunbar. Right?"

"I'm very sorry I can't be of more help," he said, and he sounded sincere. Dalby stood up, buttoned his coat and headed for the door.

Livy stood and held her hand out to him. She wanted to throttle the little messenger boy. "My passport. I'll have that, if you don't mind."

Dalby grimaced. "Of course. Once the Bureau has decided how they wish to handle this matter and you are free to leave, then the embassy will be more than happy to restore your passport."

"Mr. Dalby," she said, stopping him as his hand was on the doorknob, "if it makes you feel any better, I've done my share of dirty work for our government too."

He hesitated. "I do wish you all the best, Miss Nash."

Chapter
Thirty-One

❦

London
That evening

The Western Union courier was waiting when Ian Fleming returned to his office. He'd been home to collect clothes for work tomorrow, helped himself to a bourbon and branch water, then returned to the office.

A telegram this late at night was rare, even in a business where Kemsley's correspondents worked in every time zone around the world. Fleming tipped the young man generously and stepped into the dark office to read the message.

It came from Wilson Price, Fleming's correspondent in Washington, as well as Livy's editor there. It read: *NASH HELD BY FBI STOP PLEASE ADVISE*

Fleming slammed the telegram down on Pen Baker's desk and swore. Damn Henry Dunbar.

He grabbed the receiver on his secretary's desk and dialed her home number. She answered on the third ring. He could hear a man's voice in the background. Of course there would be.

"Pen, darling, I need you at work tonight. Yes, frightfully sorry, but we have a bit of a crisis. Yes. It's Olivia, dear. No, she's still in Washington, but listen. Before you go, I want you to stop and send a telegram to Price. Yes, tonight. I want him to drop what he's doing and do whatever it takes to find out anything about Olivia. Tell him to stand on the front steps of the FBI building all day and night if he must. Oh, and send a telegram to Fisher in New York. I want him on the first train to Washington in the morning. Same thing. Yes, my dear, I know. Everything else will just have to wait."

* * *

When Eric Dalby felt particularly taxed at work, he sought refuge in the full English breakfast served at O'Flaherty's. The day after his visit to see Livy Nash was one such morning. He sat in a back corner at a table that was little more than a shelf with two chairs. The corner felt quiet and shadowy, which suited him perfectly.

Anthony, the landlord, brought out the full plate, including black pudding, and placed it in front of the MI6 man. Dalby heard the front door open. He glanced up. Another customer. A man. Dalby had just dipped his knife into the jam when he realized the newcomer was walking to his table.

Never a field man, Dalby felt a bit threatened. He held the knife steady in his hand.

The man was still ten feet away when Dalby finally recognized him. They'd never actually met, although Dalby was more than familiar with the man's file. He looked shorter in person.

Georgi Sokolov sat down on the bench opposite Dalby. His round glasses didn't hide the lines of anxiety around his eyes.

"You know who I am?" the Russian asked.

"I do."

The landlord passed by, wondering if Sokolov might want the same.

"Just tea."

When they were alone again, the Russian spoke quietly. "We have a problem, Mr. Dalby. You understand what I am referring to?"

"I believe so." Dalby sipped his tea, trying to appear relaxed.

"We work in a profession that sometimes puts us at odds with each other. However, I have always felt that we share a mutual respect. The British are true professionals, which is why this breach in our friendship troubles me so much."

Dalby caught the veiled threat. "What exactly troubles you?"

Sokolov bristled. "I have a problem. A problem concerning one of my people, created by one of your people. So, you see, I need a solution. This situation must be made right. If you will not help me, then I will have to resort to other means."

Subtle as usual for a Russian, but Dalby recognized the implicit warning. He felt bad enough about the orders from London he'd been asked to carry out yesterday. He didn't know Livy Nash, but what he knew of her he admired. She didn't deserve how she'd been treated, and he'd be damned if he'd feed her to Sokolov.

"It's safe to say you'd be wise to use caution as well. That's about the most help that I can offer you."

The landlord brought Sokolov's tea, giving him a sideways look as he left the table. The Russian was behind enemy lines in this pub.

Sokolov took one sip and fetched a few coins from the pocket of his gray wool suit coat.

He said, "Our business is not one where we can allow a provocation such as this to go unanswered, Mr. Dalby. Enjoy your breakfast."

The Russian stood and calmly walked out.

Chapter
Thirty-Two

London

Henry Dunbar took his drink into the library of Brooks's Gentleman's Club to get away from the noise of the gaming room and the incessant chatter in the dining area. He had the room to himself. A blessing after the day he'd had. Dunbar dropped down into one of the studded leather sofas and placed his gin and tonic on the small round table next to it.

The room felt intimate and cozy. At his right stood the grand fireplace, presided over by a portrait of the wigged Duke of Portland, one of the twenty-seven men who'd founded the club in the eighteenth century. A dozen or so of the other founders watched over him from their frames on the wall behind. Everywhere else, books with leather bindings recessed into tall, oak shelves. He felt bolstered by their presence.

The drink was just how he liked it. Here, all he had to do was tell the steward, "The usual," and the rest was taken care of. He put his head back and closed his eyes for a moment. Perhaps two seconds.

He heard his name.

Dunbar blinked. Boyd, the steward, stood in the doorway. Tall, elegant posture despite his age, a calling card in his gloved hand.

"My apologies, sir, but you have a guest."

Dunbar held out his hand for the card. He read the name and felt a twitch in his eyebrow. He couldn't send him away. Not here of all places. Bad form. Tongues would wag. The "guest" knew that, of course.

"Yes, fine. Send him back, Boyd."

The steward left. Dunbar had just enough time to finish his drink before Ian Fleming joined him. He sat in the matching sofa opposite and pulled out his cigarette case.

"Another, Boyd." Dunbar held up his glass. "Bring the Commander whatever he wants."

"Bourbon and branch water. Neat," Fleming said and lit his cigarette. "First time I've ever been to your club, Henry. How quaint."

"What do you want, Ian?"

"You asked for my help. You gave us half the information we needed, and then you left my correspondent stranded. At present she is in the custody of the FBI. So, I'd say you should start with an explanation."

"Oh don't pretend to be hurt. You know how the game is played. I told you what you needed to know about the Dupont girl. And as far as Livy is concerned, you knew the risk. I was quite clear when I came to you with this."

Boyd appeared with a tray and two drinks. Then he faded away.

Fleming didn't touch the drink. He placed his cigarette in an ashtray and leaned forward. He set his jaw and glared at Dunbar.

"How long has Margot Dupont been a double?"

"Since the end of the war. I had her trained for what she was about to do. Planted her so she'd look like a POW. Perfect opportunity to get someone inside the Russian zone. And because, as former SOE, she was irresistible to them. She was picked up by the Russians and taken to another camp first. We had a contact there already set up that met with her. A guard at the camp who was working for us. So she fed the Reds out-of-date operational tripe. The Firm was off the book, so it was all useless, of course. But the Reds didn't know that. And Margot was able to be our eyes and ears in their zone. She sent back everything through this guard we had there. She was a damned good source. Then, about six months ago she went off the radar. Most of us had given her up for dead until we got that wireless signal."

"Sounds like a very brave woman."

"Right now I'm just hoping she's still alive," Dunbar snapped.

"You have a plan to get her out?"

"We don't leave our people behind."

"Really? Seems to me that's precisely what you're doing with Olivia."

"Blame yourself then, old man. I told you this was off the books. Besides that, she's created a damn firestorm over there in Washington," Dunbar said, raising his voice. He caught himself, took a breath, and leaned forward. "We'll be cleaning up her mess for God knows how long."

"She found your agent for you, dammit," Fleming snapped back.

The two men drank and smoked. Noises from the interior of the club drifted back into the library. The clinking of glasses, the rattle of silverware, the voices of men. Fleming broke the silence.

"Henry, you gave me a false bill of sale. I'm asking you now to make it right. There's only one way you can do that."

"What's done is done. The FBI might very well recommend to us Livy be tried for treason. There's also a good chance that she could be charged with murder. Should she somehow manage to avoid all that, then the Soviets will find her and make an example of her. So, I'd say, under the circumstances, Livy's not doing too badly where she is right now."

Fleming crossed one of his long legs over the other and smiled. "You must admit it is a fascinating story, isn't it? Young British woman forced to go undercover. Living the life of a double agent among the dangerous Russians until finally she surrenders her virtue to one of the Godless Soviets. All for King and Country. To rescue another young woman rotting away in a prison camp. Quite the inspiring story of sacrifice. I dare say it could also sell a lot of newspapers."

Dunbar scoffed. "Just what the devil are you playing at?"

"Precisely what I said. A story like that—filled with sex and sadism—would be a national sensation. If the wire services get hold of it, it could go worldwide." Fleming's eyes flashed and his wide mouth grinned impishly.

"*The Times* would never run that. Before they even consider it, they'd call us first, and we'd have the story buried."

"Perhaps. Perhaps not. I do have the facts to back it up. The real question is, can you afford to take that chance?"

Chapter
Thirty-Three

Nights continued to be miserable for Livy. The metal cot felt like the rack. She grew more irritable. She snapped at Glasses when she announced, "Lights out," promptly at ten.

When she'd first arrived at the Bureau facility, she craved alcohol every night. She lay in bed, her hands trembling. That continued for more than a week. But with no alcohol on the menu, the yearning calmed down. Her relapse into a bottle had only lasted two weeks.

At least the FBI had done her the favor of drying her out.

The interrogation routine proceeded without fail for the duration of her stay with the U.S. Government. Livy stuck to her vow of silence, even after her own embassy failed to help her. That might have explained the urgency she felt during the final rounds of questioning. It seemed as if some higher-up had said, "Look, we need answers out of the British girl, and we need them now."

The questions didn't change, though. Just the way they were asked. Regardless, Livy stonewalled them. Without fail. Every day.

This morning though had an altogether different feel.

After she woke up and was escorted to the washroom by Glasses, Livy returned to the converted office and found the linen stripped from both cots. Her side table, with its lamp and stack of newspapers with unfinished crosswords, had been cleared away.

The routine continued, however, and she was marched up one flight and down the hall to the white interrogation room with the table and metal chairs.

She waited. That was, of course, part of the routine too, but this morning the delay was unusually long. An hour or more went by before Livy even heard footsteps in the hallway outside.

The interrogator opened the door. Today, he wore a navy blazer over his white shirt and black tie. He carried his usual notebook and pencils, with the addition of a manila folder.

He sat down, opened the folder, and pushed it across the table to Livy.

"Read it."

She did. Quickly the first time, and then slowly a second.

The interrogator slid a ballpoint pen across the desk to her.

He said, "Sign it and you can go."

* * *

The brief affidavit explained that the Federal Bureau of Investigation had, in no way, directed the British national Olivia Nash to conduct operations in the United States, and that they were not responsible for her actions. First, her own government and now America had thrown her out with the bathwater. She didn't complain. She'd had enough.

Livy signed the paper.

After the interrogator left, without so much as a goodbye, Glasses escorted her to the washroom down the hall. Inside, Livy found the clothes she'd worn the day she arrived. The blouse and skirt had been laundered. The stain, with Yuri Kostin's blood, completely washed out. *Say what you will about the FBI, but they run a competent laundry service.*

Having worn FBI-issued frocks for two weeks, Livy felt more than a little like her old self putting on her own clothes. She wondered how long that feeling would last once she got outside.

Glasses walked her upstairs to the front doors. She returned Livy's purse, sans the Colt .32, and said, "They're waiting outside."

A new-looking Ford coupe was parked at the curb. Eric Dalby stood beside the car, along with a smartly dressed older woman. Dalby stepped forward. In his right hand he held Livy's passport.

"I'm glad to see you again, Miss Nash," he said. "This way, if you don't mind."

* * *

"We dropped by The Statler and picked up your things," Dalby said over his shoulder as he maneuvered the Ford through DC traffic. "We had to throw our weight around a bit to get them to unlock your room. The hotel has quite a number of important guests, and the staff there can be very protective, believe you me."

Livy sat in the back seat, next to the well-dressed woman. They hadn't spoken to each other. She felt a bit shell-shocked, like she'd been hibernating in a cave and hadn't seen the sun in years.

The day was bright and a bit cooler. The car drove through clean suburban neighborhoods. American flags dotted the landscape even a few weeks after the celebration of Independence Day. Men in shorts pushed lawnmowers across their lawns. She saw two little boys throwing a baseball in a park. The world had indeed kept spinning during her extended stay with the Russians and then the Americans.

It comforted Livy to hear Dalby's posh accent after feeling like an alien around her captors. Was that what they'd been? She looked down and found her left hand trembling slightly. Her breath was audible. She still felt the pain of Gennady and Kostin's blows in her jaw when she chewed. Even after two weeks, her throat felt rough, and her neck and shoulders stiffened every time she moved.

The views outside Dalby's car couldn't be more peaceful, and yet Livy didn't feel safe yet. She thought back to how she'd felt before Anka, before coming to America, before Kostin and the FBI. Had she changed after all she'd been through? She couldn't remember the last time she'd even smiled. A quick glance in the rearview mirror told her all she needed to know. The lines around her mouth had hardened. She held her trembling hand and thought about Margot and tried to imagine finally seeing her. Then she'd smile.

Traffic picked up as they headed into Alexandria on the Jefferson Davis Highway. Livy wondered if they were close to the Howard Johnson's where she'd met Keller the morning after Kostin broke into her hotel room.

Her body craved a drink, but she'd settle for an ice cream.

"Where are we going?" Livy said.

"National Airport," Dalby replied. "That was part of the deal we made with the Americans. We're sending you home."

"What changed?"

"I'm sorry?"

"Last time we met, Mr. Dalby, you told me I was a journalist and nothing more."

Dalby looked in the rearview at her. His eyes were kind. "Someone's looking out after you, Miss Nash." His eyes suddenly shifted. "A black Dodge has been with us for about the last ten minutes. Does it look familiar at all to you?"

Livy turned in her seat to get a look. The Dodge was the second car behind them, but keeping pace steadily. She could make out two big men in the front seat. Square shoulders and hats down over their faces. Would it be the Soviets or the Americans? They both had reason to make sure she was leaving, but her money was on the Russians.

The Ford had been on the same stretch of road for several miles. A railroad track ran alongside, with a service road running parallel to the right of the highway. Just beyond Livy could see a train yard with several dirty buildings surrounded by freight cars that looked in need of repair.

Dalby kept flicking his eyes from the rearview to the car's big side mirrors. The smartly dressed woman beside Livy held both hands in her lap. When Livy looked at her, she forced a nervous smile.

Definitely the Russians, Livy thought.

Dalby made a sudden right down a hill headed toward the rail yards. The Ford shook as the big car ran over the track at more speed than Dalby might've intended.

"Bit of a detour," he said. "Let's see if they follow."

Livy turned in her seat. The black Dodge was about three car lengths back, just taking the turn now.

"I assume it's me they want," Livy said. It wasn't a question.

Dalby didn't reply. Instead, he took the first left onto the service road, giving the car a bit more gas.

"Let's just get you to the airport, shall we?" he said. Livy detected more than a note of tension in the man's voice.

Dalby pushed the Ford harder. Dust kicked up around the car, partially blocking Livy's view on either side. She turned. The Dodge was right behind them now.

The woman beside her gripped the door handle. Livy took a deep breath and wished she were behind the wheel. She'd been taken for one too many rides of late.

The Ford braked. Livy looked up and saw another car about a hundred feet ahead. It too had just turned off the highway and was headed in the direction of Dalby's car. As the Ford slowed, Livy saw the new arrival turn and stop.

They were setting up a roadblock.

Chapter
Thirty-Four

❧

"Mr. Dalby, what's happening?" The woman beside Livy sounded on the verge of panic.

Dalby slowed the car to a halt. The vehicle in front parked across the dirt road thirty feet away. Livy turned to see the black Dodge behind doing the same.

No one spoke for almost a minute. Finally, Dalby turned in his seat. "Miss Nash, I'd like you to stay put, please. Lock the doors and let me handle this."

Up ahead, the doors of the car in front opened. A big man in a linen suit and fedora stepped out of the passenger side. Livy recognized the man who came from the back seat. She remembered the glasses and the cold smile of Georgi Sokolov.

"You know that man?" Livy asked Dalby.

"I do, yes."

"He's not here to talk."

"No, I shouldn't think so."

Livy waited. Did Dalby have a plan? He'd steered them off the road to confirm the tail and had ended up putting them into the worst possible situation.

Ahead, the two Russians stood in front of the car. Waiting.

"Mr. Dalby, we can't just sit here."

"Right. 'Course not."

He doesn't know what to do. Livy checked the car in back. It hadn't moved. The men still sitting inside.

She looked forward. They could only be here for one reason. To take her. Fine, then. If they were here for her, then she'd give them whatever she had left. Livy'd seen enough roadblocks for one lifetime, and she'd be damned if this one stopped her.

She leaned forward in her seat. Her voice quiet and urgent. "Listen to me now, Mr. Dalby. I've been in situations like this, and there's one way out. In just a moment, I want you to put the car in reverse and give it everything you've got."

"I beg your pardon?"

"The petrol. Reverse, step on the petrol, and aim at the driver's side tire of that car behind us. Hit the edge not straight on, understand? We're going to ram them, and it's going to shake the whole car. Then turn the wheel, put us in drive, and get us back on that highway. How far's the airport from here?

"A few miles perhaps, but—"

"Mr. Dalby, you have to trust me. I've been through this before. In the war. We get one chance." Livy looked up. Sokolov and the other man in front stepped away from the car and headed toward them. "And we can't let them get much closer. Ready now?"

"I think so. Yes. Ready."

The woman beside Livy in the back had begun to cry a bit.

"Those people are coming for me. I'm sorry you're both involved, but we'll get out of here. Right, Mr. Dalby, it's time."

He let out a long breath and then reached for the gearshift on the steering column. With one sudden jerk, he put the car into reverse and then, as Livy suggested, jammed his foot on the gas.

The Ford's big engine roared as the back tires spun, kicking up dust all around. Dalby leaned over the front seat, trying to see behind through the cloud of dirt. The engine screeched as they closed the gap, with the Dodge in the rear.

"Hold on tight," Livy told the woman next to her. She grabbed the front seat just as the Ford slammed hard into the car behind. It felt like an earthquake. The vehicle jolted and rocked. The impact pulled Livy out of her seat like a doll and flung her against the padded front seat. Dust was everywhere. The woman beside Livy screamed. But before they could reorient themselves after the crash, Dalby spun the wheel hard. The entire car whipped around one hundred and eighty degrees, bashing into the Dodge again as the Ford righted itself, pointing in the direction of the exit they'd taken off the main highway.

Dalby had done it all perfectly. At least until the car stalled.

Livy glanced over her shoulder. Through the dust, she saw the Dodge, battered and spun around. Smoke poured from of its hood. Behind them, Sokolov's car had just started and was moving after them.

"Mr. Dalby!" Livy shouted.

"Not to worry."

He turned the key, bringing the engine back to life, slammed the gearshift into drive, and stepped on the gas hard. Livy's head whiplashed, throwing her body into the back seat. Dalby didn't let up. The Ford bumped and skittered over the dirt road and then turned right, back to the main road. The big car bounced as its wheels caught on the asphalt. Ahead lay the Jefferson Davis Highway. Traffic looked light, but Dalby didn't slow down. The car hit the railroad tracks with two hard thumps as the Ford bounded into the line of cars. Horns squealed all around them as Dalby forced his way into traffic.

He smiled into the rearview at Livy. The color had drained from his face, but his eyes were bright.

"Not bad," Livy said.

"Can't have you missing your flight, can we?"

*   *   *

About twenty minutes later, the Ford pulled into the departure area of National Airport. The Dodge coupe—with a sizable dent in its front end—followed them the rest of the way. The Russians kept a healthy distance, but nevertheless did nothing to disguise their intentions. If they couldn't have Livy Nash, they apparently wanted to make sure she left town.

The Ford stopped in the departure zone amid other cars pulling in and out, all discharging passengers. Dalby jumped out and headed down the walkway in the direction of a uniformed DC policeman. A minute later, a man in a gray suit joined them as Dalby pleaded his case. Livy couldn't resist turning around to catch another glimpse of the battered Dodge.

"You all right then?" Livy asked the smartly dressed woman next to her.

"I've never been through anything like that. But I'm fine. We'll get you on that plane."

The car door opened, and Dalby slid back into the driver's seat. The car surged away from the curb.

"We're getting you as close to the plane as possible," he said. "They've given us permission to park on the tarmac."

Livy nodded and thanked him, but she wondered if her life had forever changed. The Russians wouldn't stop chasing her once she boarded that plane. They'd have someone at the airport in London. They'd have someone at her flat. They wouldn't stop until they had revenge for Kostin's death, which meant she was about to enter an altogether different prison on the other side of the Atlantic.

They drove behind parked planes as they made their way across the runway to a big DC-3. Already, passengers walked single file out of the terminal to the stairs descending from the opened door of the twin-engine plane.

The Ford stopped about fifty yards away. Dalby got out first, opening the boot and pulling out Livy's own suitcase. The well-dressed woman came around to Livy. She handed her a folded ticket and checked to make sure she had her passport. Dalby put the suitcase in her hand.

Livy wasn't use to this kind of caretaking. She'd been beaten and held captive for the better part of three weeks, so she kept her mouth shut and grudgingly allowed them to baby her.

"I'd say you should take it from here, Miss Nash." Dalby had to almost yell. The noise of the planes drowned out all other sound. "Bit of a walk, but we'll be right here the entire time. Someone will be waiting for you at London airport. With any luck, you may even be able to get some sleep during the flight."

The wind whipped through Livy's hair. The question had nagged her since that awful day at the American *dacha*. She'd pushed it away, rationalized countless answers, but now she had one last opportunity to get an answer before embarking on the long journey home. So she turned and grabbed Dalby's hand, holding it tight and looking him in the eyes. "Mr. Dalby, I need to know something. Was Margot Dupont one of ours?"

He hesitated and then leaned next to her ear. "One of ours? Let me put it like this: if I have my way, she'll be in line for an Order of the British Empire from the king."

Livy didn't know what to say. After all she'd been through, for one moment, her heart felt almost full. She nodded and turned toward the plane.

* * *

Livy sat alone on the last row of the DC-3 as it began its descent into London Airport. Exhaustion had overtaken her during the flight. Shortly after takeoff, she'd allowed the steady whirring of the big propellers to help her drift off to sleep. The airline seats had proven far more comfortable than that bloody contraption the FBI had called a bed.

Now, as the plane lowered its altitude in preparation for landing, she wondered what home would be like. Not exactly the sort of trip where one heads back to the flat, puts her feet up on the ottoman, and catches up on old newspapers. For she was no longer the girl reporter who'd been a spy during the war. She'd killed an MGB officer, the man handpicked to be Berlin *rezident*.

What did that make her? A marked woman? Disavowed by her country and sent packing by its closest ally. She'd never been good at seeing her future clearly. Things happened and she reacted. Now, with her world so cloaked in shadow, Livy figured she had no choice but to take each moment as it came. Like it might be her last.

After the plane landed, she was the last to disembark. She walked across the tarmac, collected her bag from the cart, and stepped cautiously into the terminal building. A young man about her own age walked just ahead of her. He had the familiar slow gait of the weary transatlantic traveler. Suddenly his pace quickened, and he put his arm around a beaming young red-head who stood just inside the gate.

Livy found herself distracted enough by their reunion that she almost missed seeing the man who stood beyond. He leaned, one might say jauntily, against a kiosk bearing the familiar sea-man logo of Player's Navy Cut cigarettes.

As he saw her, Ian Fleming smiled. He didn't stop grinning until he took her bag and said, "Welcome home, Olivia. We've been lost without you."

Chapter
Thirty-Five

They put her in a safe house in Greenwich. Fleming had insisted she couldn't go back to her Camden Town flat, so after her arrival at the airport, she took a seat in the back of a blue Bentley that wound its way all the way across London to a small flat nestled near the local Greenwich library. Fleming got her settled in and introduced her to Mrs. Ashton, a rather stern-looking woman of about sixty, who reminded Livy of her aunt from Blackburn, the one that griped every year that Christmas dinner has been overcooked.

Livy mostly slept and ate for the first two days. The bed in her upstairs room was comfortable enough, and, despite her dour demeanor, Mrs. Ashton proved to be more than an adequate cook. After dinner they took an evening stroll in nearby Greenwich Park. The walks, which made Livy feel quite a bit like Mrs. Ashton's dog, always gave her the impulse to run. However, she knew if she were to flee that even if Mrs. Ashton didn't catch her, the tall slender Special Branch man who always shadowed them on the walks would certainly track her down.

The whole routine became unbearable by the fifth day. Livy couldn't sleep at all the night before, so when she woke up, she marched down to breakfast and informed Mrs. Ashton that she wouldn't stay in the house another day without news about her friend Margot Dupont. "I'll not be kept here in this cottage jail cell one more day unless someone tells me what the hell is going on."

Mrs. Ashton grinned, cleaned the dishes, and then disappeared for the rest of the day.

The next morning at breakfast, Livy came down and found her reticent companion had set a third place at the small table in the kitchen.

"You have a guest, dear," she said. "In the front room. Take all the time you need."

Livy's heart leapt, and she turned quickly toward the front of the house. She couldn't help but be disappointed to find a man about her age sitting in one of the armchairs. He bolted up when she entered, and smiled. Not a bad-looking sort at all. Tall, with wavy blond hair and green eyes. He wore a blue RAF uniform, and Livy recognized a squadron leader's stripes on his sleeve.

"Miss Nash, it is such a pleasure," he said, extending his hand. Livy shook it. He had a broad smile and a gleam in his eye. "I haven't even introduced myself. Frank Woodward. I'm just so thrilled to actually see you and shake your hand."

Livy nodded, waiting for some explanation of the purpose of the very friendly Squadron Leader Woodward's visit.

"Sorry, I'm so clumsy. Haven't been myself since I heard the news, you know. Oh wait. Let me go back a bit. You see, I'm Margot's fiancé."

At first Livy thought she'd missed something. This didn't make sense. How could Margot be engaged?

"Look, sir, I'm not quite sure how to—" Livy began.

"Frank, please."

"Right, Frank, then. Where is Margot? Is she home? I'm a bit lost here."

"Of course you are. What am I thinking? Please sit down and let me explain." Woodward took the chair opposite. "Where to start, um, well Margot and I met in France during the war. We worked in different SOE circuits, but well . . . we became rather close near the end of it all. When France was liberated, we were able to spend quite a good deal of time together. She took me to Lyon, showed me where her mother had grown up. Then, of course, she had to report back. That's the last time I saw her, actually. Round about January 1945."

This wasn't what Livy had hoped for exactly, but she felt closer to her friend than she had in years. She didn't budge while Woodward continued.

"Of course she couldn't tell me what she was going away to do. I understood the nature of her work and all that. I told her I'd wait for her, and when she came home that I'd be here. Then time went by, and I never heard anything. I asked, of course. But every time, I was stonewalled. Finally, about a year ago, I went round to talk to a Miss Atkins who worked at the Old Firm up on Baker Street. She told me they'd listed Margot as "missing, presumed dead." So for the last year—well, things were pretty bad, as you might imagine. Kept telling myself I had to move on and all, but I'd made Margot a promise, and if there was even a chance that she . . ." His voice trailed off. He looked away, gritted his teeth, and cleared his throat.

"Then, about a week ago, they told me they knew where she was and that you'd found her. Of course, they didn't tell me the whole lot. Don't have clearance for that, I'm sure. But I convinced them to let me come and see you . . . and thank you. So . . . thank you." Woodward's face lit up, and Livy saw tears at the edge of his eyes. "I know you and Margot were friends. They told me you took risks to find her. Great risks, they said. So, I'm just very grateful, Miss Nash. Just knowing that she's alive, you see, makes all the difference in the world."

Livy nodded, fighting back her own emotion. She'd felt so alone during it all. The whole ordeal. She wished she could tell Woodward what had happened to her. Tell him she'd thought of Margot every minute and that those thoughts had gotten her through. But she couldn't say any of that, so she reached out and took his hands and held them. They sat there, in silence, until Mrs. Ashton called them in to breakfast a few minutes later.

* * *

Woodward didn't stay to eat, and Livy barely touched her food. She pushed it around the plate and took only a few sips of her tea. After Woodward's departure, she felt back to square one.

"Not hungry, my dear?" Mrs. Ashton said. Her plate had been clean for minutes.

Livy felt every muscle clinch. The thumping headache that had been her constant companion in FBI custody had returned. She knew her stay at the safe house was for her own protection, but she couldn't take like this another day.

"I still want to know what's going on." She threw down her napkin and bolted out of her chair. "I'm tired of being kept in the dark, and I'll be damned if I'm going to be held hostage by my own people. So you do whatever it takes. Tell them the fiancé didn't appease me. I want answers or I'll walk out that door first thing tomorrow. Understand?"

She didn't have to wait long.

That afternoon—around teatime—both Henry Dunbar and Ian Fleming arrived. They looked like Livy felt. Frustrated and restless. Fleming ushered them into the front room, where Livy had met Woodward. He closed the door and sat beside her on the loveseat. Dunbar across from them.

Livy got to the point. "I want to know about Margot. All of it."

"What exactly do you want to know?"

"What was she doing over there all this time? Working for us?"

Dunbar rubbed his thick mustache and leaned forward. "Her role in the Soviet zone was much like yours in America. She was picked up as a prisoner after the war and offered the Russians information. We prepped her for it, of course. What she gave them was all old Firm material. Codes, communication, the lot. They grew to trust her, and she was able to be our eyes and ears in their zone. Even in the camp where they kept her, she saw things. Troop movements. The other prisoners in the camp. Who came and went. But we lost our go-between six months ago. We knew they moved Margot, but had no idea where. You found her for us, Livy."

"Not asking for your praise, Colonel. I just want to know what's going on. All of it."

"Well, the rest is a bit hazy on our end. Once we heard from you, we knew where to look for her. We paid someone from the town near Sachsenhausen to have a look around for us—a baker who made deliveries to the camp. He tried to get eyes on her. It took him two trips, but he finally spotted Margot. Apparently, she'd become sort of the mistress of the commandant. I'd imagine she was forced into that situation. To maintain cover and keep herself safe. Thing is, a rescue operation is out. We go in there, and all hell is liable to break loose."

Livy put her head down. Tears pushed at her eyes. "What are you saying? We just leave her there?"

Dunbar leaned back in his chair and glanced at Fleming. Something seemed to pass between them. Livy turned to her boss. He didn't look at her. Instead, he removed a gold case from his jacket, withdrew one of his specially blended cigarettes, and pushed it into his holder.

Dunbar went on. "We've no intention of leaving Margot there. I've talked to their people, the ones here in London. Dalby has done the same in the States. The Reds want an exchange of prisoners."

Just like that Livy's spirit surged. She took a deep breath and rubbed her eyes. Then she knew. It all made sense now. Fleming wouldn't even look at her. Henry Dunbar's very presence in the same room with her spoke volumes. She knew what he was going to say next.

"They want you Livy."

The silence hung in the air for what felt like minutes. *How much more do they want?* Livy wondered. How much had she already sacrificed? But now they wanted more. They always do.

Fleming broke the silence as he lit his cigarette and took a deep draw before speaking.

"And just as I told you earlier, Henry, they can go to hell. Olivia has done enough. It's up to you now to bring that poor girl home, but Olivia is staying put."

"Colonel?" Livy sat up, her back ramrod straight, her voice clear and strong. "What will happen to Margot if we don't do this?"

Dunbar shook his head. Livy saw the toll this was taking on him. She hadn't seen the man in over a year, but he looked like he'd aged a decade.

"We'll keep trying to get her back, of course. See if they would accept someone else, but the Reds were clear with their demand. About who they want, that is. It's about Kostin, you see. They mean to make an example to us. Of us. Show we can't go around killing their people."

"You didn't answer the question."

"Dammit Livy, you know the bloody answer. Nightshade won't last much longer over there if we don't move on this."

Livy nodded and slumped back into the loveseat. Fleming put his arm around her shoulders, but she didn't respond. Dunbar had used Margot's code name this time. He was already distancing himself from her inevitable fate.

Livy felt just so tired. Washington, Kostin, the "dacha," Nadia, her frantic escape, and then the FBI. She'd come so far, and what did she have to show for it? Margot still a prisoner? How could Livy possibly go forward? She tried to imagine a life beyond this day. For her. For Margot's fiancé. How could she leave this job—of all of them—unfinished? She wiped her eyes. Her hand came away moist. By God, she'd not cry now. She had one more question.

"What will they do to me then?"

Fleming jolted up. "Olivia, you can't possibly consider this!"

"Please tell me, Colonel. Be honest."

Dunbar's focus changed. His eyes locked with hers. His voice was clear and calm. The man seemed prepared for this moment. "More than likely, they'll put you on trial for murder. They'll make it look legitimate and fair, of course, but make no mistake, it would be a show trial at best."

Livy tried to imagine what lay ahead, but it was pointless. What mattered was now. *Finish the job.* That's what she did. It's what made her who she was. And she realized there was only one thing she truly wanted in the world right now.

"Would I be able to see Margot first?"

Chapter Thirty-Six

One week later
British Zone, Occupied Germany

Livy Nash sat in the back seat of a black Vauxhall saloon, staring out the window at the German countryside. This was her first time in the country. She'd only gotten as far as the mountains of Southwest France during the war. It was almost midnight, so she couldn't see distances, but it appeared that here there were fewer reminders of the great Allied bombing that had rained down. Berlin would be devastated. She wondered if they would take her there.

"You can still call this off, Olivia." Fleming sat beside her, smoking. The back of the car filled with the musky scent of his cigarettes. "You don't have to do this."

Livy nodded. She'd barely moved since the car had picked them up at the nearby RAF base. She held her hands in her lap. Her eyes still focused on the passing landscape. She'd spent the night before reading her copy of *Hamlet*, and found comfort in how the prince faced his inevitable fate.

"There's a special providence in the fall of a sparrow
. . . the readiness is all."

Not that she was ready to die. Far from it. She saw this as the
only possible way to finish her job. Livy wanted to see Margot—
if only for a moment—and know that her friend's long ordeal
was finally over. She'd spent the flight to Germany thinking
through it all. Preparing herself. Livy'd been in an enemy prison
before. Her training had taught her how to stay alive in such
circumstances. Her experience in a Nazi cell had nearly killed
her, but now she thought back on it as a reminder of her own
resilience. Even now, as the car cruised toward its destination,
her mind felt calm and her heart settled. Like Hamlet, Livy
knew she had to make this right. The readiness—for whatever
lay ahead—was all.

Henry Dunbar turned around in the front passenger seat. A
fair-haired Royal Army sergeant drove the car.

"Just about two miles now," Dunbar said. "We wait for them
to make the first move, then we'll exit the car. Once we have a
visual on Nightshade, I'll give you the signal to go. Are we clear?"

Livy nodded. Only a few minutes now. She turned to Fleming and placed a hand on his navy jacket. His blue eyes met hers.

"Is it true what they said about you during the war, sir? All
those creative schemes you came up with?

Fleming's brow furrowed. "I think you know I'm still bound
by—"

"Of course," she said. "But the stories I heard—they give a
girl hope." Livy gave him a brief smile. Fleming started to speak,
then stopped himself. He took a long drag on his cigarette,

exhaled the smoke, and his wide mouth curled into a grin Livy had seen many times before.

The Vauxhall slowed. "We're here," Dunbar announced. Livy looked out the front window. They'd come to the edge of a forest. Beyond, tall trees lined either side of the road. Dunbar had told them earlier the exchange would take place at the point where the British and Soviet sectors met. The car stopped. The driver turned the headlamps off but left the engine idling. No one spoke. Everyone focused ahead on the road, except for Livy, who turned away and closed her eyes. She put one hand on her stomach and felt her breath. She counted each rise and fall, trying to block out the fear that invaded her mind.

Dunbar's voice broke the silence. "Look sharp everyone."

Livy turned to the front. Headlamps cut through the darkness ahead and approached through the shadows of the forest. Livy shielded her eyes as the lights came closer. Suddenly they dimmed. She blinked and could make out the shape of another car that had stopped about fifty feet away, turned at an angle to the Vauxhall.

For what seemed like minutes, nothing happened. No one spoke. The two cars sat as if each was waiting for the other to make the first move.

The passenger side door of the car ahead opened. Then both back doors. Three figures stepped out into the night. Livy strained to make out their features, but they were only silhouettes. Still, one shorter, smaller figure stood out. Livy sat up and tried to get a better look.

"It's time," Dunbar said. As if on cue, he and the driver opened their doors. Fleming nodded at Livy as if to say, *"Let's go."* His normally bright eyes were hooded and narrow. Livy opened her door and stepped into the night. A breeze made the air bite, but she felt nothing. Her eyes were glued to the car ahead and the small figure beside it. Someone from the rear of the other car turned and took the smaller person by the arm, bringing her—it was a woman; Livy could see that now—to the front.

Dunbar turned to Livy. Fleming came around to her side of the car and took her hand in his. Together, they walked to the front of the Vauxhall. Livy's eyes straight ahead.

Dunbar asked them to stop once they'd reached the spray of the car's headlamps. "Just her now," he said.

Livy turned to Fleming, her hand still tight in his. His sad eyes looked beyond her as he spoke.

"I should never have sent you, Olivia. It was selfish and wrong . . ."

"Sir, please," she said, her voice a whisper. Livy took a breath. "Now, go and impress me. I'll be waiting."

Fleming glanced down at her. He nodded. "My dear, I'll think of nothing else. Night and day."

Livy almost smiled. She turned away from him and looked straight ahead. The woman at the front of the other car began to walk toward them. Slowly, Livy took her first steps away from the Vauxhall, away from her life, away from England, and headed into the unknown.

Her gaze fixed on the woman walking toward her. The lights of the car lit her from the back, so shadows masked her features. But Livy recognized the gait. The quick steps. Always in a hurry because she was late. The gap between them closed. Now twenty feet. Livy could make out her hair now, which was a bit longer.

Just fifteen feet to go. She saw recognition flash across her eyes—across Margot's eyes. It was her.

"Livy?" The slight Lyon accent tinged with surprise.

Now so close. Livy held out her hands and Margot took them. The two women held each other for a moment. Tears pooled in Margot's eyes.

"I don't understand. What are you . . .?" Livy stopped the question with a long hug. She held her friend tighter than she'd even expected. Margot sobbed, her body convulsing against Livy's chest; then she pulled back.

"You all right then, luv?" Livy asked.

"Yes . . . I am, but what are you doing here? I don't understand."

Livy held Margot so close. She felt her friend's breath as Margot's tears dripped onto the back of her hands.

"You're almost home. Those men'll take good care of you."

"Livy, tell me what's going on."

"I have to go now."

And she could see the thought flash across Margot's features. In an instant she understood, and her grip on Livy's hands tightened.

"Don't, luv," Livy said. "You have a lovely fella waiting for you back in England. And a life. You let me go now, and don't say another word."

"Livy, what are you doing?"

"I've got to go. And so do you." Livy pushed Margot's hands away and started to turn. Her friend grabbed her coat and held it. Livy smiled at her and put one hand on Margot's cheek.

"*À bientôt,*" Livy said and removed Margot's hand from her coat gently. "See you home soon."

With that she turned her back on her friend and took the first steps toward the waiting car. Margot was alive and going home. A great tempest rose deep inside Livy. She wanted to wail into the night, but the luxury of time was not hers.

She could now make out the faces of the people who waited for her. A tall soldier in a Red Army uniform stood at the driver's side. Another man in a dark suit waited at the passenger door. A young woman in a military uniform stepped out from the other side of the car. They watched her without expression.

Livy took a deep breath and began to walk. She had about thirty feet to go. She felt her knees buckle. She pushed forward, each step an effort. She tried to focus on her breath, but it came in rapid bursts. Still, she kept the emotion in check. Twenty feet now. She wanted to turn and see Margot one more time. But she dare not. One look and she wouldn't be able to take these last few steps, and by God she'd not be a coward. Not now.

The young woman on the other side came forward in a hurry. She hooked her arm under Livy's armpit and took her the last few feet. Then, she turned Livy around, facing the Vauxhall. She could see Dunbar close to Margot, speaking quickly to her. Then, they all turned and looked across the road at Livy.

Tears ran down her cheeks. She had to let that much out. The road had been so long, but she'd finished the job. Margot was safe and would soon be back in England. Livy then felt hands gripping her arms and the steel of handcuffs, clapped tight around both wrists. She looked straight ahead, taking in every moment. Dunbar led Margot to the back seat. She stopped at the door and glanced at Livy one final time before disappearing inside. Fleming took his place beside her as Dunbar hurried around to the passenger side.

The Russian woman put a hand on Livy's elbow. "We have to go now," she said, her accent and voice soft.

Livy didn't respond, staring straight ahead. She watched as the big Vauxhall made a U-turn and drove away, back into the British sector. She heard the engine's roar as it gained speed, and kept her eyes on the rear lights as they grew smaller and smaller down the dark quiet road.

Acknowledgements

Thanks always to my smart, tireless agent Carrie Pestritto and everyone at Laura Dail Literary. My editor Chelsey Emmelhainz performed her magic on this one again. Special thanks to Ashley Di Do, Melissa Rechter and the folks at Crooked Lane Books.

Also I'm grateful to Reed Johnson and Dr. Sally Barbour for patiently answering my questions about all things Russian and French, respectively. Thanks also to Anthony Coppin in Lancashire.

Finally Brook, Ian and Lucy—you make everything better, including this book.